UNDAUNTED

KINGS OF RETRIBUTION MC MONTANA

CRYSTAL DANIELS

SANDY ALVAREZ

Copyright © 2017 by Crystal Daniels & Sandy Alvarez

All rights reserved.

(NOTE: This book is a work of fiction.)

No part of this book may be reproduced in any form or by any electronic or mechanical means, including information storage and retrieval systems, without written permission from the authors', except for the use of brief quotations in a book review. It is not to be shared, sold or distributed in any way except from the authors. This book is a work of fiction. Names, characters, places, brands, media, and incidents are the product of the author's imagination or are used fictitiously.

Cover Artist: Crystal Daniels

Image Provided by: Wander Book Club - Photographer: Wander Aguiar Photography

This book is licensed for your personal enjoyment only. This book may not be resold or given away to other people. If you would like to share this book with another person, please purchase an additional copy for each recipient. If you're reading this book and did not purchase it, or it was not purchased for your use only, then please return it to the author and purchase your own copy. Thank you for respecting the hard work of the authors.

TWO PENS -
CRYSTAL Daniels
Sandy ALVAREZ
- ONE STORY

To our husbands David and Esteban

1

LOGAN

I live and breathe this life. Bikes, women, whiskey. There isn't anything better. I am who I am and make no excuses. I may not be what society would call an upstanding citizen, but the way I see it, our time on earth is limited. And I don't plan on wasting any of mine. I refuse to let other people's opinions keep me from having the courage to live my life the way I choose. There is only one day a year when I throw all that shit out the window, allowing the negativity and darkness to creep in. And that day is today. The club's throwing a big party for my twenty-fifth birthday. They do it every year. They fire up the grills, bring in all the families, then as night falls, the old ladies and kids go home, and the women and whiskey start to flow.

I love my brothers, but I'd much rather lose myself in booze—which is precisely what I'm doing right now.

I have a home not far from the clubhouse, right on the lake. I got one just for the peace and solitude. There are times when I need to be alone—away from the club, apart from my brothers. Times like now. My birthday isn't a day to celebrate. To me, my birthday will always be a reminder of the worst day of my life.

"Hey, son. Happy Birthday," Jake acknowledges, patting me on my back as he takes a seat beside me. I've been sittin' outside in the cold for the better part of an hour. Lucky for me, the alcohol is not only good for drowning my sorrows but works wonders at keeping me warm.

"Thanks," I answer, dryly.

Jake has been in my life since I was eight. He married my Aunt Lily, my mom's younger sister. "Why don't you call it a night? Go home. I know you're not into any of this shit today."

I look to him and lift my beer to my lips, drinking the last swallow. "I think I'll take a bottle to my room. Tell the guys I'm out for the night, will ya?" I ask as I make my way back inside. Stopping at the bar, I grab my poison of choice before making my way to the stairs that lead to my room.

Jake understands the struggles today brings. No matter how many years pass, tragedy and pain will forever stalk me.

Once I'm in my room, I strip out of my clothes. Sitting on the edge of my bed, I twist the cap off the bottle before taking a long pull. There was a time when I would try to find the answers to all my problems at the bottom of a bottle. I started drinking heavily when I was twenty, after someone I was in love with betrayed me. That, on top of the pain I still carried from losing my mother, made alcohol become my way of self-medicating. Before too long, Jake noticed a change in me. He sat me down one night, telling me something that would make me realize the path I was choosing was wrong. "The pain of your tragedy will never go away, no matter how much you drink, son. But the memory of your mother lives on inside of you. How do you think she would feel to see the son she was raising, not living the happy life she so desperately wanted for him?"

I never could let go of the past, or it's never let go of me. I still live with the ghosts of what could have been.

Today is just another reminder of just how fucked up life is. It's also the only day I allow my old habits to seep in.

Fifteen years ago, on my tenth birthday, was the first of many losses in my life.

As a nurse, my mom worked a lot of hours, but on my birthdays, she always took the day off. She'd gotten up early that morning. She made pancakes with bacon because it was my favorite. Most mornings, she was rushing off to work while I had school, so breakfast was usually cereal or fruit. My mom had the entire day planned. We were going to meet my Aunt Lily and Jake to spend the day with them at the lake. The lake was somewhat of a tradition on my birthday. The weather wasn't warm enough to swim, but my mom would bring lunch, and Jake said he'd bring a ball for us to throw around.

I was close to my aunt. She would stop by at least once a week and help me with my homework while my mom would be working. Jake would show up with her on occasion. We'd talk about football, and how excited I was to be starting camp in the summer.

We loaded up the car after breakfast, and soon after, we were on the road headed for the lake. I'm not sure what happened. Not from memory anyway. One minute I was sitting in the backseat playing my Game, then the next, I heard my mom screaming as the car plunged over the side rail. The last thing I remember is my seatbelt pulling tight, locking me in before losing consciousness.

The next time I opened my eyes, I was in a hospital room, and my mom was dead.

I had several broken ribs, a fractured arm, tons of scrapes and cuts, and a severe concussion that kept me out of it for two days. I wasn't even strong enough to attend my mom's funeral. Bennett, our club doctor, sat with me that day.

After I was strong enough to leave the hospital, my aunt took me home to live with her and Jake.

I've lost so much, but I became a part of The Kings of Retribution MC family in the process.

Those men downstairs are more loyal than most. Jake took me in and raised me as if I were his son.

That's when I met Reid and his little brother, Noah. We became instant friends. Fuck, the three of us were always getting into shit and raising hell.

Our lives changed a few years later when Aunt Lily passed away from cervical cancer.

Two of the most important women in my life were gone. It seems losing people was becoming a theme in my life. I never knew my old man. My mom never talked about him—good or bad.

Jake became more than an uncle; he became the father I never had. Though he was dealing with his grief from losing the woman he loved, he never let that stop him from being a constant in my life. He put his heartache aside and focused on raising me with the help of the club. Through every milestone, Jake was by my side. First crush, first girlfriend, even my first fight. He was there through it all. The proudest moment he and I shared was when I earned my patch. I'll never forget the look of pride in his eyes, as he realized, through all our trials and tribulations, I'd made it.

Bennett was a big part of my upbringing. He has been with the club since day one. He and Jake grew up together. Childhood friends. Bennett is the one who taught me how to use a gun at thirteen. I caught on quick. He said I was a natural. It didn't take long before I was able to outshoot any of the brothers. I just learned early on that with determination and dedication; you could accomplish anything.

Bennett has an old lady, Lisa. They're high school sweethearts. She stood by him through two tours in Iraq as a medic and his decision to join the MC. Lisa is truly Bennett's ride or die.

Seven years ago, I thought I had everything figured out. I had the club, my brothers, and a pretty woman I loved.

It turns out; she didn't love me.

Stephanie Williams. She was my high school sweetheart. We met in my junior year. She had strawberry blonde hair and soft brown eyes. Every spare moment I had, I spent with her. Almost three years together.

Up until the day I turned twenty.

I rode out to her parents' house, where she was still living. I went to pick her up for the party the club was having. I knew I was a couple of hours early, but I was anxious to see my girl. That time of day, she was usually out back in the guest house her parents let her stay in. I parked my bike and made my way around to the gate that led to the back of the property.

What I wasn't prepared for, was catching the girl I loved sucking some other guy's dick as I passed the large living room window.

I enjoyed beating the shit out of the punk, but it did nothing to ease the pain of betrayal I was feeling.

It turns out the money was more important to her than I thought. Once daddy threatened to cut her off, she started seeing one of the guys that worked for his firm. She fuckin' kept me around because the prick couldn't satisfy her in bed. Her words, not mine. She told me she could never marry a biker anyway.

Fuck love. I decided from then on that I didn't want or need it.

Some of the other brothers have divorces under their belts with women who thought they could handle the club life, but in the end, they couldn't deal.

Not everyone is lucky enough to have what Bennett and Lisa have.

Jake had that once with my Aunt Lily. Even though it's been years, I've never seen him interested in another woman. I know he gets his release like the rest of us brothers do, but that's it. He always goes home alone at night.

Although, I have noticed he's developed a bit of a sweet tooth the past couple of months. I'm guessing a certain little redhead that opened a bakery in town might have something to do with his slight donut obsession lately.

It's just not for me. I'm not looking for a permanent woman. I'm happy with the way things are now. No strings attached pussy. They all know the score beforehand. We have a good time. Then it's time for them to go.

Fuck. I take pride in knowing I paid my dues and earned this VP patch I wear on my cut today. Sure, there were plenty of times along the way when my dumb ass almost fucked it up. My brothers never let up, though, and sometimes taught me the hard way to rein that shit in. Which believe me, I did. The day my brothers voted me in and gave me the title was one of pride.

I'm the man I am today because of them.

I still suffer from insomnia and the occasional nightmare that I've been dealing with since I was ten. I'm not sure if they're actual memories or something my mind has conjured up. I found that smoking a little weed helps with insomnia from time to time, but I don't partake in it as much as I used to.

I live and breathe club life. Being a Kings of Retribution MC member holds much more meaning than just wearing the cut and having a title.

I have killed and would lay down my life for any one of those men because they are my family.

This is who I am. I don't need more.

Halfway through the bottle, I feel my eyes getting heavier, and I give in to the liquor-induced sleep.

2

BELLA

"Alba, stay right here with me and be very quiet. Okay?" I tell my little sister as I sit her down on the closet floor.

She looks up at me with her big blue eyes. "Bella, I'm scared."

"I know. Me too," I admit to her as I quietly close the closet door, and lock it just like Mommy has taught us.

"Where are those little shits?" Daddy yells.

"Nick, leave the girls alone."

"Shut the fuck up, you bitch."

The sound of a sharp, smacking noise makes me jump—he slapped her.

Alba starts crying, so I hold her telling her it's going to be okay. We cling to each other tighter as we hear Daddy banging on the door.

"Open this door, goddammit!"

I startle awake, my heart pounding, as sheer panic grips my insides until I realize it was just a dream. Sometimes the dreams can be so vivid that there's a blurred line on reality, and it takes me a while to not feel the suffocating feeling of dread known as anxiety, a black hole that can swallow me whole.

Our father passed away when Alba was only five, and I was six. She doesn't remember much about him at all, and I have only a few memories of him. None of which are good. No child should have to live with that kind of evil clogging their brains. It doesn't help when you have the type of parent that repeatedly trades one horrible man in for another.

A few years after my father died, Mom met and married husband number two, who was a good man, but he soon realized he didn't want the burden of two small girls to raise.

About six months after he left, she decided that we needed a change, so she got in touch with an old friend that lived in Polson, who offered for us to stay with her until we could get our own place.

Mom packed us up, and we left Wyoming, the only home we had ever known.

After getting settled in the new town, Mom found a job at a diner. Three months later, she moved us into a two-bedroom apartment. We've moved to a few different places since then, but we've been in this house the longest—going on two years now.

She met Lee last year. He came into the diner one day and asked her out. Within six weeks, he was living with us. A couple of months after that, they married. My mother can't seem to break the cycle. She has blinders on when it comes to the opposite sex. She's not good at being alone. It's like she needs a man to feel good about herself, and in return, they all bring her down. Hopefully, one day, she'll open her eyes.

It didn't take long for Lee's true colors to show either. As soon as they married, he suddenly developed a back problem and couldn't work anymore. Mom struggled to pay the bills and keep Lee stocked with beer that he demanded all the time.

As soon as I was old enough to work, I got a job, and now with Mom's hours cut back at the diner, a lot of the burden is being put on my shoulders.

Lee is a low-life scum of the earth type of guy, if you ask me. The man wakes up drinking and passes out at the end of the day from all the booze. He also has a nasty temper and hasn't been afraid to use it on my mom in the past. I've seen the proof on her arms before. He's careful not to leave evidence on her face for everyone to know the kind of man he is.

Let me rephrase that. He isn't a man, more like a piece of shit.

He also keeps Mom's bank account drained every month. The lazy fucker can't even hold down a damn job long enough to collect the first paycheck.

I roll over and look at the clock glowing on the nightstand, which reads 6:00 a.m. I wish I could say I'm getting up to go to school, but after graduating, I didn't have an option to do the whole college thing. I needed to keep working so I could help pay the bills, help keep a roof over my sister's and my heads, and make sure we have food to eat and clothes to wear because our mom struggles enough as it is.

My goal is to save enough money so I can get my own place, bringing Alba with me. I want her to have the chances I didn't, like going to college and living and experiencing life, soaking up as much as she can without all the negativity that our current situation is offering.

I close my eyes. "Just a little while longer," I say out loud.

Rolling out of bed, I walk out of my room, dragging my feet down the hallway to the bathroom. On the way, I pass my mom's room, where I notice her sitting up in bed watching TV.

"Morning, Mom," I say as I walk in and hug her neck.

Even after all she has been through, she's still a beautiful woman, and I wish she wouldn't waste herself staying with Lee.

"Hey, sweetie," she says, cheerfully. "Are you working today?" she asks while she reaches for the remote, changing the channel to the local news.

"Yeah, I have the morning shift at the store today," I tell her as I sit down on the edge of her bed.

"Okay, sweetie," she responds, patting me on my leg, as she starts watching the weather report.

I get up and make my way out of her room when she stops me by calling out. "Oh, wake your sister up. I don't need her missing the bus again. Lee doesn't like it when I use his truck to run her to school."

"I'll take her to school on my way to work. Lee needs to quit being such a dick about that truck. Hell, you pay for the damn gas in it anyway," I say, irritated.

I hear her let out a heavy sigh. I know she wants me to keep my mouth shut, but sometimes something needs to be said.

I decide to drop the subject.

"I love you, Mom," I murmur, walking out of her room.

Finally, in the bathroom, I reach into the shower and turn the water on, letting it warm up. I walk back, checking to make sure the bathroom door is locked because I don't trust Lee to not 'accidentally' walk in while I'm in the shower.

I strip out of my black sleep shorts, letting them pool around my feet. Then I pull my tank top over my head, chucking it on the floor. I walk over to the counter, grab my phone, and pull up my playlist, hitting play before stepping into the shower.

Taylor Swift and The Civil Wars' voices fill the air, singing "Safe and Sound," as the water cascades down me. For just a few short moments, the melody helps me to escape.

When I finish my shower, I head back to our bedroom, the one I share with my younger sister. Alba is eighteen years old and a senior in high school.

She is, in many ways, my complete opposite.

You wouldn't know just by looking at us that we're sisters. I'm petite, only standing five-feet-two-inches, with long, deep brown hair, and hazel eyes I feel are too big for my face. I'm also mouthy, opinionated, and stubborn.

Whereas Alba is five-feet-seven-inches, legs for miles, long blonde hair, and blue eyes. She always has her nose buried in a book and is a bit of an introvert. She is also very timid, shy, and would rather be reading about romance and adventures than going out and find one of her own, but I'm not one to be preaching because, besides a couple of high school boyfriends, I haven't done much living myself.

"Alba...Alba," I say as I poke at the lump that is now mumbling some form of the English language.

"Time to get up. I'm taking you to school today on my way to work," I inform her while making my way over to my dresser.

I rummage through my drawer until I find a pair of black lace panties and a matching bra and start to pull them on when Alba whines.

"Come on, Bella, just a few extra minutes. Please?" she says while curling tighter into the sky-blue comforter on her bed.

She is not a morning person, so I entice her a little bit.

"Alba, if you're up and out this door with me in one hour, I'll bring home that new release you saw at the bookstore last weekend."

That gets her attention. She sticks her head out of her blanket burrito.

"You add a bag of peanut butter cups, and you have a deal."

"Deal."

She unwraps herself from the blanket and starts to get ready for the day. I walk over to the closet to find something to wear, grabbing a pair of dark blue skinny jeans and slipping on a green sleeveless blouse.

My phone chimes with a new text message, so I walk over to my nightstand, pick up my phone, and then sit on the bed, pulling up the text. It's from Mason.

I ran into him about a month ago at the coffee shop downtown while shopping with my sister. He asked if he could take me out sometimes, so we exchanged numbers. We went out a few times. On a Friday, he called wanting to go to dinner and a movie, so I agreed. The whole night he was super handsy, and the asshole also conveniently forgot his wallet, so I ended up paying for everything. I decided to give him another chance after he apologized, but that was a huge mistake.

I throw my phone down, not bothering to respond to his text. I reach down, picking up my favorite pair of brown boots, pull them on and walk over to the full-length mirror putting on some mascara and my favorite lipstick.

Fifteen minutes later, I grab my phone and shove it into my back pocket.

"Grab your shoes and put them on in the car, Alba. We gotta get going!" I shout as I walk into the kitchen, grabbing my keys and smock off the counter.

On our way to the front door, we're stopped by Lee, who is blocking off the door leading to the garage.

Jesus, the man reeks. It smells like he bathes in beer.

"Lee, I don't have time for any of your shit this morning. I need to get Alba to school and still make it to work on time."

He stands there, letting his eyes linger on the both of us, causing my skin to crawl, and Alba to shrink behind me before he speaks.

"Your mom needs some money to go to the store. I need to eat."

What the fuck. I know I just spent most of my last paycheck to get groceries, and mom just got her check not long ago.

"What the hell, Lee. Where did all the food go that I just bought? Huh?"

The asshole stands there with a smirk on his face. No way in hell he's getting my hard-earned money.

"Look, I'm tapped out. And if I did have it, I sure as hell wouldn't be giving it to you."

That pisses him off.

"That smart mouth of yours is going to get you into trouble one day, Bella," he hisses as he goes to sit at the kitchen table, and passes the refrigerator on the way for another beer.

Popping the top, he says, "One way or another, you two are going to earn your keep."

I usher Alba out the door, pausing just long enough to look back at him. "You know, Lee, how about you get off your ass and find a job? Mom may not want to see it, but I know where all the money is going."

I've heard enough gossip in the checkout line to know he's been seen with some shady people in town.

The little smirk he was wearing turns into a scowl.

I shut the door and head to my car. My sister has a look of concern as I climb in. "Nothing to worry about," I tell her, starting the car and pulling onto the road.

We're about two blocks from the high school when Alba speaks up.

"Bella?"

Reaching over, I turn the radio down.

"Lee gives me the creeps, the way he stares at us."

"Yeah, he makes my skin crawl too, but hopefully in a few more months I can afford a small apartment, and we won't have to worry about him anymore. I wish Mom would stand up to his bullshit, and dump his ass."

"Me too," she agrees.

I'm sitting at a traffic light when a motorcycle pulls up beside me in the other lane, followed by at least five others behind him.

I can't take my eyes off the lead biker. Damn, he's hot.

I don't realize I'm staring so hard until my sister breaks the spell.

"Oh my God, Bella. You're totally perving on that biker over there!" She laughs, "And is that drool?"

"Girl, look at that! Hell, yes, I'm perving!" I turn my head to catch one more look at him, and just my luck, he catches me.

His lips turn up just enough, letting me know he caught me checking him out.

I shyly smile to hide my embarrassment as they all rev up and ride away.

3

LOGAN

Friday night after I'm done closing the garage, I head over to Kings Ink, the other business we run in town, right across the street from the shop.

I need to finish the sleeve on my left arm. Gabriel, our Enforcer, runs the place. He's also the best artist in Montana. He has people come from all over the state, wanting him to work on them, but no matter how busy he is, he always makes time for his brothers.

Gabriel and I prospected together when I was eighteen, and he was nineteen. I remember the first time I met him. I had just turned eighteen and was prospecting when Jake took a trip to Florida to visit his mom. When he pulled up to the compound, after being gone a week, he had some guy with him. The only explanation he offered was, "This is Gabriel, he's the new prospect," and for me to show him how things worked.

My first impression was *he's going to fit right the fuck in*. Our club is full of big, crazy looking motherfuckers, and Gabriel is definitely a big motherfucker.

Hell, I stand at six-foot-two. He stands at least six-foot-four, with short black hair, eyes so dark they look almost black, and what looks to be a permanent scowl on his face. I wasn't so sure I was looking forward to hanging' with him, but as time went on, Gabriel slowly started opening up.

After weeks of grunts and one-word answers, he started talking to me, telling me about his past and how he met Jake.

Jake met Gabriel after he witnessed him rob a gas station. While pumping his gas, he watched the whole thing happen. Afterward, Gabriel jumped into his car and took off. Jake followed him to some piece of shit motel about five miles from the place.

Prez, being the crazy motherfucker that he is, just walked right up to that motel door and knocked.

Gabriel opened the door to the motel, gun drawn.

"No need for that, son," was what Jake said to him.

I once asked Jake what made him go after some kid robbing a gas station.

"Had a gut feelin'," was his explanation.

Jake always says you should trust your gut.

He was right, because I couldn't ask for a better brother. Gabriel told me he and his father left Cuba when he was only ten, leaving behind his mother and sister.

Six years after coming to the U.S., his father died.

After hearing his story, I soon realized that he wasn't a bad guy at all. He just had a chip on his shoulder. In many ways, I could relate. We both lost important people in our lives but had gained something as well.

After a while, I could see the change the club was having on him. He was beginning to see this as a family, a brotherhood. Having a family again was precisely what Gabriel had needed.

As prospects, we were made to bunk in a room together, and one night I noticed him sitting up in his bed writing in a notebook. I also had seen that he was never really without it. Every spare moment was spent scribbling in that damn thing. So, one night, I asked him what he was writing. He studied me for a moment before handing it over. Every page was filled with amazing fuckin' drawings.

The next day I grabbed his notebook out of the dresser and took it to Jake.

I remembered Jake mentioning that Bobby, an older club member who ran the tattoo shop, was looking for someone to start helping around Kings Ink.

Bobby was getting older, and his eyes were not as sharp as they used to be; therefore, he needed someone to start taking the reins slowly.

It took Jake about five seconds of looking at Gabriel's work to know exactly what I was thinking.

Later that day, Jake approached Gabriel, telling him he wanted him to apprentice alongside Bobby at the tattoo shop.

Fast forward seven years, Gabriel now manages Kings Ink and is the most renowned tattoo artist in the state, and I manage Kings Custom Bikes.

Walking in the tattoo shop, I see him working on some chick's hip.

Looking up, he gives me a chin lift. "Be with you in a minute, brother."

"No problem, man," I say, taking a seat in one of the chairs in the waiting area by the front door.

When Gabriel is done, he walks the girl over to the reception desk so she can pay.

I look over and notice the chick eye-fucking me as she licks her lips. She's a hot little piece—blonde hair, tight little body, and big tits.

As she walks past me to leave, she hands me a piece of paper with her number on it. Looking up from the paper in my hand, I see Gabriel grinning at me.

"What?"

"Man, get your ass in the fuckin' chair."

Standing, I slip the paper in my pocket. "That was a hot piece that just left, man."

"She's alright. I fucked her a few months back."

"No, shit?"

"Yeah, man. That pussy's loose as fuck, and the bitch is too damn clingy. Don't bother."

Fuckin' figures.

Gabriel is about to start on my arm, but my phone rings. Pulling it from my pocket, I see it's Jake. Swiping the screen, I answer, "What's up, Prez?"

"Where are you at?" he barks.

"I'm with Gabriel, why? What's up?"

"You two get your asses to the club now, and come straight to the basement," he spits out before hanging up.

Standing up, I look at Gabriel. "Sounds like there's a situation."

We lock up the shop before climbing on our bikes, and make our way to the clubhouse.

Fifteen minutes later, we're walking down the basement stairs. We see one of the prospects guarding the door. He gives a chin lift and lets us by. Opening the door, I see a man tied to a chair. Jake is sitting in another chair directly in front of our tied-up friend, and Quinn is leaning against the wall at the other end of the room.

"Hey, Prez. Who do we have here?"

"Caught this motherfucker snooping around our warehouse. Prospect found him trying to break in through the back door. Knocked his ass out and called me."

"Is he talking?" I ask.

"Nope, doesn't seem to speak any English."

Our eyes cut over to Gabriel. This is where he comes in.

Jake stands up, moving his chair out of the way, as Gabriel steps in front of the idiot who had the nerve to fuck around on our property. "Nombre? *Name*?" Gabriel asks him. The man spits at his feet, earning him a punch to the mouth, splitting his bottom lip. "Nombre?" he asks his name again.

"No te estoy diciendo mierda. *I'm not telling you shit*," the man spits out.

"String him up!" Jake orders.

Quinn pushes off the wall, walking over to help me. There is a large wood beam that spans the entire length of the basement about ten feet off the floor. Grabbing some rope, I toss it over the beam while Quinn grabs the now struggling man. I thread the rope through his already tied hands and walk behind him to pull until his feet barely touch the floor. Then I wrap my end of the rope around an anchor bolted to the floor.

Visibly shaking, our nameless friend is starting to realize he's fucked with the wrong club. Gabriel comes back over after removing his cut and t-shirt. This pussy looks like he's about to piss his pants.

Suddenly, the man shouts. "Mi Nombre es Manuel, por favor. *Please, my name is Manuel.*" He starts talking in rapid-fire Spanish, back and forth with Gabriel.

"He says, Los Demonios sent him. They found out where our warehouse is, and Manuel here was supposed to call them once he broke in. They promised him a cut if he did it."

"Those mother-fuckin' cocksuckers think they can steal from us?!" Prez roars.

We buy guns from the Russians and store them in our warehouse across town. Then every few months, we run them to the Canadian border, selling them to a couple of low-level Asian street gangs. That's how the club makes a good chunk of its money.

Now we've got Los Demonios sniffing around our dealings. Jake looks over to Gabriel, giving him the signal.

"We can't let him live. You fuck with the club, and there are no second chances. Make an example of him."

With a nod, Gabriel reveals the knife he carries at his side, and in one swift move, slits Manuel's throat. We stand there and watch the life drain from his face.

"I want his body dumped at those sons of bitches' compound. Let this be an example as to what happens when you fuck with The Kings," Jake rages.

"Quinn, get the prospects here to clean this shit up. Gabriel, you're with me. Let's get this shit done," I bark.

An hour later, we approach the Los Demonios clubhouse after loading Manuel's body in the back of the van. It looks like there's a party. We can hear loud music, and a few people are strolling around outside. It doesn't look like they have anyone at the front gate—stupid fucks.

We pull right up, and no one even notices. I jump out and go around to the back of the van, opening the door. Gabriel comes up beside me, and together we drag the body out. We drop him to the ground, leaving him there.

Hearing a commotion, we turn to see men running from inside the clubhouse toward the front gate, guns drawn.

Stepping on the gas, we haul ass before they can get close enough. Once they see our little present, they will know exactly who they fucked with.

Game on motherfuckers.

I need to swing by the warehouse to check the fence that borders the property. I need to know where that bastard could have gotten through. I fire off a text to Prez, letting him know what Gabriel and I are doing.

I walk up to the front of the warehouse and see Austin, the prospect that caught that piece of shit.

"Hey, kid. Good job tonight," I say, slapping him on the back.

"Thanks, Logan. Just glad I caught him."

"Alright, man. Gabriel and I are going to walk the fence line to see if we can spot where he slipped through."

Starting at the west end of the property, I walk along the fence, and about seventy-five feet in, I see it.

Son of a bitch.

There's a big, gaping hole in the fence, and the cutters lying on the ground. That fuckin' idiot even left the damn evidence. Why in the fuck didn't the sensors get tripped? That's something I'm going to have to talk to Reid about. He keeps all our technical shit on the up and up.

The hole in the fence is an easy enough fix, so I put the prospect on it while we finish the grounds check.

After finishing up at the warehouse, Gabriel and I make our way back to the clubhouse.

I'm tired as fuck and need a drink. Walking in, I head straight for the bar. With the prospects at the warehouse and front gate tonight, Liz, one of the club girls, is behind the bar.

"Give me a beer and a shot of whiskey," I tell her, taking a seat on the stool next to Jake.

"Got everything sorted out?"

"Yeah, Prez, it's done," I confirm before downing my shot.

"I had a feeling those damn Mexicans were going to give us trouble when they moved their piece of shit club to Dixon."

"Well, now they know what they are dealing with when fuckin' with The Kings."

Jake stands after he finishes his beer and raps his knuckles on the bar, "I'm going home."

"Take it easy, Prez. I'll see you in the morning."

No sooner do I get those words out of my mouth, I hear, *POP, POP, POP.*

Windows shatter in a spray of bullets, and everybody hits the floor.

I reach into my cut and grab my gun. Looking around, I see Jake and Gabriel crouched under a broken window, rapidly returning fire.

I hear screaming coming from over by the hall and see Cassie, another one of the club girls, standing there.

"Get the fuck down!" I holler at the stupid bitch.

She drops down and crawls behind the bar with Liz. Over by the pool tables, I see Bennett lying on top of Lisa, shielding her from the bullets.

Moments later, everything goes silent.

I pick myself up off the floor and run to the front door, opening it just in time to see two cars race down the street away from the clubhouse.

I look to my right and see Gabriel standing there with murder in his eyes.

"How the hell did those cocksuckers get the drop on us? Isn't there a prospect at the goddamn gate?" I roar.

All eyes look toward the gate and see a shadowy figure lying on the ground.

"Shit!"

I take off running.

Blake looks to have been shot. "Fuck, someone get Doc."

Bennett crouches down next to Blake, looking at his wound. "Let's get him inside, now," he demands.

Reid races over to help carry him into the clubhouse, and we lay him on one of the pool tables as Bennett comes in with his medic bag. He cuts the prospect's shirt off to get a better look at what he is dealing with.

"It's his shoulder. It looks to be a clean shot. He took a pretty good blow to the head, knocking him out," Bennett states. "The kid's going to be fine, possibly a mild concussion, but won't know until he wakes up."

I release a breath I didn't know I was holding.

Looking around at all my brothers, I feel relieved they are all okay, but as I gaze around, I realize I don't see Gabriel.

I turn to Jake. "Prez?"

He looks over at me.

"We need to go after Gabriel."

Understanding, we rush outside and mount our bikes, and peel out of the compound in the direction of Dixon.

We only get about two miles down the road when I see his bike off to the side in the ditch, along with one of the cars I saw speeding away from our clubhouse earlier.

Jake and I jump from our bikes at the same time.

Gabriel is standing there with his knife in hand and breathing hard. On the ground in front of him are two dead Demonios.

Not knowing where my brother's head is, Jake and I wait him out.

I haven't seen Gabriel lose control and rage out like this in some time. It's best to wait and let him come back on his own.

We watch as he slowly turns around. He looks from Jake to me, giving a chin lift. "Prez. Logan," then proceeds to get on his bike and heads back home.

"That is one crazy-ass motherfucker," I murmur.

Jake and I are both silent a moment before turning around to assess the big-ass mess Gabriel left here on the side of the road.

"I'll call some brothers to come to clean this shit up before the cops show," Prez announces.

It's after three in the morning when I return to the clubhouse completely exhausted. The glass has been cleaned up, and the windows boarded. Besides a couple of people lingering around, it's pretty quiet. I decide to stop by Blake's room to check on him.

I owe it to him to show my gratitude. Opening his door, I see Lisa sitting in a chair next to his bed.

I'm not surprised to see her here. She's always taking care of us.

"How's the kid doing?" I ask.

"Bennett gave him something for the pain, so I'm sure he'll be out for a while. He's okay, Logan. Go get some rest, sweetie."

"Thanks, Lisa."

I finally make it to my room. The only thing I want right now is a shower, then bed.

I am standing under the spray of hot water, trying to relax my tense shoulders. It's been one hell of a fuckin' day.

After I dry off, I climb into bed. I lay here with my thoughts going a mile a minute. I can't help but worry about what's to come next.

I reach over into my nightstand, pull out a joint, and light it up. After taking a few tokes, I'm able to relax. The only thing that puts my mind at ease right now is knowing that, no matter what happens tomorrow with this shit-storm, my brothers always have my back.

4

BELLA

"Bella?" I hear my sister's voice as I open my eyes. "Wake up. It's 7:30 am. I missed the bus, and I can't get Mom to answer her door and take me to school."

"Shit," I fuss as I jump out of bed. "I'm supposed to be at work at eight this morning to help open."

I fly around the room, throwing anything on. I'm pulling on a pair of black leggings when Alba murmurs, "Sorry, Bella."

"It's okay. It's not your fault; I overslept." I reach into the closet, yanking a purple tunic off the hanger. "Meet me at the car. I'll be there in a minute."

She heads out of the room as I'm slipping on my black flats.

As I go past my mom's bedroom, I stop and knock on the door. She doesn't answer, so I open the door and walk into the room. I find her with her legs curled under her, staring at nothing.

"Mom? You okay?"

She turns her head, looking up at me. I can see a welt the same size and shape as a handprint across her cheek, and I gasp.

"What the hell, Mom? That fucker hit you?"

She doesn't say anything. She gets up, kisses my cheek, and walks out of the room.

"Mom, you can't let him do this to you. It's not right!" I plead with her as I follow her to the living room.

Grabbing her by the shoulders, I make her look at me. "Mom, I need to run Alba to school, she missed the bus. On top of that, I'm going to be late for work. Promise me you'll call the police if Lee comes back."

Her eyes glaze over with unshed tears, but I don't get a response from her.

I lean forward and hug her. "I love you, Mom. You deserve better."

I hate leaving her alone like this.

"I promise. I'll call the police if he shows up," she quietly whispers.

"Call me if you need to, okay?"

I watch her slowly nod her head before I turn to leave.

I make a quick walkthrough of the house. Lee is nowhere to be found, so I head out the front door but notice his truck is still in the driveway.

"Bella, I really am sorry," my sister whispers as I climb in my car.

"It's okay. None of this is your fault. I'll write your excuse and sign for Mom. She wasn't feeling well, that's why you couldn't get her to answer her door earlier," I lie.

Once I've dropped her off at school, I continue toward downtown to the grocery store. I'm thirty-five minutes late already, and I just realized I should have called my boss, Travis, to let him know I'm on my way.

I go to dig my phone out of my purse and realize I don't have it. I left it sitting on my nightstand at home.

I hear a loud pop before the car pulls hard to the right. I managed to swerve off to the shoulder of the road. I cut off

Undaunted

the engine and get out to see what has happened. Great, a flat tire.

"Fuck my life," I mumble.

As I'm trying to get the tire out of the trunk, I hear the rumble of a motorcycle behind me. The guy pulls up, puts the kickstand down, and climbs off his bike.

He's wearing aviator glasses and has sandy blonde hair. When he gets a little closer, I can see the cut he has on. It reads SGT AT ARMS, on the top right.

"Darlin', that tire looks bigger than you are. Let me help you."

"Thanks, that would be great." He carries the tire around to the front, leaning it up against the car.

"The name's Quinn."

"Bella," I say as I reach out to shake his hand.

"Well, Bella. Let me get your tire iron and jack from the back. I'll get you fixed up."

I watch him swagger back to the trunk of my car. "Feel free to check out my ass, pretty girl," he says, making me smile.

Quinn brings everything needed to change the tire and gets to work. Me? I am just hoping like hell I do not lose my job today.

"Hey, darlin'?"

I look down at him as he kneeled, pulling my flat tire off.

"You sure have yourself a fine car, or at least with some lovin', it will be. A '68?"

I look at my car. It's an Acapulco Blue 1968 Ford Mustang automatic. I saw this car sitting out in front of the Pull-a-Part junkyard and stopped in one day to ask about it. For more than a year, I paid old man Roy every week. I also helped clean his office and sort his files from time to time. In return, he held on to this beauty until I could pay it off. After my last birthday, I stopped by to give him my payment for the month. He handed me the key, saying, 'consider it paid.' I only got to visit a couple of times after that day before learning that he died from a heart attack in his sleep. The sweetest old man I'd ever met. Thanks to him, I have this car.

"Yeah, '68. She may not look like much and runs like shit, but when I can do more, she'll be beautiful."

I smile just thinking about cruising the mountain roads with the top down on it.

"How did you luck out and find her? I haven't seen any good classics around this area in a while. I have a GT Fastback of my own."

"A nice old man helped me out."

I lean against the car and watch Quinn finish tightening the lugs on the spare when some clouds start to roll in.

"Looks like I finished just in time. A storm is heading our way," he says, walking to the trunk, placing the flat tire and tools back in, and closing it.

"Thank you, Quinn. I would still be trying to change that thing if you hadn't come along."

He wipes his hands on a bandanna that he pulled from his back pocket. "Hell, my pleasure, darlin'. That spare will not last you long, though. You come by the shop, and I'll hook you up with a new tire, and maybe look under that hood while we're at it."

I look at him, contemplating his offer, which must show all over my face. He reaches in his back pocket, pulls out his wallet, and hands me a card.

KINGS CUSTOM BIKES is printed in bold black ink with a skull wearing a crown and wings in the background.

"I work there, just a few blocks down the road. You come by soon and ask for me. I'll take care of you. Okay?"

"Okay. I think I'll do that. Thanks again, Quinn."

"Not a problem. It was good to meet you, Bella. I'll see you around, darlin'."

I watch as he mounts his bike, pulls his aviators over his eyes, fires up the engine, and cruises down the road.

Undaunted

It doesn't take me long to get to the store.

"Shit. I'm so late," I grumble as I pull into the parking lot. I hope that Travis will understand why.

He isn't exactly a good guy. My boss can be a creep. Always staring at me and finding little ways to touch me.

Mila, one of my good friends, who also works at the store, sees me walking in and calls me over.

"Bella, where have you been?"

I sigh. "Everything has gone wrong this morning, Mila. Long story. I'll tell you at lunch."

Mila chews her lip before informing me, "Listen. Travis is looking for you. He said if we see you, tell you to head straight to his office."

"Thanks, I'll catch up with you later."

Standing outside his office door, I'm about to knock when Travis comes barging out, almost knocking me to the floor.

"Ah, so you finally decided to show up," he sneers at me.

"Travis, I'm sorry. I had some family stuff come up, and I got a flat on the way here too."

Putting his hand up, he cuts me off. "Bella, if you don't mind, I'm about to break for a smoke, step outside with me so we can discuss this."

I follow Travis through the door that leads to the alleyway between the grocery store and the bakery, preparing myself for a lecture.

He lights up his cigarette and blows the smoke out, "I can't have you being late, Bella. You've been working here for over a year now, and you've been late many times."

"Travis, I can explain—"

Interrupting me again, he says, "I don't need to hear another excuse. You're replaceable Bella, just like the rest of them in there."

"Please, Travis. I need this job. I promise not to be late again."

Blowing smoke in my direction before dropping the cigarette

to the ground, Travis reaches forward and places his hands on my shoulders. When he touches me, I instantly feel uneasy.

"I can overlook this and not write you up if we can come to some sort of...arrangement to help you keep your job," he smiles, as his clammy hands run down my arm, completely catching me off guard.

"What?!"

His grip tightens a little. "Come on. Put that pretty mouth to use, and you can keep your job."

I jerk from his hold, "Don't touch me! I'm not putting my mouth anywhere on you!"

He grabs at my wrist as I try to pull away from him again.

"What the fuck is going on back here?" A deep voice booms from behind us, causing Travis to release his grip on me.

I turn toward the man walking in our direction. He's huge. Easily over six feet tall.

"You okay, sweetheart?" he asks me, not taking his eyes off Travis, who has backed up a few feet behind me.

Coward.

My boss speaks up. "Everything is fine here. I was firing an employee." The tone of his voice giving away how nervous he is.

"Didn't sound like you were firing her." The stranger accuses then turns to me; his eyes go soft for a moment.

I realize I'm crying as I feel the tears run down my face.

"Sweetheart, go on inside."

I look between him and my now ex-boss and decide not to question anything. I pull the door open and walk inside.

I walk back through to the front of the store, avoiding all the looks people are giving me. Mila has concern written all over her face but has a line of customers now. If it weren't for that, she would be over to me in a second. I'm sure I look a mess as I walk out the doors of the store and out into the parking lot to my car.

As soon as I unlock it and get in, I lose what little control I have left, letting the tears flow.

I had my boss proposition me in the back alley to keep my job, and now I'm unemployed. All I can think about is how I am going to take care of Alba and myself now.

Lost in my thoughts and self-pity, I hear a tapping on my car window. I look up to see the stranger that helped me out in the alleyway. I roll the window down, and he kneels to eye level. That's when I get a much better look at him. He has light brown hair peppered with gray, and a thick bushy beard that I'm pretty sure hasn't seen a razor in a long time.

But it's his eyes that make me feel at ease. His dark blue eyes are kind, a stark contrast to the rough look that the rest of him has.

"Name's Jake. I wanted to make sure you're okay, sweetheart."

I wipe my eyes and rub my hands down my pant legs. "I'm okay. Unemployed, but okay. Thanks for stepping in back there. I..." Sighing, I rein in my anxiety. "I don't know what I'm going to do now. I needed that job. I have a sister to care for."

"You didn't need a fucking job at a price he was asking, did you?" Jake gruffs out.

"No, I don't."

He looks at me a moment longer, then stands up and pulls something from his back pocket. He hands me a business card. Taking it from him, I look at it and realize it is the same card that Quinn the biker gave me this morning when he helped change my tire. KINGS CUSTOM BIKES.

I look up at him and notice he's wearing a cut with a patch that reads PRESIDENT.

This is the second biker that has helped me out today.

"Listen, I'm kind of in need of front desk help at my shop. I do not promise anything, but I'm willing to give you a chance. So, if you can be here," he points to the address on the card, "first thing Monday morning, then I'll take you on and see how you do."

I'm at a loss for words for a second before clearing the cloud from my brain.

"Yes! I'll be there. Just tell me what time."

"9:00 am."

With that, he walks off toward the bakery next door.

5

LOGAN

We have been cruising the streets day and night, looking for any sign of Los Demonios. Those fuckers have caused significant headaches for all of us in the past few days. We've got a run coming up soon. I don't want them to cause any issues, which is why we've all been working twice as hard to flush them out. On top of that, the men are tired. Everyone has been on watch duty.

When I got to the shop, dragging my tired ass behind me this morning, I decided to approach Jake and ask him to let the brothers unwind at the clubhouse tonight. He agreed everyone needed to let loose, so the prospects have first watch along with a couple of others who volunteered.

It's been a long-ass week, and all I want is some whiskey in my veins and my cock in some pussy, and that's exactly what I get when I ride out to my club's compound, and the party is already in full force.

WAKING THE NEXT MORNING, I see the sun is just beginning to come through the window in my room. I roll over to the side of my bed in search of my pants to retrieve my phone. Seeing it's only 6:30 am, I've got plenty of time for a shower. When I go to get out of bed, I feel an arm snake around my waist. Jerking my head over, I look behind me and see Cassie.

"Come back to bed, baby."

"What the fuck you still doing here?"

"I fell asleep," she purrs.

"You know the fuckin' rules, Cassie. Get the fuck out."

I get out of bed and head to the bathroom. "I want you gone by the time I get out."

After I've showered away the smell of cheap perfume and booze, I walk out of the bathroom and notice Cassie has left. Bitch is starting to get too fuckin' clingy. It looks like I may need to find some new pussy.

Sometimes women come here and think becoming one of our club girls is their way into becoming an old lady. They soon realize that it's not going to happen. Some of them even go as far as trying to get pregnant, lying about birth control, and poking holes in condoms. I don't play that shit. I'm not looking for an old lady, and the last thing I need is a kid.

After getting dressed and pulling on my cut, I head out into the main room that houses our bar, several pool tables, a few couches, and a small stage that we use for various forms of entertainment.

I see Austin behind the bar putting on a couple of pots of coffee. As a prospect, he has the displeasure of having to be up early to tend to the brothers and clean up from the party the night before.

I see a few of my brothers sitting around drinking their coffee before they too head to work. Gabriel is sitting in his usual chair in the corner of the room, where he can see everything going on around him.

Undaunted

I grab a cup of coffee and take it outside. I need some fresh air. I walk over to one of the picnic tables sitting out front and sit by myself for a bit before heading into work.

Walking into work, I see Quinn is already here.

"Morning," he says.

"How's it going, man? Jake here yet?"

"Yeah, in his office."

I make my way to the back where his office is. Seeing his door already open, I walk in.

"Mornin', Logan."

"Hey, Prez. I need you to order a filter intake kit and some shocks for that Dyna that was brought in yesterday."

"Sure, I'll put the order in today."

"Thanks, Jake."

I turn to leave, but he stops me. "Logan."

I turn back to face him.

"I hired someone to work the front desk. She'll be here on Monday morning."

Confused, I ask, "What for? We've never had anyone work the front."

"We do now."

"Okay, Prez," I say, shrugging my shoulders. I'm not going to question his intentions on this. I know Jake, and if he has hired someone to work here, it's not without reason.

Walking back out into the bay area of the garage, I see Quinn under the hood of a Nissan. We are a custom bike shop, but being the only local garage, we also offer basic services such as oil changes and car repairs.

"Jake tell you about the new hire? I for one, think it's a great idea. I need something besides your ugly fuckin' mug to look at all day." Quinn snickers.

"Shut the fuck up and get to work, asshole."

"What's up your ass this morning? Would it have anything to

do with Cassie leaving your room this morning, looking like she wanted to murder someone?"

"The bitch is starting to get clingy, and she needed to be put back in her place."

"Yeah, man...a bit of advice. You need to watch that one. She's got her sights set on you, brother, and these women will do some crazy shit to get a brother to claim them. Club girls are some fuckin' shady bitches," he says before getting back to working on the Nissan.

AFTER GETTING OFF WORK, I decide I'm not in the mood to go to the clubhouse tonight. I want some fucking peace and quiet. Some of the brothers like to drink and party to unwind. Not me though. I need quiet so that I can think and get my head on straight. Coming home, I realize I have nothing to eat, so before going to the store, I grab a quick shower. When I'm done, I pull on my cut and grab my truck keys.

In the store, I make my way down each aisle, grabbing all the shit I need. Standing in the checkout, I notice the chick in front of me.

Standing there with her back to me, I let my eyes roam over her body. She has dark brown wavy hair and can't be more than five-foot-two. My eyes drift further south until I stop, getting a good look at her ass. Fuck, she's small but curvy.

The blonde girl standing beside her, notices me openly checking out her friend and elbows her. When she turns around, the most beautiful hazel eyes, framed by long dark lashes, lock on mine. Suddenly I feel like I've been punched in the stomach. Fuckin' gorgeous.

I watch her eyes appraise me, taking in every inch. When her

Undaunted

eyes meet mine again, I see a flash of desire, liking what she was looking at.

I give her a knowing smile, before I drop my eyes to her cleavage, taking in the rest of her.

Her cheeks turn red, and she quickly turns back around.

While I'm loading my stuff in the back of my truck, my mind is still on the hazel-eyed beauty. My cock goes half hard just thinking about those perfect fuckin' lips, and how they would taste. It's been years since a woman has grabbed hold of my attention like this. Not since that bitch Stephanie, and even she didn't affect me this way. No, the beauty in the store knocked me on my ass with one look.

Being a grown man, I now realize what I had with Stephanie wasn't true love. What hurt the most about losing her wasn't about losing love; it was about the betrayal.

Pushing those thoughts away, I climb in my truck and make my way home.

That night as I'm lying in bed, I can't get my mind off the girl from the store. Fuck, what is it about her?

A two-minute encounter, and she is already under my skin. I should be kicking my ass for not getting her number. Truth be told, it's for the best. I refuse to let another woman in, giving her the power to destroy me. And I have no doubt this woman would slay me.

Closing my eyes, I imagine her on her knees, her perfect fuckin' lips wrapped around my cock.

Reaching into my boxers, I wrap my hand around my cock and began stroking myself. I imagine her hair wrapped around my fist as those big, lust-filled eyes look up at me while she takes me to the back of her throat.

It doesn't take long before I'm growling out my release. Fuck, I can't even remember the last time I came so hard.

After taking a moment to get my breathing under control, I get up and make my way to the bathroom to clean myself up.

Going back to my bed, I sit on the edge, and run my hands through my hair while staring out my window, and watch the wind stir the lake waters.

What the hell is wrong with me? I've never had a woman affect me like this. All it took was one look, and now look at me, fuckin' jerking off like some goddamn teenager.

Lying down in my bed, I look over at the clock and notice it's after midnight already. Shit, I've got to be at work early tomorrow to finish up that bike. I need to get my head straight. The last thing I need is to be distracted by some woman. Tomorrow I'll get me some new pussy and forget all about this chick.

When my eyes become heavy and sleep finally takes me, visions of hazel eyes are the last thing I remember.

THE NEXT MORNING, I step out on my porch with a cup of coffee and breathe in the fresh morning air. The sun is just starting to come up, painting the sky in a mixture of purple and orange, casting its reflection on the lake.

Buying my house was the best investment I ever made. I saved for years while living at the clubhouse, and as soon as I had enough, I jumped at the chance to get a place to myself out here.

When you live the kind of life I do, you need a quiet place like this to come home to. My home is my sanctuary, and I won't share it with just anyone. One day I'll have someone to share all this with. At that thought, visions of a brown-haired angel come to mind. *Angel*. That's what she looked like, with her big expressive eyes and full lips.

Sighing, I push those thoughts from my mind and head inside to get ready for work.

Undaunted

Pulling up at the garage, I park in my usual spot. Walking through the bay doors, I can hear female laughter. I stop in my tracks when I see the dark-haired beauty from the store standing beside Quinn.

6

BELLA

My sister and I stop by the store on the way home after picking her up from school to grab something for dinner. When we make it the checkout line, I notice Mila is working the register.

"Hey, Bella. Where have you been? I sent you a few texts. I haven't seen or heard from you since last week. I've been worried about you."

I'm such a lousy friend. I know I should have texted her back, but I didn't feel like explaining anything to her over the phone.

"I'm sorry, Mila. I should have at least told you I was okay."

Mila is a good friend. She listens without judgment and knows what it's like to bear so much responsibility. My situation isn't exactly like hers. She's a single mom of a beautiful three-year-old girl. She lost the father of her child in a tragic accident before her daughter was born and took care of her grandma, who has Alzheimer's. She's a strong woman. We confide and lean on each other for moral support.

"I'm glad you're okay. Everyone found out what happened the other day. Travis deserved that black eye he got."

Black eye? I'm just about to ask her what the hell she's talking about when I'm interrupted by my sister.

Elbowing me, she lightly whispers, "Bella, there's a fine guy behind us, checking you out."

I turn to look behind me, and he has his eyes glued to my ass. The first thing I notice is the cut he's wearing. The patch reads VICE PRESIDENT. The guy is tall, at least six-foot-two, closely cropped brown hair with just the right amount of stubble on his face. Checking the rest of him out briefly, I see he's built and toned in all the right places. I study the colorful array of tattoos that cover most of his arms.

My breath falters for a moment when our eyes meet: one blue eye and one green. I let my eyes travel down to his mouth, which happens to be turned up into a cocky grin. Slightly embarrassed, I give him a small smile then turn around to pay for my things.

"You have my number. Let's meet for coffee next week," I say, smiling warmly at Mila.

She smiles back. "Great, I'd like that."

As my sister and I walk out of the store, I can still feel the biker's eyes on me.

On the drive home, I can't stop thinking about the man from the store. I've never seen eyes with such intensity.

"Bella, that guy was hot."

"Practical Magic."

"What?" Alba says as she reaches for the bag of chips in the back seat.

"You know? My favorite movie. Practical Magic? Where the little girl casts the spell for her perfect man?" I glance toward my sister, waiting for it to click. "In the movie, she wished for him to have one blue eye and one green eye."

"Okay," she says slowly. "I still don't see what that has to do with anything?"

"The guy at the grocery store. He had one blue eye and one green eye."

My sister gives me a look when it finally dawns on her. Smiling, she comments, "It's fate."

The rest of the ride home, I can't stop thinking about the biker. I can't say I'm a believer in fate, but I can say I'm a dreamer. Maybe both beliefs aren't so different.

When we get home, my sister and I spend the rest of the night hanging out and stuffing our faces with junk food while binge-watching Golden Girls. I also insist on watching Practical Magic before finally making myself go to sleep because tomorrow is my first day at my new job.

THE NEXT MORNING, I pull into Kings Custom Bikes, which is ran by the local MC. Jake said to be here by 9:00 am if I wanted the job, so I made sure I would be here a little early.

Most people would call me crazy for taking a job offer from the local MC. Everyone in town is aware of some of the activities that the MC partakes in, me included, but people turn a blind eye for the most part. Even our local police seem to brush most of the activities they hear about under the rug.

Sitting in my car, I notice that one of the bay doors is open. I see a guy working on a bike, so I step out of my car and throw my purse over my shoulder. I walk across the parking lot and head in his direction. The guy looks up when he hears my boots crunching on the gravel. I instantly recognize him from last Friday morning and smile.

He stops what he's doing and smiles too. "Well, hey there, darlin'. You come by to let me replace that spare tire?" He stands up and starts cleaning off his hands with a rag then shoves it back into his pocket.

Undaunted

"I'm here to start my first day of work."

He cocks his head to the side "Well, damn. You're the newbie Jake told us about last week. About time we get something pretty to look at around here. Well, no one will be showing up for another forty-five minutes or so. Most days we open at 9:00 am, but this morning we won't be opening until 10:00 am. Got some club shit that needed taking care of. In the meantime, why don't you let me look at that beautiful car you have over there? I'd like to see what you have going on under the hood."

"I'd like that. Thanks," I tell him as we make our way back over to my car.

He lifts the hood. "Doesn't look too bad. I can see some hoses need replacing, and your radiator cap looks half-ass broke." He walks around, trying to get a closer look. "I'd like to start her up, maybe take her for a spin to hear what she sounds like."

Quinn is showing me how the motor's chassis is a bit rusty and starts laughing at the fact that I'm having to climb up to look inside to see where he is pointing to.

"I want to help. That is if you would be willing to teach me?" I ask him while climbing back down off the bumper of the car.

"Seriously? Never known a woman to get herself dirty under the hood of a car." He looks at me skeptically.

"I like being able to do things for myself. I can handle it." I sass him, putting my hands on my hips and cocking my head.

Wearing a big ass smile, Quinn chuckles. "You won't be getting any complaints out of me. Shit yeah. If you want to get your hands dirty, that's fine by me." He shakes his head, laughing, "Can't believe I just agreed to get dirty with a pretty ass thing like you, and it doesn't even involve getting my dick wet."

I laugh along with him. I'm going to like Quinn. He's easy to be around and makes me laugh.

About that time, Quinn looks over my shoulder, and I turn around to see what has caught his attention.

I watch as a bike pulls into the parking lot. The man parks, gets off his bike and walks in our direction. As he gets closer, he pulls off his shades. My eyes connect with the guy from the grocery store. The one that I couldn't stop thinking about last night.

My pulse is racing, and it feels as if my heart is about to come out of my chest. My sister's mention of fate comes to mind. Quinn walks up, greeting him.

"Hey, brother. Come on over here and meet this pretty thing who happens to be the new hire Jake told us about."

"Logan, this is Bella. Bella, this is Logan. He manages the garage."

"Nice to meet you, Logan."

Logan, who still hasn't taken his eyes off me, reaches out his hand, and I offer mine. A jolt of energy surges through every fiber of my skin like static electricity as soon as we touch.

Quinn clears his throat. Only then does Logan release my hand. The loss of his touch has my body instantly craving more.

What is wrong with me? I don't even know this guy.

"Bella, how about I give you the grand tour while Logan here figures out how to use his words."

I look from him then back to Logan.

He goes to place his hand on my lower back to lead me through the bay door when Logan barks out. "I've got this, brother. Why don't you go open the rest of the bays? The other guys will be here in fifteen."

"You got it," Quinn offers, then walks off.

I'm left standing alone with Logan.

"Alright, Angel. Why don't we look around and get you situated before the guys show up?" I feel a small flutter in my stomach at his endearment.

He places his hand on the small of my back and leads me through the garage into the central part of the building. Stepping inside, I take in my surroundings. Nothing unusual about the

Undaunted

place. It looks like your typical mechanic shop. Posters of custom bikes of assorted styles are hanging on the deep red walls, and the shelves are all silver diamond-cut metal.

"Over there," he points to the counter by the window, "is where you'll work most of the day. Whenever a customer comes in, you'll greet them and find out what they need. Unless they're here to settle a final bill, you'll have to ask them to wait, then send for one of us out in the garage. Okay?"

I nod as he leads me down a short hallway and opens the first door to the right.

"This is where we keep all our customer files and invoices along with the printer and fax machine." Guiding me back out into the hallway again, he shows me another door.

"This is Jake's office. If he's here, remember to always knock first before going in. Okay?"

"Always knock, got it," I smile. I'm trying hard to concentrate on everything he is telling me, but with his hand still making contact, I'm finding it hard to focus on anything else.

We walk back through the garage, to a door that's found on the far end.

"Through here is the break room if you'd like to use it."

I walk in and notice that it's a completely furnished room with a small kitchenette along with a small, round dining table. Off to the right is a large couch with a coffee table and a big ass TV hanging on the wall.

"This looks more like a small apartment," I tell him as I walk around. I look over my shoulder at Logan, who's leaning against the door frame with his arms crossed watching me.

"By chance, is there a soda machine or coffee anywhere? I could use some more caffeine this morning." He points to the counter next to the refrigerator.

"There's a coffee maker there, and we always keep water, soda, and beer in the refrigerator. The guys unwind after work sometimes back here, so you'll find that it's usually stocked."

I smile. It seems like a laid-back place.

"Well, I think I got a good feel of the place, but I would love to see Jake and speak with him for a moment when he gets here and thank him again for the job."

Logan reaches in the refrigerator, grabbing himself water and hands me a soda.

"He'll be here soon. Let him know what you like to drink and eat, and he'll make sure to stock it."

He leads me back out through the garage and back into the main building. I walk over to the front counter, setting my purse down behind it on a shelf, and then turn the computer screen on.

Leaning in over my shoulder, Logan points to the screen. "The system we use is pretty simple, but if you have any questions, Jake can answer them. I don't mess with this shit."

Logan continues to stand. He smells so good. His scent isn't overpowering. He smells simply of fresh, clean soap and leather.

"Where's the restroom?"

"You can use the one in the break room. It's the door to the left side of the TV," he informs me.

I move past him, lightly brushing my back against his front, and make my way to the bathroom. Once inside, I lean against the door and close my eyes while taking a deep breath.

Looking in the mirror, I give myself a mental pep talk. *Get yourself together, Bella.*

I walk back out front and notice Jake talking with Logan and a younger guy I haven't met yet.

Turning their attention toward me as I make my way to the counter, Jake speaks up first. "Hey, sweetheart. Glad to see ya. Heard Logan here showed you the ropes. Anything else you need to know, you ask me. There are donuts in the break room, help yourself."

Undaunted

"This here's Blake. Write down anything you might need for the break room, he'll go get it," Logan says, introducing Blake.

"I don't need anything special. Whatever is in there is fine."

"He's going either way, best to tell him or he'll pick up random chick food."

Most guys think all women want salads. This chick likes real food. I'll take pizza and burgers over veggies any day.

"Okay. Give me a second to write a few things down."

Once I'm through, I hand my small list to Blake.

The rest of the day goes by smoothly. I only had to bug someone once on a specific order. Quinn was the one to show me how to enter in all the specs.

Before closing, I make my way back to Jake's office. Knocking three times, I wait for him to answer.

"It's open," he barks, sounding irritated, so I slowly open the door peeking inside. He peers up from what he's looking at, and his features relax a bit when he notices it's me.

"You got a minute?" I question.

He leans back in his chair, rubbing his beard. "Sure, sweetheart. Come on in."

"Jake, I just wanted to thank you for giving me a chance with this job. You have no idea how much I needed it."

"You did good today. Keep on doing as you have been, and we're square."

I feel a little lighter after thanking him. I walk around and hug his neck. He tenses for just a moment but seems to relax. I make my way to the door, but he stops me.

"Bella, if you need something just let me or one of the guys know. It's dark outside, so no walking to your car alone. Got it?"

"Yeah, Jake. I'll let someone know I'm leaving."

He nods his approval, and I shut the door when I leave.

Logan is standing by the front counter when I come back out.

"Walking you to your car tonight," he states, unknowingly making my skin hum with his gravelly voice.

I grab my things from behind the counter before walking toward the door he's now holding open.

We make our way across the parking lot, and I unlock my car.

"Hand me your phone," Logan demands.

I look at him and raise an eyebrow, silently asking why. He has his hand held out, waiting for me to comply.

"Putting my number in your phone, beautiful. I want you to text me when you get home. Let me know you made it safe."

I should feel strange with his demand, but I don't, so I hand him my phone without hesitation.

There is no ignoring the spark that is felt when the tips of our fingers brush slightly as he hands my phone back. With a husky tone in his voice, Logan says, "Get in the car, Bella."

I get in and start the engine. He takes a few steps back as I pull out the lot and head home—the whole time, my pulse racing from being near him.

I make it home and pull into the driveway before I get out of the car I reach over into my purse and grab my phone. Pulling up Logan's number, I type out a text.

Me: *I'm home*

Logan quickly answers back.

Logan: *Goodnight, Angel*

7
LOGAN

Angel: I'm home
Me: Night Angel
Angel: Goodnight Logan

It's been two months since Bella started working at the garage, and each night ends with her text letting me know she's home. Though I've enjoyed getting to know her, it's hard as hell keeping our relationship on a friend level. Bella is not the kind of woman you take to bed, then forget. She's too fucking good, too sweet for me to treat her that way. The problem is, I can't seem to take any woman to my bed lately. My cock knows what it wants, and it's not club pussy. My heart and my head are playing tug of war with each other. My heart is telling me to take what I want, make Bella mine. My head is telling me to stay fucking clear and not to go down that road again. Am I a bastard for sometimes sending mixed signals? Hell yes. Do I care? Fuck no. I never said I wasn't a selfish man.

Smiling, I put my phone back in my pocket, and motion for the prospect to bring me another beer. I came to the clubhouse after work to have a few drinks with my brothers and to sort shit out with our run this weekend. Tensions have been high ever since Los Demonios were caught trying to break into our warehouse. Dealing with all this bullshit right now is another reason I'm keeping Bella at a distance. I can't risk anything happening to her.

I've just finished my third beer when Gabriel takes a seat next to me at the bar.

"Look, man. I've got to ask. We got this run tomorrow, and I want to make sure your head's in the right place after all the shit we've been dealing with lately."

"Yeah, brother. I'm straight," he answers, looking me dead in the eyes.

Satisfied with his reply, I stand up and take one last pull of my beer. Time to call it a night, so I head upstairs to my room and take a quick shower before laying my tired ass down for the night.

FUCK. I can't sleep. I've been lying here staring at the ceiling for the past couple of hours. I'm feeling too uneasy about the run we have coming up. Ever since Los Demonios moved their club into Dixon, they have kept to themselves. They're mostly into selling drugs and pussy, but as long as they don't bring their drugs to Polson, we don't give two shits about what they do. The Kings have an understanding with our local police. We help them keep Polson clean, and in return, they look the other way when it comes to our less than legal operations.

What has me pissed the fuck off is their sudden interest in our operations and why those pussies thought they could come into our territory and try to steal from The Kings.

I sit up on the edge of my bed. Sighing, I run my hand through my hair, deciding that if I can't sleep, I may as well take a shower and start my day.

After spending a good fifteen minutes under the spray of hot

Undaunted

water to relax my muscles, I dry off and pull on a pair of jeans, my boots, and a long-sleeve black Henley. I slide my cut on, lock up my room, and head to the kitchen.

I see Reid sitting at the table. Looking over, I notice a fresh pot of coffee sitting on the counter. I fix myself a cup before taking a seat across from him. We sit in silence for a moment before I speak.

"You still not sleeping?"

"You know how it is," he says, shrugging his shoulders.

"Yeah, brother. I do."

We've all got our demons keeping us up at night. My brother is struggling right now. Reid was in an accident almost four years ago, causing him to lose his leg, but that's not what he struggles with. He lost his little brother in that car accident. I lost one of my best friends. The whole club was devastated when Noah died.

Changing the subject, I ask, "Do you have today's route mapped out for us?"

Reid is the club's Road Captain, and he plans all our runs. We take a different route every time, making sure we stay off the police radar.

"Yep, we're all set, brother. Let's take a prospect with us today," he suggests. "You know, with all the shit that's going down, we could use the extra eyes."

"Let me run it by Prez."

Lisa comes walking in with Bennett, "Hey, boys. I'm going to make some breakfast. You hungry?"

"Hell yeah. You know we're not about to turn down your cookin'."

After I finish two helpings of eggs, bacon, and toast, I take my empty plate to the sink where Lisa is washing the dishes.

"Thanks, Lisa," I say, kissing her on the cheek.

"Anytime, sweetheart. You boys stay safe out there today."

I leave the kitchen and made my way down the hall toward Jake's office.

When I pass Cassie in the hall, I try to ignore her, but she reaches out, grabbing my arm to stop me.

"Hey, baby. I'm going to miss you," she purrs while running her hands up my chest. I take her wrist and move her hand off me.

"Not now, Cassie."

"Come on, Logan. Why don't you let me take care of you before you go?"

"Fuck, Cassie! Go find some other brother's cock to suck, that's what you're here for," I bark at her, completely fucking annoyed at the way she's been acting lately.

"You're acting this way because of that bitch, aren't you?"

"What the fuck you are you talking about?"

"I'm talking about that little bitch you work with."

Suddenly, I see red. In one swift movement, I wrap my hand around the bitch's throat and push her against the wall. Her eyes got big, shocked by my actions.

"Bella is none of your fuckin' business. You, Cassie, are a club girl, and your only business is laying on your back or getting on your knees. Is there any part of that you don't understand?"

After nodding her head quickly, I let her go.

"Now get the fuck out of here."

How does the bitch even know about Bella? She's probably been snooping around, pissed that I haven't touched her pussy in months.

Once she scurries away, I continue to Jake's office. I knock on his door before going in.

"Hey, Prez. Got a minute?"

"Sure, kid. What's up?"

"I was talking with Reid, and he suggested we take Austin with us today. With all this shit going down lately, I think it's a good idea."

Jake leans back in his chair, folding his arms over his chest, contemplating my request.

"Alright. Take the prospect. Call on the burner if there are any signs of trouble."

Leaving his office and walking into the common room, I see the prospect cleaning up from the night before. "Austin!" I holler from across the room. "Get your shit and be out front in five."

He doesn't say a word, just lifts his chin, and does what he's told. Making my way outside, I see Reid leaning against his bike smoking a cigarette. Looking around, I notice Quinn isn't here.

I turn to Reid. "You seen Quinn?"

He looks at me with his head cocked. "Do you need to ask? You saw the redhead he had hangin' all over him last night," he says with a grin.

Fuck no, I don't need to ask. I head back inside, going straight to the dipshit's room. I open the door without knocking, and sure as shit, he's banging the hell out of the redheaded bitch while wearing dreadlocks and an eye patch.

Shaking my head, I let out a sigh. "Hey, Johnny Depp. Wrap this shit up. We leave in five."

Quinn pulls out of the chick, not even bothering to cover himself, and slaps the girl on the ass. "You're fuckin' lucky I was finished, bro. There is no way in hell I was leaving this fine pussy and riding with a case of blue balls," he says as he walks over to the chair sitting by the bedroom door and starts pulling on his jeans.

Deciding I've seen enough, I tell him, "Don't forget to take off the dreads, brother."

I turn around and head back outside, leaving him to finish getting ready.

As I'm fishing a cigarette out of my cut, I look over and see Quinn mounting his bike. I can't help fuckin' laughing at him because the fucker is still wearing the eye patch.

He shrugs his shoulders and starts his bike.

Quinn is who he is and makes no apologies. We all like to bust his balls from time to time, but he knows he has no judgment from his brothers.

"Listen up," I raise my voice above the rumble of the engines, "you all know the shit we have going down with Los Demonios. We need to keep our eyes open today. Stay observant. They're some shady motherfuckers."

Our first stop is the warehouse to load the guns into the van I have the prospect driving. We usually would have three brothers on this run, that way things look less suspicious, but with the recent threat to the club, we have five men today.

Pulling up in front of the warehouse, I see a couple of our guys sitting outside.

"Alright. Let's get this shit loaded. I want to be back on the road in an hour."

Forty-five minutes later, we're loaded and ready to roll when Gabriel pulls me aside.

"Just got a call from a friend in Dixon. He's doing me a favor by keeping an eye out for any Demonios today. He told me he saw about seven of their men riding through today in three trucks headed in this direction. My guess is they are about thirty minutes out. What's the plan?"

"We stay ahead of them. Plus, they don't know our route. We can't miss this delivery. We do, and then our buyers will be looking to take their business somewhere else. I'm not willing to risk it."

"I'm with you, brother," he says.

I motion to everyone as we prepare to head out. "Let's roll."

The plan is to meet up with the Asians in Eureka. We don't go all the way to the border because of checkpoints. That's their problem, not ours.

Two hours later, we make it to our agreed meeting place. Looking at my phone, I see we are about twenty minutes early.

Climbing off my bike, I decide to have a smoke while we wait.

Feeling irritated, I recheck the time. It's been forty-five minutes, and still, our buyers are a no show.

"I don't fuckin' like this. Something's off."

"Agreed, man," adds Reid.

"This shit reeks of Los Demonios."

Throwing my cigarette down, I grab the burner from my cut. "I'm going to call Prez. See what he wants to do."

I barely get those words out of my mouth when two trucks come flying up the dirt road. I reach into my cut for my gun.

"I wouldn't do that if I was you," a man, with a heavy Spanish accent, says. Taking my hand slowly out of my cut, I turn around to find a man with a gun to Quinn's head.

"Sorry, boss. Chaparro '*Shorty*' here, got me while I was taking a piss."

"Cállate cabrón, *Shut up asshole*," the man says, then clocks Quinn in the eye with the butt of his gun.

"Son of a bitch! That wasn't necessary, man," Quinn tells him while holding the side of his face.

"Now, here's what's going to happen. My men and I are taking those guns. If I see any of you reaching for your piece, you'll be going back home with one less gringo."

I motion for all my men to take it easy. I look specifically at Gabriel, and I can see the wild look in his eyes.

I shake my head at him.

Now is not the time for him to lose his shit.

Thirty minutes later, they have our guns loaded into their trucks, and it's taking everything I have not to put a bullet in the motherfucker's head, but I won't risk Quinn's life.

"You know you won't get away with this," I say, gritting my teeth.

"Fuck you puta, *bitch*," he laughs. "Looks to me like we are."

My men and I just watch those sons of bitches take our guns.

I'm about to call Jake when Quinn approaches me with anger and regret written all over his face.

"Look, Logan. This is all on me. I fucked up, brother."

"Damn straight. You fucked up. Had you been paying attention, that motherfucker wouldn't have gotten the drop on you."

Quinn hangs his head at my sharp words, but it needs to be said, and he knows it. Sighing, I tell him, "Shit, man. Regardless, it happened. At the end of the day, the most important thing is that we're all going home in one piece"

Back at the clubhouse, Jake calls emergency church. We need to figure out our next plan of action. Once we all make our way into the room and take our seats, Jake regards Quinn. "You okay, brother?"

He nods his head in response.

"Alright. Once Logan informed me of what happened, I called our buyer. It turns out they got a text telling them the meetup time had changed. That's why they were a no show."

"You believe him?" I ask.

"Yeah, I believe him. They've been dealing with us a couple of years now without incident, so I don't see them risking their business to start up any sort of a relationship with an unknown MC."

"So, what do we do?" This is coming from Reid.

"We wait for now," Jake says. "If we go in hot, letting our anger cloud our judgment, things will get sloppy. So, we play this smart. Let them think they're getting away with fucking us over. In the meantime, we contact the Russians. Let them in on what's going down. I have a feeling they're not going to take to kindly to Los Demonios fuckin' with their business. I know you don't like waiting, letting those pussies think they've won, but it is what's best. Are we all in agreement?" Jake asks.

With collective 'ayes' from all the brothers, Prez slams the gavel. "It's decided. We wait."

Undaunted

Walking out of church, I stride up next to Quinn and slap him on the back.

"Come on, man. Let's go grab a beer."

Some heavy shit went down today, and my brother is feeling the weight of it. Even though he fucked up, he needs to understand that what happened out there could have happened to any of us. Hell, we all fuck up from time-to-time, but at the end of the day, you suck it up and roll with it.

"Not tonight, brother. I'm going to go for a ride. Clear my head."

"Alright. I'll catch up with you tomorrow."

As he's walking away, I call out to him. "Hey, Quinn."

Turning, he looks back at me.

"You know you can call me if there's anything you need, man?"

"Yeah, brother. Thanks."

I take a seat at the bar next to Reid, "Quinn doing okay?" he asks.

"Yeah, just going to sort his shit out."

Quinn is known for cutting' up, cracking' jokes, and always fuckin' with one of us. Behind that humor is a man that is very passionate about his club. Seeing him so torn up about today doesn't surprise me. I know he'll be okay once he clears his head.

Needing a shot of whiskey, I turn my attention to who's behind the bar and see our prospect, Blake.

"What can I get you, Logan?"

"Give me two shots of whiskey and a beer, man."

Several shots and too many beers later, I decide to crash in my room. Too fucking tired and drunk to bother with a shower.

I strip off my clothes, put my piece on the nightstand, and climb into bed. Looking at the time, I see it's a little after one in the morning. I know Bella is asleep by now, but after the day I've had, I want to hear her voice.

Grabbing my phone off the table beside my bed, I find her

name in my contacts and press the call button. It rings four times before I hear her sleepy voice.

"Hello?"

I let out a deep sigh because this is precisely what I needed.

"Hey, beautiful."

"Logan, is everything okay?"

"Everything is fine, babe. I just wanted to hear your sweet voice and tell you goodnight."

With a raspy giggle, she says. "If you'd have waited a few hours, you could have told me good morning."

"Yeah, I guess you're right," I say, chuckling. "I'm going to let you get back to sleep. I'll see you at work on Monday. Goodnight, Angel."

"Goodnight, Logan."

8

BELLA

The weight of Logan's firm muscular body pressing against mine has my whole body buzzing. Pulling my hair to one side, his lips make their warm descent down the bottom of my neck and over my shoulder. The feel of his hands caressing my skin as they run over the curve of my hips has me desperately wanting more.

Rubbing my ass against his hard length, his cock slips between my legs, and he begins sliding the head of his cock along my wet folds. A whimper escapes my lips just before he thrust into me from behind. Reaching his hand around, he starts to work my clit rhythmically.

"You're gonna come for me, Bella," his words rasp in my ear, causing my skin to tingle. "I want to feel your tight pussy come all over my cock."

Beep, Beep, Beep, Beep.

Opening my eyes, I groan as I reach over to shut my alarm off. I blow out a frustrated breath. My body is still tingling, and my panties soaked. I've been waking up the same way for weeks now. Logan consumes my every waking thought, and now he's taken over my dreams as well. He still hasn't moved our relationship past being friends, even though he sometimes gives me the impression that he wants more. Of course, I'm too much of a chicken to make the first move.

Looking over, I see Alba's bed is empty, which is surprising because my sister is not an early riser. It's a struggle getting her butt up every morning.

Walking out of our room and into the hall, I stop in my tracks when I see Lee hovering by the bathroom door with his hand on the knob. My stomach clenches because I know Alba is in there.

Rushing over, I get right up in his face. "Get the hell away from that door."

"What? She's been in there awhile. I just wanted to make sure she's alright is all."

"You're disgusting," I seethe.

Lee's face goes red, "Your mouth is going to get you in trouble, little girl. I would watch it if I were you."

The bathroom door opens, and Alba lets out a startled yelp. "Bella, is everything okay?"

"Yeah, everything's fine. Come on," I say, grabbing her hand and leading her back to our room.

"Are you going to tell me what that was all about between you and Lee back there?"

"It's nothing for you to worry about."

After eyeing me for a second, she goes about getting ready for school.

A few hours later, I'm in the break room at work, making lunch for everyone. It's become my thing. Logan has even started eating with me every day unless he has club business.

I look forward to our time together, getting to know one another. We mostly talk about everyday things like when my sister and I moved to Montana and what high school I went to.

In return, he told me about growing up with the club and how much his brothers meant to him. I find myself so comfortable with Logan that I'm sitting here telling him about my father and the abuse my sister and I suffered as children.

My father is a subject I never talk about. The memories of beatings and verbal abuse are too much at times and can trigger panic attacks.

I'm stunned at Logan's reaction after telling him about my father. His body is vibrating with anger as he stands up from the table and starts pacing the break room, then he stops, turns, and punches a hole in the wall.

"Son of a bitch!" he roars.

I sit here a little confused by his actions. He must have taken my confused look for something else because he immediately drops to his knee in front of me.

"You have no reason to be afraid of me, babe. I would never hurt you."

"I know, I'm not scared of you. I don't understand why you're so upset."

"I'm upset because the thought of any man putting their hands on you—on a child—makes me want to kill the motherfucker."

"It was a long time ago, Logan. I'm fine now."

"Where is the piece of shit now?" he asks through clenched teeth.

"Dead. Died when I was six."

"Good," he says, before returning to his chair.

I jump, when Quinn's voice startles me from behind. "What's for lunch? Sorry, sweetheart. Didn't mean to scare you."

"It's okay," I chuckle. "I made meatball subs."

Wrapping up a couple and placing them in a sack, I hand them to Quinn. "You mind taking these across the street to Gabriel for me?"

"You got it, darlin'."

Hearing my phone ring, I pull it from my back pocket. I see it's

Mason calling...again. Sighing, I shake my head. This shit's getting ridiculous. You would think that after months of my not returning his texts or answering his calls that he would take a hint. He has been getting more persistent lately. It's like the more I ignore him, the harder he tries. He went from a text or call here and there to several a day. It was his last voicemail that had me a little concerned. He was calling me a tease and demanding I pick up the phone. Just thinking about our previous date sends chills down my spine.

"Everything okay, Bella?" Logan asks.

"Of course," I say, setting my phone on the table then bringing our plates over before sitting down. I'm about to take a bite out of my food when my phone chimes again—this time with a text. After setting my sandwich down on my plate, I go to grab my phone, but Logan beats me to it.

"What the hell, Logan? Give me my phone."

"What the fuck?" he hisses, totally ignoring me, "Who the fuck is Mason, and why in the hell is he demanding you call him back?"

"It's not any of your business. Now give me my phone back."

His face reddens, nostrils flare, and his hand grips my phone so hard I'm afraid he's going to crush it.

"When I see some motherfucker, with a pissant name like Mason, calling and texting your phone, it is my business, babe."

"Um...I'm pretty sure it's not," I snap back.

My phone chimes again, and from the murderous look on Logan's face, it's not good. Logan swipes his finger across the screen.

"Shit. Logan, please don't do that. Just leave it alone."

"Fuck no, Bella. I'm not ignoring this shit."

"Is this Mason? No, motherfucker, you can't talk to Bella. If you call her phone one more goddamn time, I will personally beat your fuckin' ass," he says, then hangs up. "I'm only going to ask you one more time, Bella. Who the fuck is Mason?"

What the hell has gotten into Logan? Since when has my personal life become his concern?

Giving up on trying to get my phone back, I slump down in my chair and let out a heavy sigh.

"He's a guy I went to school with. A few months ago, I saw him at the coffee shop in town, and he asked me out. I thought what the hell and agreed."

I look up and see Logan clenching his teeth. "We only went out a few times. I remember him being a decent guy in school. On our first couple of dates, he was nice and respectful, but it was on our third when he changed."

"Changed how?"

"Well, we went to dinner and then he was going to take me to a concert. He said a local band was playing at a bar in town, but he'd left the tickets at home. I didn't think anything of it at first. We drove to his house, and he invited me to come in for a minute, so I wasn't waiting in the car. Once we were inside his house, it was like a switch flipped. Suddenly, he was all over me. Mason was telling me it was time to give it up and quit being a tease. I was so scared. I didn't know what to do. He was strong and so much bigger than me. Somehow, I managed to knee him in his balls. When he went down, I ran out of the house. I kept running until I reached a gas station down the street. I called a cab to take me home. A few days later is when the calls and texts started, and he's been doing this for a couple of months," I tell him.

"I'm not a tease, Logan," I say, looking up at him, "I didn't do anything to lead him on."

"It's not your fault," he says, pulling me into him and holding me.

I lay my head on his chest, breathing in his scent, and it instantly calms me. A few minutes later, I lift my head and look up at him. Logan brings his hand up, cupping both sides of my face. He brings his face down closer to mine, and our eyes lock. My breath hitches, and my lips part. My heart feels like it's going to beat out of my chest. This is it. Logan is finally going to kiss me.

"You guys better have saved me some lunch," Quinn's loud voice echoes as he comes walking into the room, breaking the connection.

Seeing that he has just interrupted us, Quinn stops in his tracks. "Aww fuck, I sure got shitty timing. Well, don't let me stop you guys. Please continue."

That causes me to giggle, and Logan reluctantly releases his hold on me. "It's okay, Quinn."

"Fuck no, it's not," Logan growls.

Quinn, of course, ignores Logan and sits down with us, giving me a wink.

7:00 pm rolls around, so Logan and I are closing the garage down for the day since Quinn and Jake left about an hour ago. After filing the invoices for the day, all that's left to do is take the garbage out.

Walking out from behind the reception counter with my small bag of trash, I see Logan closing the bay doors.

"Hey, I'm taking the garbage out!" I yell over my shoulder.

"Give me a minute, and I'll do it."

"I got it."

"Babe, I said I'd get it. Just as soon as I get this broke-ass door closed," he grunts as he manually starts to pull down the second bay door.

"I'm capable of toting this small bag of trash by myself. I don't need you to carry it for me," I sass while admiring his backside and the way his muscle flexes as he pulls the garage door down.

"Woman—" I hear his fading voice say as I continue to finish the task at hand.

After grabbing the trash from the break room as well, I head to the back door. Opening it, I walk over to the garbage bin and toss both bags inside. As I turn to make my way back, I'm slammed up against the wall of the garage with so much force my breath gets knocked from my body.

Before I can get my bearings back, a hand covers my mouth, keeping me from making a sound.

"Did you think siccing your biker-boyfriend on me was going to scare me away, you little bitch?" Mason sneers only an inch from my face.

I start struggling to get out of his hold, but it's no use, so I do the only thing I can think of. I bite down as hard as I can on the hand that's covering my mouth, drawing blood.

"You fucking bitch!" he roars, right before backhanding me across my face, knocking me to the ground. A second later, he's on top of me, and his hands are everywhere.

I refuse to let this asshole do this to me, so I start fighting back with everything I have.

"Stop fucking fighting me, you stupid cunt!" Mason says right before I see him rear back. This time with a closed fist.

I close my eyes and brace myself for the punch, but it never comes.

9

LOGAN

"What the hell is taking that woman so long?" Checking my watch—it's been at least 5 minutes since I watched her walk toward the back door—I make my way to the back of the garage to check on her when I hear her scream through the door, "Get off me!"

What the fuck? My stomach clenches at the sound of her distress.

I start running toward the back door that leads to the alleyway. That's when I see Bella struggling with someone that has her pinned on the ground. His hand rears back, and he's about to punch her when I grab the fucker and pull him away from her, then slam him against the wall and watch his body crumple to the ground. Reaching down, I grab a handful of his hair, pulling his sorry ass up. I press him against the dumpster only to bury my fist into his face repeatedly until he can no longer stand on his own. My knuckles are cut from connecting with his teeth.

Letting him go, I walk over and kneel to help Bella to her feet. "Babe, you okay?" I ask as I'm looking her over. Her shirt is torn and hanging from her shoulder. When I make it to her face, I'm met with a red mark on her cheek, combined with tears running down her face.

I'll be damned if a man lays a hand on her while I'm breathing. Fueled by rage, I walk over to the little punk that's trying to get back up and give him a boot to the side of his bleeding head.

"I'm going to assume you're Mason. The little cocksucker who's been harassing Bella."

I stand him up and punch him in the ribs, causing him to groan in pain.

"Man, she's a fuckin' tease," he coughs out.

That earns him another fist to the face. Blood gushes from his nose as he falls to his knees.

"You broke my nose," he whines.

"I'm going to do more than break your fuckin' nose."

Bringing him to his feet, I slam him against the brick wall of the building, this time wrapping my hand firmly around his throat.

"Logan! Watch out!" Bella screams, just as Mason brings his hand up, slicing my arm with a knife.

Grabbing his wrist, I twist his hand back, making him drop the weapon, and I tighten my grip on his neck, causing his face to redden.

Reaching into my cut, I pull out my gun and press the tip of the barrel against his temple. "You're eaten up with stupid, aren't you, motherfucker?"

"Logan, he's not worth it! Just let him go!" Bella bellows.

I cock my gun, my adrenaline pumping. "This fucker put his hands on you. I'm not letting that go. Get inside, Bella."

She walks up and touches my arm. "Logan...look at me."

When I don't, she tries again. "Logan," she says calmly. "Please. He's not worth it."

How can anyone want to hurt her?

"I can't let this go, Angel."

She nods. "I know. But don't kill him. I'm more worried about what will happen to you. What if someone hears a gunshot and calls the police? I don't want you to get in trouble."

Shit. After getting mauled by this prick, the only person she's thinking of is me? Not herself, but for me.

I decock and lower my weapon.

"Bella, go inside and find something to tie him up with."

She goes to say something, but I cut her off.

"Woman! Get your sweet ass inside, and do what I said."

Reluctantly, she walks inside, and as soon as she does, I turn back to the son of a bitch I'm still holding against the wall.

"I may not be ending your worthless life, but you're going to wish I had before the night is through." I shove him, releasing my grip on his neck.

Grabbing at the side of the brick wall, he gasps for air. "You won't get away with this," he spits out.

I let out a laugh. "Is this the part where you tell me your daddy is so and so?"

I give him a few more blows to the ribs, causing him to stumble a few feet before falling to his knees, trying to catch his breath again.

"I think maybe I'll let some of my brothers have a little fun with you tonight," I taunt, walking up behind him.

Spittle comes flying from his mouth as he starts to plead. "Please...I swear, I won't bother Bella again. Please."

I hate whiners.

Mason watches as I pull my gun back out.

"Shit, man. You said you weren't going to kill me," he cries, putting his hands up.

I look down at him and shrug my shoulders. I proceed to take the butt of the gun, knocking his ass out with a blow to the back of the head. He collapses to the ground as Bella returns, holding a couple of rolls of duct tape.

Undaunted

Her eyes scan from my pistol to the ground where Mason is lying.

"Logan?" she questions.

"He's not dead. Just knocked his ass out."

I walk over to her, take her face in my hands and rub the pad of my thumb over the raised welt on her face, before leaning down and lightly brushing my lips on the mark that fucker left on her cheek.

Stepping back, I look at her. "I'm sorry he put his dirty hands on you. It won't be happening again."

I take the tape and begin to wrap it around Mason's wrists and ankles. Once I've finished, I pull my phone out to make a call. It only rings once before I hear Gabriel's voice.

"Yeah?"

"Hey, Brother. Got a loose end that needs to be taken care of over here at the bike shop."

"I'm across the street. Be there in five," he declares, hanging up.

I'm leaving his ass out here, so before I head inside, I bend down and tape his mouth, just in case he wakes up. Bella is still standing there, watching. "Come on, Angel. Let's get inside." I put my hand on the small of her back and lead her toward the break room. "Let's get you cleaned up. I'll make us some coffee."

Just before I walk her to the couch, she breaks away from my touch and walks over to the kitchen to grab the first aid kit from under the sink.

Walking back to where I'm standing, she grabs my hand before leading me to the table. The jolt of electricity from the contact is hard for both of us to ignore, and she lifts her eyes to mine, letting me know she felt the same thing.

I can feel her pulse racing as my thumb traces across her wrist.

With a shy smile, she clears her throat before speaking. "I'm going to clean that cut you have on your arm before anything else."

I look down at my arm. "I'm okay, babe. I've had worse."

Sitting the kit down on the table, she opens it and starts pulling out some of the contents, setting them on the table in front of her.

"I'm sure you have. Please, sit down, Logan. Let me take care of you."

Fuck me. I feel a tightening in my chest again. I sit down, extending my arm, and Bella begins to lightly dab the antiseptic on the cut with some gauze, cleaning it up. The sting causes me to flinch slightly.

Lifting her eyes to me, she whispers, "Sorry," then lowers her head, blowing air across my skin to soothe the burn. Bella looks at me through her long thick lashes. Fuck, there is nothing I can do to hide the effect she has on me.

"Doesn't look deep enough for stitches, but I'll put a few butterfly bandages on to keep the wound closed."

Not trusting my voice, I nod. She goes about putting the bandage on, then wraps some gauze around my forearm, before applying some tape.

"Thank you, beautiful. I haven't had someone take care of me like that in a long time."

I see questions in her eyes, but she doesn't ask. I love that about her. Bella does things, wonderful things for people, and doesn't require anything in return. She listens without judgment, and she doesn't push for any more than I'm willing to give.

I lead her to the couch, sitting her down. "I'm putting on a pot of coffee. I'm also going to walk into the storefront and grab a t-shirt off the rack for you. I don't want you sitting around with that torn shirt you're wearing."

Coming back into the break room, I walk over to the sink with a clean washcloth and soak it under some warm water before ringing it out and walking back over to Bella.

I kneel, placing the shirt on the couch and pull her toward me, positioning myself between her legs.

"Let me clean you up."

Never breaking eye contact with her, I wait for her to give me the go ahead before placing the warm washcloth to her face to wipe away the dirt and dried tears. The welt is starting to bruise a bit, so I'm careful not to rub too hard on her cheek. I can feel the tension build at the thought of that prick marking her face this way. Bella senses it and places her hand over mine.

"I'm okay, Logan."

Looking at her, I'm once again hit with a strong urge to kiss her. I never thought I would need more in my life than the club and my brothers. I've never felt so unsatisfied with not having more until now. Until this beautiful woman in front of me made me crave it. Crave her.

Letting my hand fall from her face, I reach over and grab the t-shirt I laid next to her. "Here, put this on while I go grab us both a cup of coffee."

She looks down at the shirt, then back to me. "Um, I'll just go to the bathroom and change."

"I'll keep my back turned until you're changed. I promise I won't peek," I say, smiling at her.

Her face flushes, returning a smile of her own.

I turn and head toward the counter. I reach up and take two mugs out of the cabinet and proceed to pour the coffee, taking my time, until I hear her softly say.

"You can turn around now."

I turn, with both mugs in my hands, as she walks to the table. The t-shirt swallows her. An image of her in nothing but my shirt flashes through my mind.

"Thanks for the shirt, Logan."

She sits down, taking the mug I sat in front of her. I sit down, joining her, and we enjoy the silence for a moment before my cell rings.

Looking at my phone, I see it's Gabriel, and swiping the screen I answer. "You find the package out back by the dumpster?"

"Yeah," he replies.

Bella shifts in her chair, intently watching me.

Not taking my eyes off her, I continue with my phone call. "The fucker jumped Bella tonight. He stays alive, but have some fun with him first. Find out his address and dump him after you're done."

She visibly relaxes in her chair a bit after hearing what I said to Gabriel and finishes her coffee.

Gabriel doesn't ask any questions. He only lets out a huff before hanging up.

"Thank you," Bella whispers, peering at me over the rim of her coffee mug.

Leaning forward, I do what I've wanted to do all night. Hell, for days. I grab her face, and brush my lips against hers, then pull away and peer into those beautiful eyes.

"Only this one time. He's alive because you asked, but I won't do it again, babe."

Licking my taste off her lips, she nods. "I understand."

"Good. Now, let's get you home. I'm driving you in your car. I'll text Reid to pick me up from there. You're exhausted and don't need to be behind the wheel tonight."

I shoot off a text to Reid with Bella's address and finish locking up the shop. I lead her to the car, helping her in and buckling her up.

"Logan, I'm a big girl. I can buckle myself in."

"Shut up, woman, and let me take care of you."

After I finish latching the buckle, I close her door and walk around to the driver's side. Once I sit down, my knees are crammed so far under the steering wheel it's painful.

I hear Bella's soft giggle beside me as I slide the seat back far enough to get my legs comfortable. I love the sound of her laugh. It makes me smile.

About twenty minutes later, we're pulling up in her driveway. I look over to see she's sound asleep.

Reid has just pulled in behind us as I'm getting out and making my way to the passenger side to open the door.

"Babe, wake up. You're home."

She opens her sleepy eyes and reaches up, touching my face. "Thank you, Logan. For everything."

I usher her out of the car, close the door, and hand her the keys. I bend down and kiss the top of her head.

"Goodnight, Angel."

"Goodnight, Logan."

I watch her walk inside and close the door before climbing into Reid's truck, where he's wearing a goofy fuckin' grin.

Looking at him, I say, "What?"

"You didn't kill someone for that girl tonight," he states.

"Yeah," I respond, folding my arms across my chest.

Reid stares back ahead. As he takes off, he says, "Good."

10

BELLA

Glancing in the rearview mirror of my car on the way home from work, I look at the fading bruise on my face and run my finger over my skin. It's been a few days since Mason attacked me at the shop, and since then, the guys have assured me that he won't be a problem anymore. My sister happened to be sound asleep that night when Logan dropped me off at home, so she had no clue what had happened until she saw my face the next morning. She's been texting me every day since then at least an hour before I leave work to check on me and make sure I'm not alone.

I'm pulling up to my house, and the driveway is full of cars. Lee and his scummy friends are here. Dread settles in my stomach, knowing my sister is home alone with them. I forgot that my mom had to work late tonight. I know she told him not to come back. Mom kicked him out after their last fight. He's been gone for several weeks. I bet she doesn't even know he's here at the house.

Parking my car on the street, I jump out and make my way to the house. I can already hear the loud music coming from inside.

Opening the front door, I'm immediately hit with the stench of cigarettes and sweat. I spot the low-life himself, sitting at the kitchen table with three of his friends. I ignore their eyes, leering at me as I head straight to mine and Alba's room.

When I open the door and don't see her, my heart starts racing, and I begin to panic. I feel a light breeze that has me looking to my right, noticing the window is open. Rushing over, I look out into the night. That's when it hits me. She's gone to the park. Walking back through the kitchen, I pass Lee as I make my way to the front door.

"Where are you off to, Bella?" he says with a drunken slur.

I don't bother responding to him. That prick is an afterthought. I walk out, slamming the door behind me.

When I arrive at the park, it's so dark I can hardly see it. I dig in my purse for my cell phone to use as a flashlight.

This is the place Alba comes to feel safe when things get too overwhelming at home. She knows this is the first place I'd look if I needed to find her. I know exactly where she'll be—the top of the tube slide.

Climbing the steps of the jungle gym, I make it to the top and see the glow of Alba's flashlight she carries on her keychain. She's sitting just inside the opening with her legs crossed, with the light shining on the book cradled in her lap. I stand there for a minute, looking at my little sister. She shouldn't be here. She shouldn't have to climb out of the bedroom window and walk to a park at night to hide because she doesn't feel safe in her own home.

She senses me and turns her head.

"Hey, Bella."

"Hi."

"Lee showed up," she says.

"I know, I was just there. You weren't in the room, so I knew I'd find you here. You know you can call me anytime, even when I'm at work."

"I know, Bella, but you just started that new job, and I didn't want you to get in trouble having to leave early because of me."

"Alba, you come first, you hear me? No job is more important than you."

"But—" she starts to protest.

"No buts, Alba. Next time you call me, okay?"

"Okay, I promise," she sighs while swiping at a tear that rolls down her cheek.

"Come here."

I sit down beside her. She scoots closer to me, laying her head in my lap for me to stroke her hair.

"It's going to be okay, Alba. I've got this new job now, and it pays more than the grocery store. I'm able to save money, and soon I'll be able to afford to get us our own place."

I'm a little nervous driving into work the next day. My sister has school break coming up in a few weeks, and after what happened last night, I can't risk leaving her home alone all day knowing Lee could be hanging around. I need to ask Jake if I can bring her into work with me while she's out of school.

In the short time I've been working at Kings Custom, Jake has been nothing but kind, yet asking him such a huge favor has me a bit nervous.

I arrive at the same time as Jake, and I see him getting off his bike. Of course, he also has a pink box in his hand. Every morning I've worked here, he has been stopping at this cute little bakery in town. It opened about six months ago. They have the best pastries. I suspect that his obsession with donuts has something to do with the pretty baker that owns the place.

"Good morning, Jake."

"Mornin', sweetheart."

Undaunted

Walking in, I see Logan and Quinn are already here. They usually come in early to set up for the day.

"Hey, Prez. What's with the donuts every day?" Quinn questions, with a knowing smile.

"I like donuts," Jake tells him.

Quinn, being Quinn, wasn't letting it go.

"Yeah, they are pretty kickass. In fact, they're so good, I'm thinking of going to town, so I can personally tell that sexy as hell, redheaded baker exactly how much I enjoy her sweet treats," he says that last part while wiggling his eyebrows.

He must have a death wish, because as soon as those words leave his mouth, Jake punches him in the face.

"You go anywhere near Grace, and I'll personally rip your goddamn balls off!" Jake declares with fury in his voice.

I stand there, stunned. I look over at Logan, and he's smiling. I turn my attention back to Quinn, who is now picking himself up off the floor. He's wiping the blood from his lips with the back of his hand, but also has the biggest damn grin on his face.

"You son of a bitch!" Jake growls, before stomping off to his office.

"I can't believe you did that to him," I fuss.

He winks at me and turns back to the bike he was working on.

I turn, looking back at Logan just as he walks off, muttering 'idiot' under his breath.

Later, I make my way to Jake's office. Hopefully, he's cooled down from this morning and is not in a pissed off mood. I see his door closed, so I knock.

"What!"

I poke my head in. "Hey Jake, you got a minute?"

When he sees it's me, his face softens. "Sure, sweetheart. What do you need?"

I let out a deep sigh. "My sister is out of school for spring break in a few weeks, and I wanted to ask if I can bring her into work with me during the day that week? I promise she won't be in the way. You won't even know she's here."

"Ah, not that I mind her being here, Bella, but isn't she old enough to be left alone?"

He's right. Alba is eighteen, well past the age of needing a babysitter.

Seeing that I'm reluctant to answer his question, he asks. "Is there a reason why your sister can't stay at home?"

I avoid looking at him. Wondering should I tell him about Lee? "Bella, look at me."

When I do, I see the concern on his face.

"Now, tell me why you can't leave her at home by herself."

I plop down in the chair sitting in front of his desk. "My stepdad, let's say he's not a good man, and he keeps showing up after my mom has told him he's not welcome. I don't trust him," I state.

By the dark look on his face, I don't need to say anymore.

"I'll tell you what. You bring your sister in with you when she's out on break. I also want her here every day starting today after school, as well. If we're busy and you're not able to pick her up, then one of the brothers will. You good with all that?"

I feel a huge weight lifted off my shoulders. I lean over and put my head in my hands, releasing a huge breath. By the time I look back up, Jake has knelt in front of me.

He looks me straight in the eyes. "You're not alone anymore, Bella. You have me, and you have the club."

Trying to blink away the tears, I nod. "Thank you."

Walking back to the front desk after leaving Jake's office, I run into Logan.

"What the hell, Bella? Why the fuck are you crying?"

"I'm fine," I sigh. "I promise."

"You're not fuckin' fine. Tell me why you're coming out of Jake's office with tears in your eyes."

"I had a minor problem, and Jake was helping me out. That's all."

"What kind of fuckin' problem? Don't even think about lying to me, babe," he growls.

"I was asking him if I could bring my sister with me to work while her school is on break. I don't trust our piece of shit stepdad."

"Why the fuck not? What's that motherfucker been doing, Bella?"

"Nothing...yet. He's just a creep, and I don't trust him."

I can see Logan's body tense, and his fists clench at my words. Wanting to calm him down, I put my hand on his arm.

"Look, Jake's helping me out. He said Alba could come in with me and every day after school."

He reaches up, tucking a strand of loose hair behind my ear, and says, "From now on, if you got a problem with that motherfucker, you tell me. Okay, Angel?"

This is the first time Logan has touched me since our kiss. For some reason, he seems to be putting distance between us. Like right now. I know he wants to kiss me. I see it in his eyes. He's confusing me with all the mixed signals lately. I have no clue which way to go with him.

IT'S SUNDAY, my day off. I decided to get out and take Alba shopping. With what Jake is paying me, I can afford to buy us some new clothes for the upcoming summer. Both of us haven't had new stuff in a while since money has been tight trying to help my mom catch up with bills. We've been doing a lot of shopping at second-hand stores, but my sister has never complained and has always been grateful for whatever could be provided. It feels good that I can treat her today, so I've brought us to the vintage boutique downtown, and then later, I'm taking her to the bookstore.

"I'm thinking of getting a tattoo for my birthday," I say while browsing the racks.

"Really?" Alba beams, her head popping out from behind a blue shirt she's holding up.

"I swear, Alba. If you get another blue shirt...."

"Don't change the subject, Bella."

My sister is obsessed with blue. I believe everything she owns is blue.

"I want to come with you," she demands.

"Of course, you're coming with me. You think I would do it without you?" I smile at her.

"Where are you getting it done? Doesn't the club have a place?"

"Yeah. I was talking with Quinn about it the other day. He said to go have Gabriel work on me."

"Ooh, I like that name. He has the perfect sexy billionaire book name."

I roll my eyes at her comment. "You, and your books."

A flash of red reflecting through the storefront windows catches my attention as a bright red Camaro pulls into the parking spot next to my car. I watch as two women get out and walk toward the store. The bell over the door chimes and watch as they both march in. One has short bleach blonde hair, and her friend has medium length black hair. The blonde is wearing a crop top showing her stomach and a jean skirt that barely covers her ass cheeks. Her friend is dressed the same. Both outfits scream "look at me", and the strong smell of perfume that follows them is repulsive.

As we continue to shop, I notice the blonde giving me a nasty look. I have no idea what her problem is. I don't even know her.

"Do you know that woman?" Alba asks, glancing back over her shoulder at them.

"No."

"Well, she looks like she wants to pull your hair out."

Just then, the blonde and her friend walk over to us. The sound of her clearing her throat makes me cringe. She's standing there with her hand on her hip and a sneer on her face.

"Bitch, you need to stay away from my man."

Has this little twit lost her mind? "Um, I don't know who the hell you're talking about."

"I'm talking about Logan. He's my man, and I want you to stay the fuck away from him."

Does Logan have a woman? What the hell? All the texting, the phone calls. The kiss. That's why he's been a little distant. You know what, I could care less about her being with Logan. Who am I kidding? I'm lying to myself. I do care. I want Logan. It turns out he doesn't want me.

Collecting myself, I stand a little taller and look at her. "Look, Logan and I work together, that's it. So, whatever you think is going on between us, isn't. He's not interested in me."

"Oh, I know he doesn't want you, because he was just telling me the other night how good my pussy is," she says while her friend snickers beside her.

I hold my hand up to stop her from talking any further. "You know what? I think it's time for twat one and twat two to go on about their business."

I feel Alba pulling on my arm. "Come on, Bella, let's just go," she pleads with me.

If my sister weren't with me, there would be no way I'd back down from this bitch, but my sister is not a fighter and always avoids confrontations. She is the only person I would show this much restraint for. So, as much as it pains my ass, I grit my teeth, and we walk away.

Coming out of the store, I walk over to the bitch's car, take the keys in my left hand and proceed to drag them across the hood of her car and down the driver's side.

Sliding into my car, I look over at Alba. She has her mouth hanging open.

"What?" I say innocently, shrugging my shoulders. "Don't let people walk all over you, Alba. I may have walked away from that skank just now, but when she comes out and gets a look at her car, the bitch will have a pretty good idea who did it."

Keying her car might seem petty, but right now, knowing how much it's going to cost her to fix it is worth it. At least, that's what I tell myself. I partially did it because my feelings are a raging mess after hearing Logan has a woman.

I feel so stupid.

How could I have not seen that he had a woman already? Was I that blind?

11

LOGAN

"Those fuckin' Demonios motherfuckers," I bark, while we are sitting here holding church. Dealing with these assholes, getting the drop on us has all of us on edge.

"Cool your shit, Logan," Prez says. "All of us here feel the same way, brother, but we need to resolve this and do it the smart way."

I grab the beer in front of me, down the rest of it, and light a cigarette.

On top of all this shit, Bella hasn't returned any of my goddamn texts or calls all fucking weekend. I knew her sweet ass was okay because Reid saw her and her sister downtown at the coffee shop. I have no clue what has crawled up her ass. This morning, when I went to the shop for a few hours to work on one of the brother's bikes to put on a new clutch cable, she hardly said two fucking words to me.

"Reid, what intel have you found out so far?" Prez inquires, taking a swig of his beer.

"According to our contacts, Los Demonios have grown in numbers over the last year, and have been known to poach on other businesses. Their Club's Prez goes by Miguel, but the one heading up the ambush the other week is his VP, and his son, Jorge." Reid looks up from his computer that he's been typing away on, and looks at us. "Our sources informed us that there seem to be some young girls that have gone missing over the past six months from the surrounding areas. None of them from our town that we've heard of, but I can contact our guy down at the station to verify that."

"What the fuck does that have to do with anything, brother?" Prez asks, irritated.

Reid puts his hands up, "I'm getting to that. We also have confirmation that Los Demonios have their slimy hands in the skin trade, and have for some time now, which would explain the disappearances of the girls. Just trying to give everyone a better picture of who we are dealing with here."

Quinn chimes in, "That's some bottom-feeding scum there."
Motherfucker.

Looking around, I see that all my brothers have the same look. One thing we don't do is mess with kids or women. To hear that those bastards, who fucking stole from us, deal in skin makes my blood boil.

We aren't by any means the good guys, but fuck. Skin trading is low as shit.

I drag my hands down my face. "Brothers, we need to find out exactly where they're holing up. These bastards are good at fucking hiding; that's for sure, but we have one thing they don't have—the Russians."

I look to Jake, because he got the call, so he needs to fill them in.

"I got a call from our supplier, the head of the Volkov family that we do business with. One of their associates got a call from the eyes they have here in the States and made them aware of our little problem. It seems these fuckers have hit a few others that they do business with. And since they are becoming a nuisance for them as well, they would like to aid in taking care of this mutual problem we're having."

The Russians getting involved means securing more resources and firepower. I look around at all my brothers. They've soaked it all in. I see the thirst for retaliation in their eyes.

"We don't need the Russians help," Gabriel grumbles.

"With the numbers Reid reported, we do," I deadpan.

"Sure, we could pull sources from the other chapters, but they need their men too. The word is, our chapter down in Louisiana has been seeing activity from these assholes around the south for some time now. Hasn't affected them yet, but can't chance it either," I tell them all.

"Now, we bide our time for the moment. We need to find out every location they have because when we take them out, we want to take as many as possible. So, for now, we keep a low profile. Let them still think they have the upper hand. With the numbers they have, we will need to keep a closer eye on our family. We need brothers cruising the roads during the day. See something, say something. I don't want to put anyone on lockdown just yet. Can't be raising any suspicions." I look around at each of them as I speak.

Gabriel is sitting over in a corner with his jaw twitching.

"Alright, brothers. I'm gonna hand it back over to Prez."

The tension in this room is off the charts as Jake's voice booms over everyone else's, "Okay...listen up. I know sitting on our asses is not what you want to hear, but I expect you to do it anyway. No jumping the gun or trying anything on our own. Keep that shit reined in. You happen to catch one of those dirty sons of bitches lurking anywhere, bring him to the basement. Then, and only then, will you be given a chance to have some fun."

"Get ready for war, brothers!" Jake slams the gavel down, and church is over.

We all file out into the common area.

"Logan," Prez calls out, as he saddles up to the bar.

I walk over and pull up a stool for myself beside him.

"Jake," I sit, motioning to the prospect to bring a beer.

"I'm going to need you to stick around the club more often. You have a room here, so since you and some of the other brothers don't have old ladies or kids, I'm going to be posting you, and whoever else you need, here and over at the warehouse overnight as well."

He's right. Those of us not tied down don't have as much to lose.

"You got it, Prez. I want Quinn and Reid on night watch at the warehouse. That's where most of Reid's computer equipment is anyway, and I want Gabriel here with us. We'll put some of the other guys on watch during the day. We have the shops to run and don't want to risk burnout on anyone," I tell him.

"Sounds good," he agrees, downing the shot put in front of him.

"I'm not too keen on the Russians wanting to be a part of all this, but I get it. They've been putting up with Los Demonios for a while now. I don't like the idea of someone else dictating what we do and when we do it, though," I gruff out.

"Look, we need the extra men they can send. Those fuckers outnumber us. The Russians dropped themselves in our laps, and I'm not fucking up our association with them."

I know he's right. It doesn't mean I have to like it.

"You're right. Better to have them on our side than against it." I down the last of my beer.

"I'm gonna head out. I'll be back later."

Jake nods his head and continues with his drink.

On the short ride to my house, I can't help but think about Bella. If all this shit weren't going on, I would have already had her in my bed.

Which is why I'm still pissed that she won't talk to me.

"Fuck."

I scrub my hand down my face as I pull into my driveway. Getting off my bike, I walk through the door that leads from the garage into the laundry room and make my way to the kitchen. I might as well grab a bag of my shit. I'm going to need it since I'll be staying at the club awhile.

I don't waste much time gathering my things, before loading up and heading back toward the club. It's starting to get late, and I need to make sure the men know where they need to go by nightfall.

I decide to try and call Bella again.

Still no fucking answer.

First thing tomorrow morning, we are going to get some shit straight and find out what the fucking deal is with her avoiding me.

As I'm pulling up to the club, I notice that the guys have decided to cut loose tonight with a party. The music is loud, and I can smell food cooking on the grill out back. I figure, what the hell, they need to unwind a bit with all the shit going on right now, and so the fuck do I.

I grab my bag and head inside.

Walking past the bar, I tell Blake to have a cold beer and a bottle of whiskey waiting for me when I come back down.

I spot Quinn standing at his bedroom door as some blonde wanders out.

"Hey, Logan," she says, brushing by.

"Are you going down to join the party, brother?" I stop and ask him.

"No, man. I just had my fun for the night. Prez said you wanted Reid and me out at the warehouse, so I don't need to get too lit."

"Anything you need just let me know. I think I'm going to shower, then head on down and have a drink."

I turn to go down the hall to my room, when Quinn yells out to me, "Yo, Logan. Hear from Bella?"

"Not a fucking peep, brother. Don't know what's up with her."

"You'd better claim her, man, before someone else does," he adds.

I clench my fist. "What the fuck does that mean, brother? You interested?"

Quinn puts his hands up. "It's not like that with me and Bella, brother. She's become a good friend. You're my friend too, but if you keep sitting on your ass with her, someone else may swoop in is all I'm saying."

I know he's right.

"Fuck, we've got all this shit going on with the club right now. I can't risk putting her in the middle of it."

Quinn eyes me for a moment. "Look, you and I both know she can handle it, brother. That woman is exactly what you need."

"Enough with these feelings and shit. You're starting to sound like you've grown a pussy," I smirk at him.

Quinn grins. "Man, if I had a pussy, I'd be flickin' that bean right now instead of talking to your ass."

I can't help but chuckle. "Call me if anything happens tonight. Later, brother."

I've made my way back downstairs, and the party has picked up. Loud music and the smell of weed fills the air. I sit down at my usual spot at the end of the bar so that I can see everyone and everything. Blake hands me my beer and whiskey. I take my first shot. The burn feels good, so I take one more. Gabriel sits down next to me, grabs the bottle I'm drinking from, and snatches a glass from behind the bar. He pours himself a shot and downs it.

"Don't like this waiting shit."

I know how he feels.

"Look, man. I get it, but we need to do this the way Prez said.

We can't be pissing our suppliers off. We need extra manpower. Just wait it out, brother. You'll get what you want."

He sits there, gripping the bottle as his nostrils flare.

"Pull it together, man."

I take the whiskey bottle and pour us another shot. "I get it, brother...don't wait for death—hunt the fucker down."

12

BELLA

I haven't seen much of Logan in the past couple of days, though I don't mind him not being at work. Not having to look at his face every day makes the hurt and disappointment a little easier to bear.

I've missed our lunchtime conversations the most. That little bit of time we shared had become my favorite part of the day. Something about him puts me at ease. He makes me feel safe.

Since my run-in with that blonde chick while out shopping this past weekend, I haven't returned any of his calls. I've noticed the guys have been on edge lately, too. I'm getting the sense that something is wrong but haven't heard anyone talking about anything. More of the members have been riding around town more often too.

Naturally, my curiosity is piqued, but I'm also very aware that club shit is none of my business, so I haven't asked any questions about it. I'm not naive. I know they aren't saints, but to me, they're good men.

I continue to concentrate on what I'm doing. Today has been a slow day, so I took inventory of all the low and out of stock items we have in the back.

I'm standing at the computer, putting orders in when the door chimes alerting me that someone has walked in. I look up to see Lee.

What the fuck is he doing here?

He stalks up to the counter with a cigarette hanging from his mouth. I know he can't miss the look of surprise mixed with disgust on my face as I lean back from the counter.

"I heard you were seen working here for these piece of shit bikers, so I thought to myself, why don't I come down and see for myself what my stepdaughter is up to."

Shit. The last thing I need is Lee doing something to make me lose this job.

"I'm not anything to you," I seethed, "You need to leave."

Blowing smoke into my face, he leans in close. "You slummin' it with some biker, Bella? You letting one of them taste that pussy of yours? Huh?"

My skin crawls with the words coming out of his mouth. "Get the fuck out, you piece of shit," I tell him with hate, but low enough not to draw any attention to the situation from any of the guys out in the shop.

Lee drops his cigarette to the floor and smudges it out with his boot.

"Come on now, that's no way to talk to a customer. I may be shopping around for a bike."

He starts walking around, looking at magazines and flipping through the pages when his phone rings.

"You'd have to have a job and money to do that," I say, crossing my arms and glaring at him.

I can't hear what he is saying into the phone because it's in hushed tones, but whoever it is has wiped that smugness right off his face.

Quickly hanging up, he shoves his phone into his back pocket and walks out without another word.

I breathe out a sigh of relief as soon as he's gone.

I'm thankful that he left, but it only adds to all the other shit that's been going on lately. He's been gone from the house more than usual, which I'm not going to complain about. Still, something isn't right. I'm not sure what, but my gut is telling me something is up.

I shake all those thoughts off and finish the orders I started before breaking for lunch. I walk to the entrance and flip the lock and insert the sign that points to the bay doors in case an actual customer shows up.

I'm hungry since breakfast consisted of nothing but coffee this morning. After taking my sister to school, I didn't have time to stop for anything else. She has exams this week and can't be tardy. She has a great shot at graduating with honors, and I'll make damn sure nothing screws that up for her.

I'm walking through the door leading to the garage on my way to the break room with a peanut butter and jelly sandwich on my mind when I hear Quinn holler out from near the third bay door, where he's airbrushing graphics onto a gas tank.

"Hey, Bella. What do the Mafia and pussy have in common?"

I smile and hang my head because I know another dirty, inappropriate joke is about to come out of his mouth. I love that about him. Quinn is one of a kind.

"I don't know, Quinn. What do they have in common?"

"One slip of the tongue and you're in deep shit!" he says with the biggest grin, laughing at himself.

I laugh. "Quinn, that's nasty!"

He shrugs his shoulder, continuing with his work. He doesn't know it, but he just helped lift my mood.

"Quinn, I'm heading to the break room to make a sandwich.

Undaunted

You want something while I'm in there?" I ask as I finish making my way across the garage.

"Hell yeah! Can you make one of those grilled sandwiches you made for everyone the other day? That shit was good."

I love to cook. It helps to calm my nerves when my anxiety gets the best of me. They've all been great to me ever since I started working here, and Alba shows up often after school, and nobody complains about her hanging around. So, she and I cooked for them before closing last week.

You would have thought those men had never eaten before by the way they devoured their food. They definitely like to eat.

Logan was here that day.

I'm in the break room slicing the bread while Alba mixes the sauce when he walks in to grab a drink from the fridge.

"Smells good," *he says.*

I look over at him and can't help but smile. The deep tenderness of his voice gives me butterflies in my stomach.

"My sister and I are making Reubens for everyone. Even made enough to run across the street to Gabriel. Just my way of saying I appreciate this job and the MC."

He's standing there, looking at me. I start to feel flushed from his intense stare.

Alba walks up and hands me the sauce, making me break eye contact with him.

Logan stands, holding his bottle of water, with one of those cocky smiles of his.

I hear him whisper, "Perfect," *just before walking out the door.*

"Yo, Bella. How about that sandwich, darlin'? You got some more of that good-tasting shit?"

I had completely zoned out on Quinn. "There might be some stuff to make one. I'll bring it out in a few minutes."

I walk through the break room door and head over to the kitchenette area. Opening the refrigerator, I find everything I need to make Quinn, and even Jake a sandwich before fixing my own. Once I'm through making lunch, I take Quinn's to him along with cold water.

"Thanks, Darlin'," he says, picking up the sandwich, taking a bite. "Fuck yeah," he tips his chin at me, thanking me while chewing.

"I'm going to take this other one to Jake. I haven't seen him come out of the office all day. He has to be hungry by now."

Quinn is busy devouring his lunch, so I turn and head back inside. I raise my hand to knock on Jake's door and get startled when I hear him roar.

"Motherfucker!"

I'm not sure what's going on, so I knock on the door a little louder than usual and wait.

"It's open," he barks.

Walking in, I see him standing at the window. The scowl on his face that seems to be permanently etched in his skin slightly disappears when he turns and notices that I'm there.

"Bella, what do ya need, sweetheart?"

"I haven't seen you come out of your office for anything all day, so I brought you something to eat. Thought you might be hungry."

Sitting down in his chair, he lets out a heavy sigh. Shit. "Yeah, Bella. I'm hungry. Sit down with me."

This is a first. I sit down in the chair across from his desk and set my water down.

"You okay, Jake?"

He eyes me for a moment before speaking. "Nothing the club can't take care of."

I bob my head, "Okay."

Jake takes a bite of his lunch. I can tell whatever is going on is weighing him down. He looks so tired. "Bella, I do have something I could use your help with."

I look at him over my PB&J. "Sure, Jake. What do you need?" I ask after swallowing the bite.

He sits back in his chair a bit. "I have some price quotes I was supposed to drop off to Grace, over at the bakery. I've got some club shit that needs taken care of, so I won't have time. Could you take them by after work for me?"

I've just finished the last of my food, and I take a drink of water before replying.

"Sure. I can do that. Those donuts you've been bringing in lately are amazing, and she makes the best cinnamon rolls. That gives me an excuse to pick one up on my way home." I smile.

I see the corner of Jake's mouth turn up. I leave his office, and soon after, he's heading out and dropping off the papers I need to deliver to Grace. I stick them in my purse, so I don't forget them later.

The rest of the day goes by quickly, and before I know it, it's 7:00 pm, and we're closing for the night. Logan never did show up today, so Quinn walks me to my car.

"You let him know when you get home."

"Who?" I look at him. I wasn't aware that he knew I always let Logan know when I made it home at night.

"Don't look at me like that, woman. I know Logan, so make sure you text him. Got it?"

"It's not like that, Quinn. Logan is just a good guy."

He closes the car door once I'm inside, then bends down and looks at me.

"He knows what's right in front of him, Bella."

If only that were true.

Quinn walks away and mounts his bike, waiting for me to pull out ahead of him. Once we're down the street, I turn left as he turns right.

I've made it to the bakery downtown just a few blocks from the garage and pull into an empty parking space in front of the store.

When I get out, I notice the glow of the end of a cigarette from across the street. When I look closer, I see a man leaning against the building, but since the sun has set, it's too dark to make out any of his features.

Okay, I'm officially creeped out a little.

I chalk it up to paranoia and walk into the bakery. The door chimes as I enter, and I'm hit with a sugary, sweet vanilla aroma.

A redhead comes walking out from the back, wearing a smile.

"Hi. I'm about to close for the night. What can I get for you?"

"Hey," I say, "I'm Bella. I work for Jake over at Kings Custom Bikes. He asked me to drop off these papers with the price quotes. He had some club business to take care of, so he left early today and couldn't make it."

I reach into my purse and hand her the folder.

"Oh...Okay," she says, looking a little disappointed. "Thank you, Bella. I'm Grace." She extends her hand, introducing herself. "I appreciate you coming over after work to bring these by."

Walking around the counter, she sets the papers down. "Would you like anything before you go?" she inquires.

"I would love one of those cinnamon rolls."

Smiling, Grace grabs a pink box from a shelf behind her. "These are one of my bestsellers. I'll tell you what. I'm going to give you two for one, as a thank you!"

"That would be awesome," I say, returning a smile of my own.

She rings up my purchase, and I wave goodbye, heading out the door to my car.

I glance around, looking for the guy I saw just moments ago when I arrived. I don't see anyone, so I climb into my car and buckle up.

Just before backing out onto the main road, I reach into the box, tearing off a piece of the cinnamon roll, and pop it into my mouth.

As I'm pulling out, some asshole comes up behind me with his high beams on. I move over into the other lane to let him pass, but all he does is move in behind me. "This guy is a dick."

My turn home is up ahead. Stopping at the intersection, I make another right, but whoever it is, continues to follow me. I'm starting to panic a little and instinctively grab my phone to call Logan. Shit, my phone is dead.

Okay, think!

I decide to make a left and head to where I know the MC's clubhouse is located. At this point, all I can think of is one of Lee's scummy friends is messing with me. If I head toward the clubhouse, whoever it is will change their mind once they see where I'm going.

It's only about a fifteen-minute drive, and the car is still tailing me. I've never been out to the compound before, but most people who live in the area know of it. As I'm making my turn onto the club's private road, the car starts to back off and makes a U-turn.

I keep going in the direction I'm heading, hoping that I took the right road. Soon enough, I start to see some lights. As I get closer, I can see someone standing at a gate. Pulling up, I notice it's Austin, the prospect that helps at the shop from time to time.

"Bella? What the hell are you doing way out here?" he asks.

"I need to see Jake."

He eyes me a moment. "He's here, but I have to announce you before you can go in. You sure you're okay? You look scared shitless."

"I'm not the best right now, Austin."

He nods his head and pulls out his phone.

Thank God Alba is hanging out at her friend's house for the night. She would be freaking out by now since I haven't made it home yet.

Austin leans down and startles me. "Shit. Sorry, Bella. Listen, I can't get in touch with anyone, but go on in. One of the guys can get Jake for you."

I don't question if he will get in trouble for letting me in without permission, I drive on through the gate and park my car under a tree near the end of a row of bikes out front. I sit for a moment to try and calm my nerves before getting out of my car.

The music is loud. I can hear laughing and cutting up from inside. I walk toward the only door I see. Sitting there is a big, heavier set guy I've never seen before. He's leaned back in a chair, smoking a cigarette, and he's wearing the same cut as everyone else in the club.

As I'm approaching, he looks up and lets his eyes travel over me.

"You look a bit young to be out here to party, girl."

"I'm old enough," I sass.

He grunts at my response.

What the hell is it with men and grunting?

"So? You going to let me in?" I put my hand on my hip and cock my head.

"Get on in there, girl," he gruffs as a cloud of cigarette smoke billows around his face.

Walking through the door, I'm instantly hit with the thick smell of cigarette smoke mixed with a hint of marijuana. The music is so loud you can't even hear your thoughts. I'm scanning the place, trying to spot anyone I've met before when a biker walks up to me.

"What's your name, sweet thing?"

I look up at him. "I'm looking for Jake or Logan."

The burly man runs his hand through his beard. "Well, hell. Prez is probably in his office," he points toward a door that's at the far end of the room.

Looking in that direction, I notice Gabriel's massive frame over everyone else's, sitting at the bar, and then my eyes slide to Logan, who's sitting next to him. Beside him is a tall blonde, rubbing her tits all over him and talking into his ear.

Undaunted

I'm instantly filled with jealousy. *He isn't even yours, Bella. You just want him to be.*

I feel gutted. Like someone has punched me in the stomach.

Gabriel looks up and notices me standing here. I watch as he nudges Logan, giving him a chin lift in my direction.

Logan turns, making eye contact with me.

First, I see the surprise in his expression. Then it quickly turns to concern. He jumps up from his stool and marches over in my direction. Darting my eyes around the smoke-filled room, I notice people staring, and it makes me feel uneasy.

Logan's eyes stay trained on me. "What the fuck, Bella! Why are you here? And why in the hell, haven't you returned my calls?" he barks.

I'm taken aback at the harsh tone in his voice, but can't seem to find anything to say.

I'm feeling claustrophobic as a panic attack starts taking hold.

13

LOGAN

"What the fuck, Bella! Why are you here? And why in the hell haven't you returned my calls?" I snap at her. She flinches at my tone.

Fuck. I didn't mean to sound so harsh, but the shock at her being here and seeing the panicked look on her face has put me on edge. She's white as a fuckin' ghost, and her body is trembling.

"Angel," I say, gently reaching out to her, but she takes a step back.

"I need to see Jake," she whispers with a shaky voice.

The music has stopped, and everyone's eyes are on us. Her eyes are darting around the room, uncomfortable with all the attention we're getting.

"What's wrong? Why do you need to see Jake?" I plead, trying to draw her attention back to me.

Just as she goes to say something, Prez comes from his office.

"What the hell is going on out here?" his voice clipped and alerted from the sudden silence in the clubhouse.

He notices Bella standing in front of me. Taking in her state, he

Undaunted

quickly strides over to her. Gently grabbing her shoulders, he says, "Sweetheart, what's wrong?"

"I...I need to talk to you," she murmurs.

"Okay, but first, I need you to calm down for me. Can you do that?"

Nodding, she takes a couple of deep breaths.

Shit. It hits me. Bella is having a panic attack. *Fuck.* Turning to Gabriel, I inform him, "Get everyone out. Now. Party is over."

Gabriel walks to the middle of the clubhouse and whistles, drawing everyone's attention to him, "Party's over. If you're not a member, get the fuck out."

I turn my attention back to her, "Come on, babe. Let's go to Jake's office."

I go to grab her hand, but she moves away from me again, leaning closer to Jake as we make our way to his office. What the fuck is that about? That's twice she has avoided my touch.

Jake guides her to take a seat on the couch while I grab a bottle of water from the mini-fridge. Handing it to her, Bella twists the cap off and takes a long pull.

A moment later, after she has calmed down and gotten her emotions under control, I ask her again, "Babe, what's going on?"

She looks at me, and for a split second, I see the hurt on her beautiful face, just before it's replaced with anger. She turns toward Jake to speak instead, and it pisses me off.

"When I arrived at the bakery, I noticed someone across the street, smoking a cigarette, and I started to feel uneasy like he was watching me. It creeped me out, but by the time I left, he was gone, so I just brushed it off."

Kneeling in front of her, I ask, "Did you see what this person looked like?"

She shakes her head no and takes another drink of water before continuing. "It was too dark for me to get a good look. Anyway, not long after I left, someone pulled up behind me with their high beams on and started following me. I began taking different turns in the opposite direction of my house, thinking it was one of Lee's friends trying to mess with me. When they continued to follow, I panicked and decided to come here. They followed me onto the compound's private road until about halfway down before doing a U-turn."

Jake and I look at each other, thinking the same damn thing. Los Demonios is behind this shit.

I blow out a breath.

"You did good coming here," Jake assures her. "The club's going to take care of it."

Jake stands, making his way to the door. "Church in five," he bellows, walking out of his office.

I stay in my spot, kneeling in front of her. "Where's your sister?"

"She's at a friend's house. I need to check on her, or at least call. My phone is outside in my car, but it's dead, which is why I didn't call someone first before coming here."

"How about I get Gabriel to ride out and make sure she's okay. You can use the phone on Jake's desk to call her."

She nods her head, agreeing.

"Alright, you go on and call your sister while I go sort some shit out.

I walk into church, and, as soon as I take my seat, Jake doesn't waste any time calling me out in front of everyone. "You claimin' her, Son?"

Looking him straight in the eyes, I confess, "She's mine."

After a few beats, Jake slaps me on my back. "Fuck yeah! I like her, Logan. She's strong, loyal, and caring as fuck."

I hear the murmurs of 'hell yeah,' and 'it's about fuckin' time' from my brothers.

"Alright, now that that's out of the way, let's get to why I called this meeting," Prez calls out.

All my brothers listen as Jake tells them what Bella told us moments ago. A collective round of 'motherfuckers' and 'sons of bitches' are heard around the room.

I see Reid, typing away on his laptop. Checking our security feed. "You see anything, man?"

He blows out a breath. "Nah, man, nothin'. None of the motion sensors on our property have been tripped."

The motion sensors are brand new. He added those after Los Demonios shot up our clubhouse. They should have alerted one of us before she even made it to the front gate.

Fifteen minutes later, the brothers leave church after Jake barks out orders on what our next move is, and I ask Gabriel to go by and check on Bella's sister.

After everyone has cleared the room, I turn to Jake. "I want to take Bella to my place tonight. Will you and the guys be good without me here?"

"Yeah, man. We're good for tonight. Go on and get out of here."

Before walking out the door, I turn back. "Jake, if you find the son of a bitch that fucked with my woman tonight, you call me. That motherfucker is mine," I declare.

"You got it, brother."

Opening the door to Jake's office, I find Bella, curled up on the couch asleep. She is so fuckin' beautiful. I walk over to her and gently run my hands through her silky hair. "Bella, wake up."

She slowly opens her eyes.

"Hey, beautiful. I need the address where your sister is staying, so Gabriel can check on her."

She rambles off the address as I text it to Gabriel. His reply is instant.

Gabriel: On it.

I turn my attention back to Bella. "Come on, let's go, babe."

"Go where?" she asks.

"I'm taking you to my house tonight."

"No, I'm going home," she bites out.

"Not fuckin' happening, Bella. You're coming home with me. Not risking something happening to you."

She glares at me. "Seeing as you have a girlfriend, Logan. I don't think that's a good idea."

"Girlfriend? What the hell are you talking about?"

"The woman that was hanging all over you tonight."

I think back to before she showed up, then it hit me. Shit! She saw Cassie's whining ass trying to get my attention earlier.

"Look, Cassie is not my woman. She's a club girl. She ain't shit to me, babe," I say with conviction, hoping she will let it drop, but when she narrows her eyes at me, I know that's not happening.

"Well, she told me otherwise."

What the fuck?

"Explain," I demand.

"Your little 'friend,' came up to me the other day when I was out shopping with my sister. She and her tacky sidekick informed me that you belong to her and to stay the hell away from her man. I have to say, Logan. You picked a real classy one there," she says while crossing her arms over her chest, pushing her breasts up, making my eyes zero in on her cleavage. She so fuckin' cute trying to be all angry. I'm not going to even try and hide my smirk.

"So, now you think this is funny?" she huffs, then stomps out of Jake's office.

I stand there for a minute, staring up at the ceiling before going after her. This woman is going to be the death of me. I catch up to her before she can even make it out the front door. Putting my shoulder to her stomach, I scoop her up.

"What the hell, Logan! Put me down right now!"

Reaching up, I give her a firm slap on the ass.

"You did not just spank me! You asshole!"

"Enough!" I bark.

Something in my tone causes her to stop fighting. As soon as I make it outside to my bike, I set her down, then look her right in the eyes. "I do not have a girlfriend. Whatever that bitch told you is a lie. Cassie is a club girl. Her purpose is to cater to whatever needs a brother has. That's what she signed up for. That's it. I'll deal with her ass later. You should have come to me and asked if it was true, but instead, you assumed that it was."

"I thought maybe I read too much into the last few weeks," Bella murmurs, looking down.

"No, babe. I was battling shit in my head. I don't deserve you, but I'm a selfish man. I'm finally taking what I want, and what I want is you."

I hand her a helmet before straddling my bike. "Get on." She does so, wrapping her arms around my waist. It feels so fuckin' good, finally having her on the back of my bike.

Pulling up to my house, I park the bike and hold out my hand for her to climb off. Taking my helmet off, she starts looking around.

"You live here? I've always envied people who could live out here on the lake. It must be great waking up to this every morning."

"Come on," I say, grabbing her by the hand and leading her into the house. I chuckle to myself as we walk inside because she certainly is not shy about being nosey. She looks at everything, stopping at some framed photos on the wall. They're pictures I took back in high school. I brought my camera along on a weekend ride with Reid and Noah. I tried to capture everything from the scenery, our bikes, us. I watch her run her fingers over the frames.

"These are beautiful. Logan. I recognize you and Reid, but the third guy..."

"That's Noah, Reid's brother."

"I remember you talking about Noah, the day you told me about growing up with the club. I'm sorry you guys lost him."

"Yeah, me too."

I watch as she walks to the staircase and starts making her way upstairs.

I love the look of her in my home. It feels right.

After locking up and setting my keys on the counter, I set out to find my girl.

I find her in my room in front of the French doors she has opened, which lead to a balcony overlooking the lake.

The moon is so bright tonight it's casting a glow on her face. She's so fuckin' beautiful it takes my breath away.

Turning her head, she catches me staring at her. Our eyes meet. At that moment, nothing else exists. I feel like I've waited all my life to find her.

I make my way to her as she turns to face me fully. Placing both hands on each side of her face, I run the pad of my thumb over her soft, full lips before my mouth is on hers. I run my tongue over the seam of her lips, encouraging her to open. When she does, I take full advantage.

After a few seconds of tasting her, I want more. My cock is painfully hard, straining against the zipper of my jeans, as I cup Bella's ass and lift her. She immediately wraps her legs around my hips as I walk back a few steps to sit on the lounge chair, never breaking our connection.

With her straddling me, I can feel the heat between her legs, and it does nothing but fuel my animalistic need to claim her.

Grabbing the bottom of her shirt, I slowly pull it off over her head. I then pull the cups of her black lace bra down, exposing her breasts, the cold night air instantly hardening her peaks, taunting me. Leaning forward, I swirl my tongue around her nipple.

She throws her head back with a moan, arching into my mouth further as I bring my other hand up, running my thumb over her other nipple and giving it equal attention. Her skin feels like silk against my calloused hands.

Undaunted

Deciding I can't wait a minute longer to have her, I stand up, carrying her inside to my bed, and gently lay her down.

I run my hands down her body until I reach the button of her jeans. No words are spoken as I unbutton them, peeling them off her inch by inch. I toss them on the floor, without taking my eyes off her.

Fuck me; she's wearing the most sinful, red lace panties. And they're soaked with her arousal, which causes a deep growl to leave my throat.

Leaning down, I press my face between her thighs, inhaling her scent, fueling my need to devour her.

Looking up at Bella, I see pure lust in her eyes, but there's something else I notice. Uncertainty.

"You okay, Angel?"

Swallowing hard, she answers, "Yes, but..."

"But what, babe? You want me to stop?"

"No!" she quickly answers. "It's just that, well, I've um...I haven't been this far with anyone before."

I'm fuckin' speechless for a moment. She's untouched and mine.

"Angel, you don't know how fuckin' happy it makes me, knowing no man has touched this perfect fuckin' pussy. It makes me hard as a goddamn rock thinking about sliding into you for the first time. You on the pill? I don't want anything between us, and I'm clean." I settle myself between her legs.

"Yes," she rasps.

Knowing it's her first time, I decide to take things slow. I want this night burned into her memory. Slowly, I slide her panties off; then, I gently spread her legs.

"First, I need to taste you."

I run my tongue through her wet folds, tasting her for the first time. She's just as sweet as I thought she would be, like honey.

"Perfect. It's mine. Isn't it, babe? Tell me who this pussy belongs to."

I run the tip of my tongue over her clit a few times, causing her back to arch off the bed with a moan.

"Yours," she says breathlessly.

"Damn right it is," I growl, right before I slip a finger inside her, pumping in and out while working her clit.

Gasping, she clutches the blanket, opening her legs wider as I slip another finger in stretching her.

"Logan, please," she begs.

"The first time I make you come, beautiful, it's going to be on my cock."

Bella's eyes are heavily lidded with lust as I step back and start to undress. She watches, never taking her eyes off mine.

I look down at her with the moonlight dancing on her skin, and she watches as I fist my cock, giving it a few strokes.

Crawling up her body, I stop along the way, tasting her breasts and kissing the soft, delicate skin at the base of her throat before whispering in her ear, "You ready, beautiful?"

"God, yes, Logan, please," she begs again.

Her hands start to explore my body, mapping out every inch of my skin. It takes everything in me not to lose control. I raise and grab my cock, guiding it to her entrance.

Dipping my head down, I take her nipple into my mouth, earning another moan. I ease the tip of my cock in. She's so tiny and so fucking tight. I reach down and lift her leg, opening her to me a little more, allowing me to push in further. I stop when I feel resistance.

"Breathe, babe," I tell her. As soon as she does, I thrust in all the way while she cries out, and I take her innocence.

"Fuck," I groan out.

Resting my forehead on hers, I stay still inside her for a minute, waiting for her pain to pass. Once I feel her body begin to relax, I start moving, slowly dragging my cock in and out of her sweet pussy.

She gasps and starts rocking her hips, meeting me thrust for thrust. "You feel so good, Logan," she says as I circle my hips and rock against her.

I can feel her walls tightening around my cock, letting me know she's getting close. I grind down harder, causing friction on her clit, and a deep throaty moan escapes her mouth as her nails dig into my back—the pain making my dick even harder.

Moments later, her back arches as her orgasm rips through her body, causing her pussy to clamp down on my cock like a fucking vise, triggering my release. With a final thrust, I hold myself deep inside her walls, losing myself with every long deep pulse. I hold myself up, careful not to crush her tiny frame and bury my head in her neck, as both of us try to catch our breaths.

Lifting my head, I look at her. "You okay, Angel?"

"Yes," she says with a big, lazy, satisfied smile on her face.

Leaning down, I kiss her.

"Stay here. I'm going to get something to clean you with."

A little while later, we're lying in bed. Bella is tucked into my side, tracing over my tattoos with her finger.

I pull her tighter into me, then kiss the top of her head and whisper, "Mine."

I feel her smile against my chest.

"Yours," my angel says, right before drifting off to sleep.

For the first time in forever, I fall asleep with ease, holding the best thing to ever walk into my life.

14

BELLA

I wake the next morning with Logan's head between my legs and his mouth doing amazing things. My body vibrates with pleasure as his tongue swirls around my clit, causing my hips to rise off the bed. Looking down at him through my lashes, I see Logan's beautiful eyes staring back at me. His hot mouth is licking and biting while my breaths become frantic, and my hands fist the sheets.

"Don't stop," I plead breathlessly.

"Not a chance," he growls, sliding his finger inside, pressing against my g-spot.

I'm so close. I feel it as my legs begin to shake. A whimper escapes my mouth when he pulls out of me. Not wasting any time, he slides both hands under me, grabbing my ass and pulling me closer to his mouth. Just when I think it's too much, his mouth closes around my clit, and he sucks. I throw my head back, crying out his name as my orgasm crashes over me, leaving me lightheaded and spent.

Moments later, I feel Logan slowly kiss his way up my body

Undaunted

until his mouth is on mine, causing me to taste myself on his lips. Pulling away, he peers down at me.

"Morning, Angel."

"Morning," I reply, with a lazy smile.

He climbs out of bed, completely comfortable with his nudity, as he should be. Logan is a beautiful man, with his broad shoulders, six-pack abs, and don't even get me started on that ass.

"Come on, babe. Let's take a shower before we head to the clubhouse."

"Why are we going to the clubhouse?"

"Prez called earlier. Said he needs us there."

"Okay, but I need to go pick up my sister at her friend's house soon."

"No problem, babe. Now come on."

Standing under the spray of hot water feels so good on my skin. Especially since Logan has taken it upon himself to wash me. His hands slowly roam all over my body, paying particular attention to my breasts. When he reaches between my legs, I close my eyes, letting out a moan.

Wanting to return the favor for what he did to me just moments ago, I drop to my knees in front of him. His long, thick cock makes my mouth water.

Reaching up, I wrap my palm around his shaft; his size making my hands look so small. Looking up, I meet his eyes. I've only given head a handful of times before to a guy I dated for about four months in my last year of high school. Though he never complained, I'm not entirely confident in my ability to please Logan. I'm positive he has had more experienced women.

"Go on, beautiful," he says, encouraging me.

Pushing those thoughts away, I bring the head of his cock to my mouth, swiping my tongue across the tip to catch the bead of precum and causing him to moan, then I briefly close my eyes, relishing the taste of him.

Playing off his reaction, I swirl my tongue around the head of his cock a bit before taking half of his length in my mouth, while my hand works the rest of his shaft. I never take my eyes off his. I see the substantial rise and fall of Logan's chest, and the set of his jawline, telling me he wants to take control but is letting me take the lead, allowing me to go at my own pace.

Reaching down, Logan grabs a handful of my hair as I take his cock to the back of my throat.

"Fuck," Logan hisses as he begins to pump in and out of my mouth, holding my hair so tight it stings a little. "Your mouth looks so fuckin' good wrapped around my cock, Angel."

I'm so turned on.

Reading my body language, Logan asks, "Is sucking my cock turning you on?"

All I can do is hum my response.

"Put your fingers on your clit, Bella. I want to watch you while you suck my dick."

I begin to rub my clit, and it doesn't take long before I can feel my orgasm building as he continues to fuck my mouth.

Moments later, Logan stills, as jets of cum hit the back of my throat and my orgasm crashes over me.

Reaching down, he picks me up, pulling me into him, and rests his forehead on mine. The now lukewarm water is cascading over both of us.

"Fuckin' perfect," he says, breathlessly.

LOGAN and I pull up to the clubhouse and park. Getting off the bike, I hand him my helmet. As we make our way inside, Logan holds my hand. The fact that he's not trying to hide that we're together causes my belly to flutter a little.

Last night the club had been loud, full of bikers and scantily

Undaunted

dressed women. This morning it's quiet. I only see a few of Logan's brothers. Gabriel is in his corner, drinking what I'm guessing is coffee, and Quinn is sitting at the bar with his cup.

Taking a seat at the bar, Logan motions for Austin to bring us some coffee. "Bella wants sugar and a shit ton of cream," he tells Austin.

"Well, look at you two being all cute and shit," Quinn says, interrupting us.

"Shut the fuck up, asshole. It's too early for your shit," Logan tells him.

I look over at Quinn. He winks at me, and I smile. I'm used to his crazy ass by now.

Austin sets my cup in front of me, and just as I'm about to bring it to my mouth, I see that fucking bitch Cassie slide right up next to Logan.

"Hey, Logan," she purrs, while running her hand up his arm.

Obviously, the woman has lost her damn mind. Just as Logan is about to say something, I put my hand on his chest. "It's okay, baby. I got this one." Very calmly, I stand up from my stool, getting right in Cassie's face. "You have about two seconds to take your hands off what's mine. You see, my sister being with me the other day in the store was the only reason I walked away. Make no mistake, I won't be walking away twice," I warn her.

"Logan, baby? Are you going to let this little bitch talk to me like that?"

That's it.

In one swift move, I bring my fist up, punching the whore right in her nose. I strike her so hard, it causes pain to explode in my hand.

Cassie drops to the floor, cupping her nose. Her shrieking sounds like a dying cat.

"Fuck me! I think you broke her nose, sweetheart," Quinn says.

I see Logan looking at me with an intense look on his face. He then turns his attention to Cassie, who is still on the floor. "You stay your ass there," he barks out.

Turning back to the bar, he tells Austin to get a bag of ice. "Sit. Let me see your hand, babe."

He hisses at my swelling, red knuckles as he places the ice pack on my hand.

"Watching you punch that bitch, and claiming me as yours, has my dick so fuckin' hard," he growls in my ear.

"I hate to interrupt you two, but what do you want to do with her?" Quinn questions Logan, pointing at Cassie, who now has a towel to her nose to stop the bleeding.

Logan turns his attention back to Cassie, who is glaring up at me. "You need to get your shit and leave. You're no longer welcome in this clubhouse."

Cassie stares at Logan, with her mouth gaped open. "You don't mean that? You're kicking me out because of her?" she yells, pointing her finger at me.

"Bella is my woman. You just fuckin' disrespected her. Hell fuckin' yeah, I mean it."

"Your woman?" Cassie sputters.

"Gabriel," Logan barks.

I look over to see him striding this way. Gabriel is so quiet, I forgot he was even in the room.

"Make sure Cassie gets all her shit, then escort her off King's property," Logan instructs him.

"You got it, brother." Reaching down, Gabriel grabs Cassie's arm. "Let's go," he grunts.

"About fuckin' time you dealt with Cassie's crazy ass," Quinn says out loud, as we watch Gabriel lead her out of the room.

"Yeah, brother. It was overdue."

Coming over to me and taking my uninjured hand, Logan guides me from the stool I'm sitting in.

"Come on. We need to go see Jake."

Logan and I walk into Jake's office, and when I go to sit, Logan stops me. He sits in the chair first, then pulls me down to his lap.

"Alright, Prez. What's up?"

Letting out a sigh, Jake leans forward in his chair. "After our conversation last night, I made some calls. Lee has been hangin' around Los Demonios lately."

As soon as Jake says that, I feel Logan stiffen under me.

"So, what exactly does that mean?" I ask.

"Not fuckin' sure, but I don't like it," Jake tells me. "For now, I want you and Alba staying here at the clubhouse."

"Fuckin' right, they'll be staying here," Logan says.

I don't even have to think about it. I trust both men. If they say my sister and I need to stay here, then that's what we will do.

"Let me call Alba really quick. She stayed at a friend's house last night, and I need to go pick her up."

I tap her contact in my phone. She answers on the second ring. "Hey, Bella. What's up?"

"Alba, I'm going to come to pick you up at Emma's house. I should be there in about twenty minutes."

"I'm already home," she tells me.

"When did you get there?"

"About ten minutes ago."

"You should have called me. You know I don't want you home alone."

"It's fine. Lee isn't even here."

"Hold on, Alba."

Looking at Logan, I tell him, "I need to go get my sister."

"Not by yourself, you're not. We'll go back to my place to get my truck. That way, we can grab all your shit while we're at your house."

Jake stands and opens the door, motioning for Gabriel to come into the office.

"Gabriel, I need you to go over to Bella's house and pick up her sister. Bella, tell Alba that Gabriel will be there in ten," Jake instructs.

Alba was a little apprehensive about Gabriel coming to get her, but I assured her it was okay and that I would explain what was going on when she got here.

After going back to Logan's house to get his truck, we head to my place so I can get some of mine and Alba's stuff. "How much do you think I need to pack?" I ask him as I walk into our bedroom.

"Everything. You won't be coming back."

"What are you talking about? I live here. Of course, I'm coming back. Just as soon as all this shit with Lee is over."

"I claimed you last night, Bella. That means you're mine. Therefore, you'll be staying with me indefinitely," he informs.

"I'm not just going to up and move in with you, Logan. I have my sister to think about. I would never leave her."

Logan's face goes soft, "I know you wouldn't, Angel. I would never ask you to. That's why she's coming too. My place is plenty big enough. She'll even have her own room."

I'm utterly shocked at what he's saying. "Really?" I ask.

"Of course. You're my woman, and Alba is your sister. That makes her family. I'll not only take care of you, but I'll take care of her too. There's nothing I won't do for you, Angel."

Blinking away the tears threatening to fall, I walk over to Logan and wrap my arms around him.

He places his finger underneath my chin, tilting it up, then kisses me. It's not just a kiss, but a promise to take care of me. A promise to give me everything.

"Logan, I need to go to the diner to talk to my mom," I tell him while sitting in his truck after leaving my house. "If she comes home and sees all of mine and Alba's stuff gone, she'll worry."

"So, let her fuckin' worry. It's because of her husband that you're leaving in the first place."

"Logan, I understand what you're saying, but she's still my

mother. Even though she has made some poor choices, I refuse to turn my back on her. She's been a victim too."

He lets out a sigh. "I get it. I don't agree with you, but I get it."

We pull up and park in front of the diner my mom works at.

"You go on in and talk to your mom, babe. I'll wait out here for you. I got some calls to make."

I walk in, spotting my mom behind the counter, filling drinks.

"Hey, Mom," I say when I reach the counter.

"Hey, sweetheart. What are you doing here?" She smiles.

"I need to talk to you. Can you take a break?"

"Sure. Just go sit in the corner booth, and I'll be over in a few minutes."

I'm sitting in the booth when I look out the window. I see Logan on the phone, having what looks like a very intense conversation.

"So, what's up, sweetie?"

"I wanted to let you know that Alba and I won't be home for a while. In fact, we probably won't be coming back." I'm gauging her reaction, and she doesn't look the least bit surprised. Why would she be? She knows how things have been, dealing with Lee.

"I think that's for the best, Bella. I think Lee has gotten mixed up with some bad people."

"Yeah, Mom, he has," I tell her, confirming her suspicions.

"I kicked him out for good," she tells me, staring out the window.

I'm shocked. "What?"

"Yeah. I told him yesterday that my girls come first, and I wanted him to leave."

I honestly can't believe what I'm hearing right now.

"You did that for us? For Alba and me?" I ask her.

"Bella, believe it or not, I love you and your sister very much. I let you both down. I let myself down. I won't make the same mistakes I did with your father. I did what I had to do to protect you then, and I'm doing what I need to do to protect you both now. Never again, I promise."

My dad? She did what she had to do to protect us then? A knot forms in my stomach at the mention of our father. My mom, seeing my discomfort, changes the subject.

"Is that your guy out there?" she asks, pointing out the window at Logan.

Nodding, I say, "Yeah, Mom. He's mine."

"Does he make you happy, sweetheart. Does he treat you right?"

"He makes me very happy. Logan and his club have been nothing but wonderful to Alba and me."

I smile just thinking about all those crazy-ass men.

Patting my hand, she tells me, "I'm happy for you then, Bella." I know she means it.

"Well, sweetheart. I need to be getting back to work. Call me. Let me know if you're doing okay?"

Standing up, I hug my mom.

"Sure. I'll see you later."

I watch her as she heads back behind the counter. I silently pray that she's strong enough to get her life back.

Walking out to Logan's truck, I see he is no longer on the phone.

"You get shit straight with your mom?"

"Yeah, Logan. Everything is good. She kicked Lee out permanently. Said she was done."

"Good for her, babe," he says, taking my hand in his and linking our fingers.

"Now, let's take all this shit to our house and get it unloaded before we head to the clubhouse. I know you're anxious to see your sister."

I smile, welcoming the butterflies in my stomach as he says, 'our house.'

Undaunted

I walk into the clubhouse with Logan, immediately scanning the room looking for Alba, and I notice Gabriel first because, as usual, he's in his spot. I take in the intense look on his face. Following his gaze, my eyes land on my sister, who is sitting on the couch with her book.

I let my eyes dart back and forth between her and Gabriel, who has his eyes boring into Alba. My sister is so into her book; she's clueless.

I turn to Logan, who has made the same observation as me.

"Well, fuck."

15

LOGAN

"Babe, why don't you go see your sister while I take care of some shit," I say slapping her on the ass. Bella rushes off toward Alba, not even giving me a second glance. I chuckle and shake my head when she offers Gabriel a death glare as she walks past him.

Ignoring her attempt at being intimidating, Gabriel gets up from his chair and makes his way to me. "Come on, brother. Prez is waiting for you in the basement," he says, walking past me.

"The basement? What the fuck's going on?"

Gabriel turns his head back to me with a smile. "Got a present for you, brother."

Now he's got my attention. I continue to follow him down the hall that leads to the basement, while he fills me in on what's going on.

"After I went by to check on the sister last night, I decided to go to Bella's house to see if the stepdad was home. The place was dead, but as I was leaving, I caught sight of a bike parked about a block away. Something didn't feel right about it, so I decided to double back to the house and take a closer look. That's when I found one of Los Demonios' men climbing through a window around the back of the house, and I knocked the motherfucker out. I had one of the prospects bring him here."

"Nobody thought to call me about this shit?"

Stopping and turning toward me, Gabriel asks, "Did you want to be interrupted, brother?" Fuck no I didn't, but I wasn't going to say it out loud. From the smirk on his face, he knows what I'm thinking.

"Yeah, didn't think so," he chuckles. *Asshole.*

"It's all good, brother. Nobody touched him per your request. I only put his ass in the box."

"Wait, what do you mean, per my request?"

"Did you not tell Prez last night that you wanted the son of a bitch who fucked with your woman?" he asked.

"Are you telling me the motherfucker you got last night is the same guy who was after Bella? You know this for sure?"

"Yeah, man, the pussy only lasted a few hours in the box before talking. The idiot is giving up info left and right, but I figured you still wanted your time with him, considering he fucked with Bella."

Opening the door to the basement, I'm hit with an overwhelming feeling of heat. Turning the heat up is something we like to do when putting someone in the box. The one we use is about sixty-seven inches in length and nearly thirty inches wide. So, when you put a man over six feet tall inside, he must slightly bend his knees to fit. But once the lid is closed, the fit is so tight he is unable to move or stretch out. Being in that position for hours on end, the claustrophobia, combined with joint stiffness—not to mention the heat. Yeah, few people last before giving up.

I see Jake sitting off to the side of the room, smoking a cigarette. When my eyes land on the box, Quinn is sitting on top of it with his phone in his hand playing a game. I swear he's like having a fuckin' kid around sometimes.

He looks up from his phone when he sees me walking over. "Well, hey there, brother. Glad you could finally join us."

"Shut up, asshole. Nobody fuckin' called me last night."

"Of course we didn't; we weren't about to interrupt you while you were with your woman. Look at you, man, all glowin' and shit."

I hear Jake chuckle. Gabriel is over in the corner shaking his head, but his shaking shoulders let me know he's at least trying to hold in his laughter. "Shut the fuck up before I put a bullet in your ass," I say, slapping him on the back of his head as he hops off the box.

"Alright, brothers, let's get this party started. Gabriel, get him out. I'd like to hear what the cocksucker has to say." With a chin lift, he walks over and starts to unlatch the box. Once the lid is removed, the smell of piss fills the room. Gabriel proceeds to haul the man out. The fucker is so stiff and dehydrated from the heat he can barely move on his own.

A moment later, there is a knock on the door. Jake walks over and lets Austin in. He brought bottles of water and some sandwiches. This is something else we do, because what's the fun in beating a man that's already half-dead, so we'll give the man some water and something to eat—the last meal of sorts. Though I'm sure he suspects he's not coming out of this basement alive. After Gabriel sets him in a chair, I offer him food and water, which he greedily accepts. Once he's finished and I take a seat in front of him, I notice the SGT AT ARMS patch on his cut. I also recognize him as one of the men who ambushed our run and stole our guns.

"You speak English?"

"Sí, I speak English."

"What's your name?"

"Carlos."

"Alright, Carlos, we have a lot to talk about, but first, we're going to start with the woman you were following last night."

"The bitch is the payment owed to us, her, and the sister. My Prez has big plans for them, and we already have a buyer lined up. He's coming in from Colombia next week and is expecting us to deliver. The stepdad assured my Prez that both girls are untouched."

I hear Gabriel growl from the corner of the room, and I give him a look that tells him to rein it in. It's all I can do to keep myself in check, but I need to keep Carlos talking.

"What are they payment for?" I grind out.

"That gringo, Lee, owes my club some money, and when that puta, *bitch* couldn't pay, he offered up his stepdaughters. It's just too bad my Prez wants to sell. I'd love a go at big sister. I bet her pussy—"

Carlos doesn't get a chance to finish. His words get cut off when I come out of my chair and punch him in his face. I hit him so hard his neck snaps back, and he and the chair fall to the floor, knocking him out cold.

Quinn walks over to where he's lying on the floor. "Maaaan Carlos, you got knocked the fuck out," he says with a horrible Spanish accent.

"I can't believe you lasted that long without hitting the motherfucker," Gabriel spits.

"So," Jake says when he walks over. "What do you make of what he's saying?"

"I believe him, but I don't like how he's too forthcoming with the information. I don't know Prez. Something's off."

"He's playing with us," Gabriel says.

Hearing movement behind me, I turn to see the piece of shit picking himself up with the chair and sitting back down, then using the back of his hand to wipe the blood from his busted lip.

I walk back over to Carlos. "I want to know where we can find Lee," I bite out. I'm so over this bullshit.

"Sorry, gringo, I'm all talked out," he says with a smirk on his face.

Without a second thought, I stride over to a table on the far-left side of the basement and grab the nail gun. By the time I make it back to him, I see Quinn and Gabriel cuffing him to the chair. Without a word, I press it to his right shoulder and pull the trigger.

Carlos howls in pain, a string of Spanish coming from his mouth.

"You still all talked out?"

"Bésame mi culo. *Kiss my ass.*"

This time I press the nail gun to his knee and pull the trigger—once again, hitting bone. "How about now, you cocksucker, still got nothing to say?"

Carlos is in so much pain; he has sweat dripping from his face. "I don't know where Lee is," he says through gritted teeth. "He was supposed to meet us at my club last night, but he never showed. That's why I was at his house last night. My Prez is becoming very impatient. He wants what was promised to him."

"Well, your Prez won't be getting shit, those girls are now under The Kings' protection."

Carlos starts laughing. "You gringos are so fucking stupid. Your protection doesn't mean shit. Those girls are as good as gone. You should never underestimate Los Demonios."

"Prez, we've got company at the front gate," Reid says, coming through the door.

"Who the fuck is it?" Jake snaps, thoroughly annoyed by the interruption.

"Volkov," Reid replies.

Turning to Jake, I ask, "Why the hell are the Russians here?"

"Fuck if I know. They sure as fuck didn't give me a heads up that they were coming. I told Volkov the club had shit under control."

"Well, he doesn't think so," I bite out.

"What do you want to do with Carlos?" Gabriel cuts in.

"I'm not through with the motherfucker. Chain his ass up and leave him down here until I decide I'm done with him." I then turn and follow Jake out of the basement.

16

BELLA

I walk over to my sister, who's sitting quietly by herself on a sofa reading a book. Lifting her head, she discreetly scans the room. I immediately feel guilty for having her thrust into the scary situation of having a man she doesn't know pick her up and bring her to the clubhouse around a bunch of strangers. She only did it because she trusts me, and I can tell how freaked out she is as I sit down beside her.

"Hey," I nudge her shoulder.

"Hi," she sighs, putting down her book and looking at me. "Bella, what's going on?" she whispers, glancing in the direction of Gabriel.

I decide she will be more comfortable if I take her to the room she'll be using while we stay here. Logan told me on the ride here that Alba will remain in the room next to ours. He said he already had one of the prospects get it ready for her.

First, I want to stop by the kitchen and grab something to snack on. Standing, I grab her hand, "Come on, Alba, let's get some food, then I'll show you to your room."

I lead her past the bar and into the kitchen. I smell fresh coffee as we walk in. Alba opens the pink box sitting on the table, and grabs a chocolate éclair from it, along with a napkin.

"Grab me one of those too, would ya?" I ask as I walk over to the cabinets to get some mugs. "You want a cup of coffee?"

"They happen to have cinnamon creamer?" she asks.

I rummage through the various flavors on the shelf until I find a cinnamon flavor. I hold it up to her, getting her stamp of approval with a head bob while she places our éclairs on a paper plate.

Once I've finished mixing our coffee, I motion for her to follow me up the stairs. Walking up the stairs, I turn right, leading the way down the hall.

"It's the last door on the left," I inform her before finally stopping and opening the door.

It's nice inside. It is furnished with the basics; a full-size bed, a dresser that has a flat-screen TV sitting on top, and a full-size bath of its own. Most of the rooms here I'm told are like this.

Setting the mugs on the nightstand, I sit on the bed, and Alba joins me. Before I can even get one bite of my éclair in my mouth, she speaks up.

"Okay, Bella. Spill."

Sighing, I tell her what I've been told. "Lee has been seen hangin' with a biker club that calls themselves Los Demonios. They're the rival MC The Kings have been having problems with lately. They also happen to be some pretty shady people, from what I've heard."

I get up and walk over to the window, opening the curtains to let some light in. I turn, looking back over at my sister, who's still sitting on the bed.

Alba takes a sip of her coffee, "Okay, Lee hanging with scum like that isn't anything new, but why do we have to stay here? What about Mom?"

"I wish I could tell you more, but that's all I know. I stopped by and saw Mom at work. She kicked Lee out. She said this time, it's permanent."

Her mouth gapes open in disbelief. "You're kidding?"

I nod my head, confirming what I said to be true.

"I say good riddance to his sorry ass," my sister adds.

I lie back on the bed, my sister doing the same. "Are the guys worried that something might happen to us?"

"Yeah, they just want to make sure we stay safe, and they feel the best place to do that is here." I shrug my shoulders.

"You like him, don't you?" she inquires with a smile.

I smile. I knew she would be asking eventually.

"Yeah, I like him."

"Wait!" She shoots up out of bed and looks down at me. "You're too relaxed for all this shit that's going on. Usually, you're more on edge. What gives?"

Her eyes got big, and her hand covers her mouth, but I can still see the smile underneath.

"Bella! Did you have sex with Logan?"

I can't help the smile that takes over my face and the warmth that fills my body, just hearing his name.

"He took me home last night, after everything that happened."

"Okay, back up. What happened last night?" she asks with concern.

I sigh, knowing I need to tell her, so she knows just how serious all this shit could be.

I give her the rundown of events from last night that led me out to the clubhouse. And then when I got jealous seeing the same woman that we ran into at the vintage shop hanging all over Logan at the bar.

"Please tell me you said something to that skank."

"I didn't last night, but I definitely had my say this morning." I rub my knuckles that are still sore.

Undaunted

"Ooh, I feel like I need popcorn for this," my sister says, tucking her legs under her while holding a pillow to her chest.

"Not long after arriving back here this morning, that same chick came up to Logan. While I was sitting right there, she proceeds to hang all over him. I wasn't about to have that shit happen anymore. So, I told the bitch Logan is mine. I may have broken her nose when I punched her," I tell my sister with a smirk on my face.

"I can't believe I missed that!" She giggles.

I laugh along with her. "Yeah, well, my hand hurts like hell, but it was worth it."

We both plop back and lay there stretched out on our backs, quiet for a few moments.

"I'm happy for you, Bella."

"It was perfect, Alba. At that moment, everything else melted away. It was like I was high or something. I was completely consumed by him."

Before I can get any further into the conversation, my phone chimes with an incoming text, I dig it out of my back pocket. Seeing it's from Mila, I swipe the screen.

Mila: Hey, what have you been up to? How have you been?
Me: Not much. I'm good. How are you and Ava?
Mila: Good! Meet for coffee soon?
Me: I would love that! Bring Ava too?
Mila: Great! I will. Gotta go. Call soon!
Me: Hug Ava for me. Bye!

Setting my phone on top of the dresser, I decide to get Alba's things unpacked. She gets up and starts to help.

"That was Mila. I've been so wrapped up with my new job and Logan; I haven't been to visit her and Ava in a while." Ava is Mila's daughter and the sweetest little girl. I love spending time with both of them.

I open the door to the small closet and peer inside to see if there happens to be any hangers. "Well, it looks like you'll have to keep most of your things in the drawers for now. I'll see if Logan can get some things you'll be needing, like hangers. I'm sorry about all this, Alba," I say, making my way to the bathroom and placing her makeup bag on the counter.

"It's fine, Bella. If I'm with you, I can deal with it, but I will need some more of my things from the house before I have to go back to school."

"That shouldn't be a problem. I'm sure Logan will get one of the brothers to take us, so we can grab whatever else we need. How about we go downstairs? We can meet some of the other members later, but for now, we can learn the layout out of where everything is. Find out what we can and can't do around here."

Sighing, she gives in, and we leave the bedroom, making our way down the stairs.

17

LOGAN

My brothers and I make our way up from the basement and head out to greet our unexpected guest.

I see Bella and her sister coming from upstairs, so I stride in their direction.

"Hey, babe," I say, pulling her close to me and kissing her. "You get Alba settled in?"

"Yeah, everything is good."

"Alright, Angel. I've got some shit to do, so if you need anything, just let one of the prospects know, and they'll get it for you."

"We're okay. You go do what you need to do."

Just then, Lisa steps up next to us. "Why don't you girls help me with lunch. I could use the extra help now that we have guests. It will give us a chance to get to know each other."

"Cooking is one of our favorite things to do, so we would love to help you," Bella says to her sincerely.

"You and I are going to get along just fine then," Lisa replies with a big smile on her face.

I watch as Bella and Alba walk off toward the kitchen, then

turn to Lisa. "Thanks for including them and making Bella and her sister feel welcome."

"Anytime, sweetheart. I like her, Logan. I can tell she's going to be good for you. You deserve to be happy."

"Thanks, Lisa," I say, kissing her on the top of her head.

"Now, go on and see your guest," she says, shooing me away, "your girl will be fine."

I catch up with Jake and Gabriel as they head across our compound's parking lot toward the gate. I see our prospect, Blake, standing next to a black Suburban SUV with blacked-out windows. Standing next to him is a man in a dark gray suit. I'm assuming he's the driver.

Once we reach the man in question, I immediately notice the two guns in his shoulder holster under his suit jacket. I'm also betting he has one strapped to his ankle, as well. My observation tells me that this man is more than a driver. These men are no threat to us, but I've learned to always be observant—ready for anything.

"My name is Victor," he says in a Russian accent while offering his hand to Jake.

"Jake," Prez replies gruffly, accepting Victor's handshake.

"Volkov and his son would like to apologize for their unexpected visit, but I hope to meet with you so we can dissolve our mutual problem together. This is not how we normally conduct business," Victor tries to assure him.

Jake tells the man, "I called Volkov a few days ago out of courtesy, and I don't much appreciate him just showing up at my compound unannounced."

"We can understand that," Victor says. "But Mr. Volkov also has a personal reason for this meeting as well, and feels with all that's going on, it is time for those things to be addressed."

I look over at Jake, and he has the same confused look on his face as I'm sure I do. What the fuck is he talking about personal reasons? We've only been in business with the Russians for about a year, so I don't know where this shit is leading, but to say I'm not a little bit curious would be a lie.

"Alright, Victor," Prez says. "Blake here will show you in. I'll meet you all inside."

Victor nods, then my brothers and I follow Jake back into the clubhouse.

We all walk in and head straight to the bar. Austin sees us approaching and starts pulling out beers. I grab mine, downing almost all of it in one pull.

Turning to Jake, I ask, "What are you thinking, Prez?"

"I'm not sure. I don't take too kindly to them just showing up here like this."

"We have shit under control," Gabriel adds.

"I agree," Jakes says. "But I'm going to hear them out. I don't believe Volkov would show up without cause. He's always been nothing but respectful in the time we've been in business with him. So, in return, we will show him the same respect and hear whatever it is they came all this way to say."

The clubhouse door opens and in walks Victor. Behind him are two other men, who I'm assuming are Mr. Volkov and his son. The older man looks to be in his late forties and his son probably early twenties, basically a younger version of his father. Both are wearing similar suits that reek of money.

The men walk over, stopping in front of us. I notice Jake goes deathly still, looking a bit taken aback. I glance over at Gabriel, who also has noticed Jake's behavior. I wonder what's gotten into him. He's always calm and collected.

Prez offers his hand. "I'm Jake."

"Jake, I'm Mr. Volkov. This is my son, Nikolai."

There is a collective round of handshakes between us.

"If it is alright with you, Jake, I would like to talk to you in private for a moment," Volkov asks.

"Alright, we can go to my office. Nikolai, why don't you have a drink at the bar."

I watch as Jake heads toward his office, then turn my attention to Nikolai. "Come on, man. Let's get a beer."

Nikolai and I take a seat at the bar, while the prospect gets us a beer and pours a couple of shots. He is the first to speak.

"My father and I are grateful for your club agreeing to meet with us. I assure you we don't normally do business this way."

I down my shot. "You going to tell me what the hell is going on? Your guy over there," I say, pointing to Victor, who is at the end of the bar talking with Reid, "says this is somewhat of a personal visit?"

"I'm sorry, Logan. I'm afraid that it is for my father to tell."

"Alright, man, fair enough," I say, blowing out a frustrated breath. "How long will you guys be in town?"

"We're not quite sure yet. That will depend on how things go today."

Now I'm really fucking curious. I'm also fucking tired of these cryptic answers.

"My family has an estate just a few miles from here, so we will be staying there," Nikolai tells me.

I'm about to reply to him when I feel a hand on my arm. Turning, I see Bella.

"Hey, babe." I smile, pulling her to stand between my legs. She snuggles into my chest while I kiss the top of her head.

"What are you doing, Angel?"

"We just finished cooking lunch. I wanted to say hi for a minute."

"You can come to say hi anytime you want, babe," I say, forgetting for a minute about the man sitting next to me, then I turn back to Nikolai. "Nikolai, this is my girl, Bella."

"It's nice to meet you, Nikolai," she says, offering him her small hand.

Undaunted

"You too, Myshka *little mouse*," he says.

I'm just about to ask what the fuck myshka means when Quinn comes up to me.

"Prez wants to see you, man."

"Alright. Thanks, brother."

"Well, that's my cue to get back to the kitchen," Bella sighs.

"I'll see you later, babe."

"Okay," she says, giving me a quick kiss before walking off.

When I walk into Jake's office, I notice his whole body is tense.

"Hey, Prez. Quinn said you wanted to see me?"

"Yeah, son. Why don't you sit down?"

I stride over, taking the empty seat next to our guest. Nobody is saying a word, and it's raking on my fucking nerves.

Clearing his throat, then standing, Volkov turns his chair to face me directly. His odd behavior has my full attention.

"I suppose there is no easy way to say what I'm about to tell you, so I will start by properly introducing myself. I'm Demetri Alexander Volkov."

I tilt my head at him. He looks like he's waiting for some sort of a reaction, but I have none. I look over at Jake for some clue, and his eyes are boring holes into me like he's waiting for a reaction as well.

Suddenly, I realize he said his name is Demetri. Now my wheels are turning, because my middle name is Demetri. My mother never really talked about who my father was, but she did say she gave me my middle name, Demetri, after him. I take a good look at the man in front of me. He has brown hair with a bit of gray. He's also about the same height as me, but that's not what has all the air leaving my body. The man in front of me has one blue eye and one green eye, just like me. I feel like this is some fucked up dream, but no, it's my fucked-up life. I'm positive the man in front of me, Demetri Alexander Volkov, is my father.

"You're my father."

"Yes, Logan. You are my son."

I have a death grip on the arms of my chair, needing to keep myself in check. It's crazy how many emotions one can feel all at the same time—confusion, elation, anger. Here I have been wondering my whole life about my father and always wondering why he left. Did he know about me? Was he dead?

"I can tell by the looks playing across your face you have many questions. I assure you; I will answer them all."

I'm finally able to bring myself to look at him. "How long have you known about me?" I ask because that is possibly the most important question.

I don't even know if I'm prepared for his answer. What if he's always known, and just never wanted anything to do with me. Will I be able to handle that?

"I became aware of your existence a year ago, son. Had I known about you from the beginning, I would have come for you."

"You said you found out a year ago?"

"Yes," he replies.

"Your contacting our club to do business..."

"Was my attempt to be somehow close to you," my father tells me without hesitation.

"Why wait a whole fucking year to meet me? Why not come as soon as you found out?"

"I don't have a good excuse for that. Only that the lies and deception I uncovered in my own family had me wanting to tread cautiously. I did not want to act hastily or do anything that might bring you harm."

"Bring me harm? What the hell are you talking about?"

Sighing, Demetri leans forward. "What I'm about to tell you, son, is not going to be easy for you to hear. Believe me; it about broke me."

I nod for him to continue.

"I met your mother twenty-six years ago. My family has an

estate here in Montana because we do a lot of business in this part of the country and Canada. I was here with my father. I met Rose in a coffee shop the second week I was here. One look at your mother, I was a goner."

Demetri pauses, with a faraway look in eyes, like he remembers that day like it was yesterday.

Continuing, he says, "I spent every spare moment that I wasn't working with Rose. I want you to know, Logan, I was very much in love with your mother."

"Then why did you leave her?"

Demetri closes his eyes. I can tell that it pained him to do so. I'd say that I am pretty damn good at reading people, and I have no doubt this man loved my mother. What I don't understand is why someone would leave the person they were in love with. I could never leave Bella. Nothing in this world could keep me from her.

"I left because I had an obligation to my family. I was to be married to another woman, my marriage already arranged for me. I didn't dare defy my father. That is how things worked in my family. It's been that way for generations."

"Did my mother know you were engaged to someone else?" I ask through gritted teeth. He still pursued my mother, knowing that he would eventually break her heart.

"No, I didn't have it in me to tell her. She knew I had to return to Russia. We both parted with broken hearts. On good terms, but broken nonetheless."

"How long after you returned to Russia were you married?"

"Two months. Nikolai was born a year and a half after that."

Fuck. How could I have overlooked that? Nikolai is my half-brother. I have a fucking brother.

"So, while my mother was here alone and pregnant, you were off playing family and living happily ever after," I snap at him bitterly.

"Logan!" Jake hisses at me.

Shit, I forgot he was still here.

"It's alright, Jake," Demetri says, holding his hand up. "I assure you, son, my life was far from a fairy tale."

"Can we get to the part where you find out you have a son?"

"It was after my father passed away last year. I was going through his office and came across a file with your mother's name on it. When I opened it, there were a dozen photos—Rose pregnant, Rose with a baby, and Rose with a small boy. Also, with the photos were letters. Twelve letters in total. Two were from her telling me of the pregnancy, and the other ten were each written on your birthdays. Telling me of all the new things about you each year that went by. How much you'd grown. All your likes and dislikes. How you were doing in school."

I close my eyes, trying to control my shaking hands. I had no idea she did any of that. I remember asking about my father a few times, but my mom would always change the subject.

"The letters were postmarked to our estate here in Montana. The housekeeper must have forwarded them to my father's home in Russia. He knew the whole time and kept it from me. My father knew I was in love with Rose. Had I known of the pregnancy, I would have given everything up for her, and you, Logan."

"Why do I get the feeling that that's not all of it?" I question him. I have a gut feeling that I'm not going to like where the rest of this story is going.

"Your mother's car accident was no accident at all. My father saw Rose as a threat. He did what he felt he had to do to eliminate that threat. Alexander Volkov was a heartless man, and would never let anything stand in the way of his business. I found your mother's death certificate in the files as well. I knew right then what evil my father had done. When I didn't find any record of your death, I immediately began my search for you. I was relieved to discover you were alive and well and living in Montana. I'm truly sorry, Logan. If my father were still alive, I would kill him myself," Demetri declares with anger and sadness in his voice.

I need to get the fuck out of here. I refuse to break down in front of him.

I feel like I can't breathe.

I need to go somewhere, away from all this.

Standing on shaky legs, I don't utter a word as I leave the office. There is nothing left to say. When my mom died, I was devastated, but now finding out that she was killed simply for falling in love with the wrong man?

I don't even know how to process that information.

18

BELLA

M*yshka*? I'm wondering what that means as I walk back into the kitchen. "What else can I help with, Lisa?"

"Honey, everything is cooking, so bring yourself over to the table with Alba and me for a while."

I walk over to the kitchen table and pull out a chair, and I sit down and pour myself a glass of tea. "Lisa, how long have you been with Bennett?"

"Oh, honey, I've been with that man since high school."

I'm a little curious about how she has handled this life all these years. It doesn't seem to be an effortless way to live. It's not like my life has been a walk in the park. They're a big family here, and everyone seems to be happy. I guess I'm feeling a little overwhelmed. Everyone, including me, needs reassurance sometimes. "Have you been with him as part of the club just as long?"

Getting up to grab the food out of the oven, she places it on the counter then walks over to sit back down at the table before answering my question.

"Bennett chose this life, the club, not long after he was

discharged from the Army. The club gave him a sense of purpose and brotherhood that he was struggling to find once he came home trying to adjust to civilian life. Naturally, I followed him."

When I look at Lisa as she's talking about Bennett, you can see how very much in love she is still with him.

"Was it hard, you know, adapting to this lifestyle? The MC life that is?"

Smiling, she places her hand on top of mine. "Not gonna lie. It can be tough. Takes a strong woman to love one of these men. It takes someone strong to make it through life period, Bella. Whether it's with the MC or not. Tell me, do you love Logan?"

I feel completely safe when I'm with him. He makes me smile so much my face hurts. When he walks into a room, my stomach flutters, and I get the most overwhelming feeling of warmth and peace. He was made for me.

I don't hesitate, already knowing the answer. "I love him."

"Then there is absolutely nothing you can't handle. Love will help you weather any storm, Bella." Pointing toward the direction of the main room, she continues. "That man out there loves you, and you love him. Nothing else matters."

Lisa squeezes my hand before standing up. "Alright, girls, let's get all this food laid out on the table in the common room before they start a riot. Alba, if you would bring the two pitchers of tea out of the refrigerator and Bella, go grab the potato salad and coleslaw."

We collect everything and head out to the other room. The men are all scattered, either drinking or over at the pool tables, as we carry the food to the tables and begin setting everything down. Nobody moves to serve themselves until Lisa speaks, "Okay, boys, come get ya some lunch."

Alba walks up to me with a small plate of her own. "Bella, I'm going to head upstairs and eat in my room. It's just a bit too loud and busy out here for me."

"Okay. I'll be up shortly. I'm going to see if I can find Logan."

Alba turns around and makes her way upstairs. I peer around the room, but I don't see any sign of Logan, so I decided to step outside for a moment to get some fresh air and get away from all the noise.

I've just made it out the front door when he comes charging out. His breathing is rapid, and his fists clenched so hard his knuckles are white, but it's the look on his face that has my attention. Devastation. What the hell is going on? I run over to him as he makes his way to his bike, mounting it.

"Logan!" I yell out. It doesn't take me but a second to be at his side. I reach out, touching his arm, "Logan, what's wrong?"

He looks to the sky, letting out a long sigh before he finally turns his face to look at me. "Angel, I need to get out of here. Take a ride with me."

It's more of a plea than demand or a question. He hands me a helmet, and I slip it on as I climb on the back of his bike and wrap my arms tightly around his waist, nestling into his back, inhaling the smell of his leather cut, forgetting all about the fact that I decided to wear a short skirt today.

I hear Jake call out to him as we peel away from the compound and through the gate.

We ride for what seems like forever with the sun upon our backs until we pull off the main road down a small narrow dirt one that appears to be more like a nature trail, blanketed by an endless tree canopy until it suddenly opens into a clearing. In front of us is a breathtaking lake. The water is so clear that there's a mirror image of the blue-green sky and white pillowed clouds from above.

Logan parks his bike under a large oak tree, putting the kickstand down just before turning the motor off. I don't bother trying to ask any questions, so I carefully slide off the bike, trying not to flash every woodland creature as my dress tries to fly up with the warm spring breeze. Quietly, I stand by his side and wait him out.

He reaches his hand out, grabbing at my hip. Pulling me closer, he wraps his arms around my waist. His grip tightens.

"Logan?" I barely get out before I'm lifted off the ground as he places me on his lap. I now have my legs spread on either side of Logan's, as we sit on his bike under the shade of the oak tree. His hands still firmly on my hips. "Angel." Logan leans forward, resting his forehead on mine. "I just need to hold you."

I look at him, seeing a myriad of emotions behind his beautiful eyes. The turmoil he's feeling is so intense my heart aches. I can feel his emotions seeping from his fingertips right into me. I move my head, placing my lips on the side of his face, slowly and lightly placing soft kisses along his jawline until I reach the sweet spot just under his ear on the side of his neck as my hands run across the top of his broad shoulders. Raising my hands, I cradle his face in my palms, never breaking eye contact, whispering, "Talk to me."

Running his large hand up to the small of my back, he pulls me into his body, closing the gap between us, until my chest presses against his. Gripping the back of my neck, he kisses me. An all-consuming kiss that makes you want to cry it's so good. The kind where you feel like your feet have left the earth. Logan is pouring everything into this kiss. My body—my soul is consuming all of it as if it's the very essence I need to stay alive.

His lips leave mine, only for him to whisper, "You are so fucking beautiful."

He slowly lowers me until my back is resting against the gas tank. His eyes are hooded with desire as he lets his hands slowly run down my arms, caressing my skin, igniting a fire in my flesh with every stroke. Slowly, he unbuttons my top, exposing my white lace covered breasts. "I've wanted to fuck you on the back of my bike since the moment I laid eyes on you," he rasps.

Leaning forward, he pulls the cups of my bra down before

taking my nipple into his mouth, causing my breath to quicken. I arch my back, eager for more as he moves to my other breast giving it equal attention. Running his hands up my thighs, he slowly pushes my skirt up around my waist.

"It's sinful, all the things I want to do to you, Bella."

Watching me, he shifts my panties to one side, running his finger over my slit, then starts working my clit, moving in a circular motion. I'm so turned on watching him, watching me, combined with being out in the open that it doesn't take long before I'm standing right on the edge of my orgasm. As soon as his finger slides into my opening, stroking my inner wall, I lose it. "That's it, come for me," he demands.

As soon as those words leave his mouth, my orgasm rips through my body. I don't even have time to catch my breath before I hear the clank of his belt buckle and the zipper of his jeans as he frees his thick cock. Panting, I watch as he pumps his shaft a few times, coating himself with my wetness, before gripping my hip with one hand, and positioning the head of his cock at my opening with the other. In one hard thrust he buries himself inside me, causing me to moan with pleasure.

"Fuck," he groans, "you feel so good."

With my hands clasping the handlebars, I use the leverage to rock my hips, meeting him thrust for thrust as he drives into me.

Leaning forward, Logan hitches my leg higher up his waist. The angle has me riding the line between pleasure and pain. Growling, he grabs both my hips as he pounds harder. Seeing him lose himself in me is my undoing. I come harder than I ever have before, screaming out his name. Flashes of lights dance behind my eyes as my vision blurs and my back arches. I hear Logan moan as he follows with his release.

I'm coming down from the euphoric high of the most intense orgasm I've ever had, when he slides his arm under my back, lifting me and pressing my chest to his, and softly kisses me.

"You are the best thing that has ever happened to me."

Tucking himself back into his jeans, Logan proceeds to clean me up. He helps me stand before getting off the bike himself. I go about fixing my clothes, starting with pulling my skirt down, then buttoning the long sleeve blue jean shirt I'm wearing. I'm beginning to regret my choice of wardrobe when I feel a breeze pick up. Logan notices me shiver and unstraps the rolled-up blanket from his bike, then wraps it around my shoulders. He guides me to the edge of the lake, where we sit down on the grass, and he pulls me into his lap with my back to his chest and his arms around my waist as we stare out at the clear water.

"It's beautiful out here, Logan. I've never seen this place before."

"Few people know this place exists," he tells me, "my mom used to bring me out here."

Continuing, he lets out a heavy sigh. "She died on my tenth birthday. We were heading here when she lost control of the car, going over the guardrail."

My heart sinks for him, "I'm so sorry." I couldn't imagine losing my mom.

"I got busted up pretty bad. I didn't even get to attend her funeral."

I want to spin around and look at him, but I have a feeling it's easier for him to share staying just the way we are.

"My Aunt Lily had her buried out here. Just on the other side over there." He points to the left. I look in the direction of where he's pointing, and in the distance, I notice a headstone amongst the lush green grass.

"Logan, it's the perfect resting place."

"My Aunt Lily was Jake's old lady. She told him about this place. As kids, she and my mom would come out here. It was a special place for them both. Jake bought this land for my aunt, and it's where both of them are buried."

"Both?" I question.

"Just a few feet from where my mom is buried," he points, "is my Aunt Lily. She passed away from cervical cancer three years after my mom died."

I scan to my right and see the second headstone. To lose two women he loved in such a short amount of time had to have been hard.

"Logan...What happened back at the club?"

He tenses, and his grip tightens. I don't want him to shut down on me now.

"I'm here to listen. I want to help any way I can. No judgment."

He leans down and kisses my neck. "Those men that showed up earlier...well, turns out that one of them is my father and the one I was sitting next to at the bar, drinking a beer with...is my goddamn brother."

I'm shocked for him. I turn myself around in his lap and face him. "You never knew who your father was?"

"No, Angel. I'm the product of a short-lived romance. My mom never talked about him. Good or bad. It turns out my father left her because he was supposed to marry another damn woman."

Moving me from his lap, Logan gets up and lights a cigarette. Blowing the smoke out and running his hand through his hair, he tells me the rest of the story about his father falling in love with his mom then leaving her to fulfill his family obligations. His father never knew about him. Nothing at all. His grandfather kept him a secret from his dad.

"That's not the worst of it. My very own flesh and blood, my grandfather, murdered my mom. He was the cause of the crash that killed her...and it almost killed me."

He's pacing back and forth, looking like a caged animal with nowhere to go. "I don't even know how to process all this, ya know. I mean—fuck, twenty-five years."

I listen as he tells me more about the whole unbelievable story, and I have come to realize that his father lost so much too. I'm not going to tell him that right now. That's the last thing he needs to hear.

"So, he tracked you down after finding out about you? At least he found you, right?"

Laughing, he says, "He's known about me for a whole goddamn year."

He sits back down in the grass next to me, looking defeated and tired. I reach over and take his hand in mine.

"Bella, he's the head of the Russian family we do business with. Can you fuckin' believe that? My dad is Russian Mafia. It was his way of being a part of my life until he got the guts to tell me he existed."

"But he found you, Logan. He wants to be a part of your life now."

"Yeah, well, I'm not too sure I want him in mine."

The sun is starting to set, and fireflies are beginning to glow all around us as we sit for a few moments watching the sunset flickering across the water. I stand up and walk over to a patch of wildflowers and start picking a large beautiful bundle. When I'm satisfied with my haul, I walk back over to Logan and extend my hand out to him.

"Come on."

Getting to his feet, he holds my hand in his as I begin to lead him in the direction of the headstones. Stopping in front of his mother's, I place half the flowers against her headstone before moving to his Aunt Lily's and resting the remaining half of flowers against hers.

The whole time I can feel Logan watching me. Turning back, I wrap my arms around his waist and place my head on his chest and listen to the beating of his heart against my ear. I want him to know how much it means to me that he brought me out here. "I wish I would have had the chance to know them."

We walk back to his bike. The sun has set, and the air is getting colder. Logan wraps the blanket around my waist, giving me extra protection from the night air once I'm seated on the bike. I'm on the verge of falling asleep when we finally make it back to the compound. Logan has me nuzzled into his side as we make our way into the clubhouse. We bypass everyone on our way in. From the looks on some of the brothers' faces, I'm guessing word has gotten around about the whole family reunion. He doesn't pay them any mind as he guides me upstairs. I stop long enough to peek in on my sister, who has fallen asleep reading. I walk in and place her Kindle on the nightstand but leave the bathroom light on before closing her door and heading into mine and Logan's room. I go into the bathroom to brush my teeth and wash my face before stripping out of my clothes, and slip on one of Logan's t-shirts, then crawl into bed.

Once he's done brushing his teeth, he strips down to nothing before walking out of the bathroom. I can't help but admire his toned inked body. He catches me looking and gives me his signature smile.

"Didn't get enough earlier, babe?" he grins as he slides into bed.

"Never," I smile at him.

Logan reaches over and pulls me back into his chest. It's been a long day for both of us. I yawn as I snuggle further into his embrace.

"Goodnight, Angel."

"Goodnight, Logan."

19

LOGAN

She's so fuckin beautiful, caring, and sweet, and she's mine. I watch as Bella drops her towel from her body and starts applying her favorite vanilla lotion that always has her smelling so damn good.

I woke up with the sun because her little ass was rubbing my cock, and it became too much to ignore, so I woke her up with my mouth, before sinking into her. We lay in bed for a few hours talking more about yesterday's events. Fuck, the whole damn situation is insane and the timing; I can't decide if it's good or bad. Does he want a father-son relationship, or does he have an ulterior motive? I'm not sure what to think. Out of all the chaos lately, the woman in front of me is the calm to my storm.

Bella lifts her head and blushes a little as I continue to observe her. Her eyes twinkle as she notices the physical effect she's having on me.

I continue watching her dress as she shimmies into some tight as hell jeans. "Fuck woman, you keep wiggling that little ass, and we won't ever leave this damn room."

"Doesn't sound like a bad idea to me," she says, slipping a t-shirt over her head.

I grab my gun and shoulder holster off the dresser and slip it on before reaching for my cut.

"So, beautiful, let's go over a few things. You'll be riding with a prospect today. You'll be accompanied by a brother whenever you or your sister need to go anywhere, just until we resolve all this shit with Los Demonios and that bastard Lee." I slide my cut on as she walks up to me, and I pull her in close.

"Alright, I can handle that for a while."

Walking over and sitting on the bed, she starts to pull her boots on. "You going to be at the garage today?" she asks.

"Just gonna be Austin and Quinn again, Angel. Got shit to take care of today."

Walking back over to me, she stretches her arms up, clasping her hands behind my head, pulling me down far enough so our lips can meet.

"Maybe you should go see Demetri and Nikolai."

Sighing, I kiss the top of her head. "Don't know about that. Not sure I won't lose my shit. I can't look past the fact that his father is the reason my mom is dead."

"I'm not saying you should have a relationship with him. Go find the answers you're looking for, that's all."

I know she means well. Bella is more optimistic about people than I am. I've come to find that she's a good judge of character, so maybe I should go. She amazes me, how after the hardships she's had to overcome, she always focuses on the good in life. I find it hard to trust anyone outside the club. I've seen more times than not people would rather use you for their own personal gain.

Before we're able to finish our little talk, there's a knock at the bedroom door, followed by Quinn's voice from the other side.

"Yo, brother! Everyone's looking for you. We got church in ten minutes."

Still holding Bella, I look down, "Why don't you grab your sister and head downstairs. I'll come eat something with you before you leave. Okay?"

Snaking her arms down around my waist, she rests her head on my chest, hugging me. "Okay."

Then with another kiss, I watch her walk out the door.

"Hey, Quinn," Bella says as she walks by him on her way to her sister's room.

"Hey, darlin', how's it goin'?"

Bella gets halfway down the hall when Quinn hollers out. "Hey, I got a question for you. Why doesn't a chicken wear pants?"

I hear her holler back, "I have no idea." The laughter in her voice fills the hallway.

Quinn continues, "Because his pecker is on his head!"

I chuckle. Where does he get these damn jokes from? I've put up with the endless jokes for so long, most times I tune them out, but my woman seems to love them.

Still laughing, she tells him, "See ya later, Quinn."

Stepping into the hallway, I catch him looking at my woman's ass as she makes her way down the hall, and I give him a pop upside his head. "Quit staring at her ass, dipshit."

Quinn doesn't pay me any mind. He only smiles. Walking downstairs, we head into church, where the rest of the men are gathering. Just before entering, I catch Gabriel and Reid waiting outside the door as Quinn and I approach.

Reid is the first to speak, "Hey, man. We just wanted to make sure you're good. We heard about what went down yesterday. Shit man, that's a lot to take in, brother," he says, rubbing the back of his neck. I look at Gabriel, and he doesn't speak. He nods his head in agreement before placing his hand on my shoulder. Quinn and Reid follow with the same gesture. This right here is my family. No matter what choices I make in the future, they are the ones that have always been a part of my life.

"Thanks, brothers, I'm good."

Jake is sitting in his usual spot at the head of the table when I walk over and sit down in mine. It looks like he wants to say something to me but doesn't. I'm sure he had just as many questions, if not more than I did yesterday. Clearing his throat, he starts talking.

"Alright, let's get this shit over with. First, I got the news that there was a group of Los Demonios heading South of Dixon last night. Had a couple of brothers tail them, so Reid, make sure you're on top of those burners today just in case anything should happen."

"Got it, Prez," Reid answers.

Jake reaches over and takes a sip of his coffee before adding. "Logan's woman—"

A collective sound of fists hitting the table fills the room. I do my best to hide a smile as a few of my brothers yell, "Hell yeah!"

"As I was saying, you all know Bella and her sister are staying with us for as long as necessary until we resolve the issue with Los Demonios and the connection those fuckers have with their stepdad. We need to make sure that a brother is with them at all times. I'll leave it up to Logan as to who gets put on watch for both."

I lift my chin, acknowledging the choice is mine to make.

"Oh, and there is one more thing. The issue of the asshole down in the basement. It's starting to fuckin' stink down there from him pissing himself. Logan, it's your call. What do you want to be done with him?"

I stew on it for a minute. "I'm pretty sure we've hit a wall with that one. As far as I'm concerned, he's a loose end that we don't need anymore. We'll have him disposed of before the day is done," I tell Jake.

He bobs his head in agreement. With no other objections from the rest of the brothers, he slams the gavel on the table, ending church for the day, and we all file out and make our way toward the delicious smells coming from the kitchen. I find Bella along with her sister and Lisa setting the table with platters of food.

After having breakfast with my woman and some of the other brothers, I see to it that Austin, one of the prospects, is put on watch to keep an eye on Bella and her sister. Giving him this responsibility is a big deal, so he knows not to fuck it up because there won't be any second chances given. I've also decided to take Bella's advice and ride out and see Demetri. I run down to Jake's office to see if he has the address. I find him in his office, sipping on a cold beer. I knock on the open door before going in.

He looks up from what has his attention. "Hey, son, sit down."

I pull the chair out and sit. I need to get something off my chest before I ask him for anything.

"Listen, Jake...about yesterday." I rub my hand over the back of my neck, "Sorry about running out on you and leaving you here to deal with that shit-storm by yourself."

"Son, I'm not worried about any of that shit. Hell, the whole goddamn situation took me by surprise, but you handled it the only way you could. What I want to know is if you're doing alright. That was some heavy shit yesterday."

I don't mince words with Jake. The man raised me. He's the one I should be calling dad. "I've got a better grasp of everything. Bella helped me see things from a different perspective, which is why I'm here. I want to go out and talk to Volkov. Do you have the address for his place?"

Reaching into his desk drawer, he pulls out an envelope, handing it to me. "He gave this to me not long after you left yesterday. Said to give this to you if you came asking to get in touch."

I open the envelope and pull out the letter that's inside.

Logan,

If you wish to talk, I'm at your disposal. My personal phone and address are listed below. The guard at the gate was given instructions to let you through if you choose to see me.

Your Father,

Demetri Volkov

I fold the letter and shove it into my pocket and stand. Jake stands too, stepping in front of me.

"Logan, no matter what you choose to do, I support you. That man may be your father, but I consider you my son, no matter who else makes that claim."

He pulls me in for a quick hug and claps me on the back. "Let me know how things go," he says as he steps back over to his desk, sitting down.

"I'll fill you in over a drink later," I tell him and turn to leave.

It turns out I don't have to drive too far because he's staying out on Point Road, just north of Kings Point. When I reach the end of the road, the property is surrounded by a solid ten-foot wrought iron privacy fence along with a large wrought iron gate. As I'm pulling up and preparing to stop, the gate swings open, and the guard steps out. With a deep Russian accent, he tells me I will be greeted at the door.

I pull into the circular driveway and park my bike. Victor, the guy who accompanied my father and brother to the compound yesterday, is waiting on the steps. "Your father is pleased to hear of your arrival Mr. Kane, follow me."

I take a good look around, noticing all the cameras mounted to the house, and I'm impressed. I expected to walk into a grand, over the top sterile environment, but instead, the interior matches the exterior of the large log cabin home, furnished much like my own. I'm led into the living room. A floor-to-ceiling window takes up one whole wall, giving an amazing view of the waterfront. I'm left to wait, so I walk over and gaze out at the water.

"Logan."

I turn as I hear my name. Demetri makes his way over,

Undaunted

extending his hand for a shake. He's much more casual today: jeans and a t-shirt. The resemblance between us is a bit unnerving.

"Come sit. Would you care for a drink?"

I take a seat in one of the leather chairs close to the window but facing the entrance to the room. I'm not ready to let my guard down. I have no reason, other than the fact he says he's my father, to trust him or anyone that works for him. We do business with them, and that's as far as it goes—for now.

"I'll take a beer."

Walking over to the minibar off to the side of the room, he opens the small fridge and pulls out two bottles, pops the tops off, and brings them over. He hands one to me as he takes a sip of the one in his other hand.

"You must have many more questions. I promise I will answer them all to the best of my ability."

I take a pull of my beer, wondering where to start. The questions I have are all a jumbled mess in my head. "Why not tell your family to fuck off if you loved my mom so much?" I take another drink from the bottle before setting it on the table beside me.

He doesn't hesitate to answer, and what he says is unexpected. "To save her. I was trying to save her life. My father didn't frown upon what he thought was a fling, but when he became aware I had fallen in love, he not only threatened your mother but my mother and sister as well. Said he would not only ruin Rose's life, but if I walked away from my obligation, he would throw my mother and sister out to the wolves."

Demetri walks over to the bar and sits his half-empty beer down and pours himself two fingers of whiskey into a glass tumbler. Holding it up, he offers a glass, but I decline. I'll stick to having a beer. I would rather be clear headed, ready for whatever he throws at me.

"I did what was necessary to protect the most important people in my life from a heartless bastard with the power to do and get away with whatever he promised would happen. So, as I told you yesterday, your mother and I parted ways. For her good, I married another woman that I despised. Who was just as ruthless and conniving as my father."

He may have sacrificed, but that still doesn't do much to squash the resentment I'm feeling toward the man. "You never once tried to get in touch with her the years she was alive. Why? With all the resources and power your family has, why is it you didn't have a clue about me?"

"Son—"

"Don't call me son. You haven't earned that right," I bite out.

His shoulders slump a little. "Fair enough."

Sitting back down into the leather chair across from me, he sighs. "Logan, after going back to my home country and leaving your mother here, my father had me put on lockdown, so to speak. His men were watching my every move. I was never left alone. The marriage between my ex-wife and I was purely a business merger to bring two of the most powerful families in Russia together."

None of what he says has me giving a damn. He still left my mother and never looked back.

"The day I found those files, found out what my father had done, I told you before, if he weren't already dead, I would have killed him myself. When I found the letters written to me from your mother, my Rose, it nearly did me in. When I found out I had created a life with the only woman I had ever loved..." he pauses, trying to collect himself, "not only did I find out my father hid all of this from me, but I also discovered my wife knew I had another son before we had our own..."

Before he can finish, his son—my brother walks in, holding a metal lockbox, setting it down next to Demetri.

"Sorry to interrupt, Father, but this was just delivered. I assume you wish to have it now?" Nikolai cuts his eyes to me. My younger brother looks so much like me in appearance it's fucking freaky as shit, right down to the genetic trait the three of us share, our eye colors. I stand, stretching out my arm, offering my hand to greet him.

"Logan, it's good to see you here today."

"You too, brother." And I mean it. No matter what my feelings are when it comes to Demetri, I have no ill feelings toward Nikolai. He's my brother, and I'm fucking happy about that. I sit back down in the chair I was occupying, and Demetri directs Nikolai to sit as well.

"As I was saying. My ex played a part in the deception, which is one of the many reasons I divorced her."

I cut my eyes to my brother because this is his mother his father is talking about, but he doesn't show any signs of discomfort. Nikolai cut his eyes to me, "What my father says is true, Logan. My mother is a heartless woman. I envy you. Your mother loved you."

She did love me.

I watch as Demetri takes a chain from around his neck and on the end, is a small key. Shifting to his right, he lifts the lockbox sitting on the table.

"In this box, I keep the letters along with other small mementos from when I knew your mother."

Inserting the key and unlocking it, he lifts the lid and pulls out a bundle of envelopes. "I would like to share these with you. They are the letters Rose wrote to me before she died."

Before she was murdered.

I grab the letters as he hands them to me and randomly pull one from the pile. As I open the envelope, there is a faint yet familiar smell. She must have sprayed perfume on the paper. I unfold the letter that looks like it's been read a thousand times, as worn as it is, and I begin to read it.

Dearest Demetri,

Today is Logan's fifth birthday. He's getting so big and looking more like you every day. He starts kindergarten in a couple of months. Can you believe it? Time has gone by so fast. Enclosed you will find a photo. I took it just last week at the lake. I take him to our special place as often as I can. He loves it there. I hope this letter finds you well. I miss you.

Love always,

Rose

Fuck. This whole time, she was taking me to a place that was special to both of them. I guess it was her way of giving me not only a piece of her but a piece of my father as well.

"Logan, I would be honored to have the chance to be a part of your life, but I will respect whatever decision you make."

I hear what he's saying, and I'm processing everything, or at least trying to when I hear Bella's sweet voice telling me to give him a chance. I can feel my mom nudging me to do the same.

Clearing my throat, I fold the letter, putting it back into its envelope and look at him. "Mom is buried out there. At the lake."

He made the first move. Now it's time for me to try and make mine. I hand him the letters. Before I go, I offer an olive branch. "Listen, Sunday we're having a big BBQ out at the compound. I want to introduce you to my family. It will start around noon, but feel free to show up before."

I walk out the door, not waiting for a reply, and mount my bike. I take a long ride to clear my thoughts, trying to come to peace with everything, before heading home to my woman. My family.

20

BELLA

Today is my sister's last day of her spring break vacation. She's come to work with me every day this week. I don't think she was ready to stay at the clubhouse by herself all day. Alba knows that she's safe there and gets along with all the brothers, but feels more comfortable being wherever I am. Honestly, I've enjoyed having her with me. It's been a long time since we've spent so much time together, because I'm always working. I know she will eventually become more at ease being around the club, but until then, I welcome her company.

Walking out of Logan's and my room at the clubhouse, I make my way down the hall to Alba's room. I knock once before opening the door. I see she's dressed and ready to go.

"You want to go downstairs and grab some breakfast before we go?" I ask.

"Yeah, I'm starving."

When Alba and I walk into the kitchen we see Lisa already at work cooking eggs and sausage. We dive in helping, popping bread in the toaster and making fresh coffee. My sister grabs the plates and silverware to set the table. The men will be filling in here soon. No doubt led by their noses. This has become our daily routine. We both enjoy helping Lisa in the kitchen, and with all these hungry men to feed she could use the help. I can't believe she did this every day on her own. You never hear her complain. The smile on her face shows she loves taking care of people, and it suits her too. I've quickly learned it's in Lisa's nature to be the momma bear.

As if on cue, one by one, the guys file into the kitchen, taking their seats at the table.

Bennett is the first one in, walking over to Lisa, wrapping his arms around her waist from behind, and giving her a sweet kiss on her neck. I love how they look at each other. Lisa and Bennett are the perfect examples of what true love looks like, and the fact that they still look at each other the way they do, after they've been married for so many years, is incredible.

While fixing myself some coffee I feel the energy in the room change. Looking over my shoulder, I see him standing in the doorway, his hungry eyes watching me. He strides over to the table, taking a seat. Never once losing eye contact.

"Come on and eat, Angel."

Smiling, I walk over, taking the chair next to him. I sit at the table listening to the conversation flow, loving the jokes and banter between the brothers. This is what family should be like. And I feel so lucky to be a part of it.

"What are you thinking about, babe?" Logan asks.

"I just thought that you have a great family, and you're fortunate to have them."

"They're your family now too, Bella. There is nothing my brothers wouldn't do for you and your sister."

Logan gives me a soft kiss on my lips. I turn my attention back to my plate when I hear Alba giggling. She's sitting next to one of the prospects, Blake. They are the closest in age. She's eighteen, and I remember Logan saying Blake was twenty. Glancing to the other end of the table, I see Gabriel shooting daggers at the young prospect. I swear I'm about to see steam coming out of his ears.

I've been noticing lately the way he looks at Alba, and my sister is none the wiser. You would think I would be concerned, but I know Gabriel is a good man. A bit rough around the edges but good nonetheless. I look next to me at Logan, and he has made the same assessment. He's shaking his head at his brother, silently telling him not to kill the miserable unsuspecting prospect. I chuckle to myself. This will no doubt get interesting, and I intend to sit back and see how it plays out.

After quickly helping Lisa with the breakfast dishes, Alba and I head to the clubhouse parking lot where Austin is waiting to drive us to the shop. Logan refuses to let me or Alba go anywhere by ourselves. He explained that with all the shit going on with Los Demonios and Lee it would be safer for one of the club members to take us wherever we need to go. To be honest I'm okay with it. I feel a lot safer having one of the brothers around all the time.

Logan hasn't been into work at all this week because he's dealing with club business, so it's just been Quinn and Austin working the garage. I've missed not having him there, but I understand why he's not. Part of me feels responsible for the crazy mess the club is having to deal with. I mean, if it weren't for my asshole stepdad, none of this would be happening. I confessed this to Logan last night, and he immediately squashed my guilt. He said nobody in the club feels that way and that he'd take me over his knee and tan my ass if he ever heard me say something like that again. I'm not ashamed to say that his words turned me on. Logan saw the heat in my eyes after saying that, then spent the whole night worshiping my body. I woke up this morning with a delicious ache all over.

I'm pulled from my thoughts when we arrive at the garage. Stepping out of Austin's truck, I turn to him. "I'm sorry that you've been stuck with babysitting duty, I know the last thing you want to be doing is carting our asses around everywhere. If you want, maybe I can talk with Logan about you and Blake taking turns or something."

"No!" Austin practically shouts. "It's an honor to be the one to watch over the VP's old lady, Bella, please don't say anything."

"An honor?" I asked, tilting my head; my facial expression no doubt telling him that he sounds ridiculous.

"Seriously, Bella, it means a lot to me that Logan asked me to be the one to look out for you and your sister, so please don't say anything. Besides, you and your sister are fuckin' great and easy to look at," he says with a grin.

"Come on, let's get to work," I say while rolling my eyes. Austin follows behind me, chuckling.

The day passes quickly, and it's time to close for the day. I went across the street to Kings Ink at lunchtime and talked to Gabriel about wanting a tattoo. He told me to come by after work, and he'd fit me in.

I wasn't expecting to get it done this soon, but I already knew exactly what I wanted, so why wait.

Alba helps me clean the break room while Quinn and Austin close the bays. When we're done, we grab our things and wait for Austin. He's in the back taking out the trash. Ever since Mason attacked me, I haven't gone out there anymore. I know he was dealt with and will never hurt me again, but I'm more cautious about my surroundings, especially at night. I've let what happened to me be a lesson learned. Logan never told me exactly what they did with Mason, and I haven't asked. He only assured me that he was not dead. That was all I needed to know. If Logan says I'm safe from Mason, I believe him.

I see Austin making his way from the back. "You ladies ready?"

"Yep, Gabriel is expecting me." We're making our way to the parking lot when Quinn jogs up to us.

Undaunted

"Hey, Prez just called, says he needs the prospect. It looks like you ladies will be stuck with me."

We say a quick goodbye to Austin, then the three of us stroll across the street to Kings Ink. Quinn opens the door to the shop for Alba, giving her his trademark smile and wink. My sister blushes crimson red then ducks her head before walking in. When he ushers me in, I give him a look that tells him to quit messing with my sister. Quinn isn't deterred, giving me a cocky grin.

I'm sitting on a stool next to Gabriel who is finishing up the stencil for my tattoo. I told him in detail what I wanted, and he wasted no time getting to work.

I try to make small talk with him but realize I'm talking to myself. His attention is on Alba and Quinn, who are sitting next to each other across the room. They look to be having a normal conversation, but I don't think Gabriel likes it too much. When Alba laughs at something Quinn says, the pencil in Gabriel's hand snaps in two.

"You okay, big guy?" I ask him. I look over at my sister and Quinn again before turning my attention back to Gabriel. "You know he's just trying to fuck with you, right?"

Cutting his dark eyes to me, he mutters, "I don't know what you're talking about."

"Look, I'm not the only one who has noticed the way you look at her. Logan sees it too."

Gabriel's body goes tense, and his jaw tightens. I reach out, putting my hand on his arm. He jerks slightly at my touch but doesn't move away. "It's her age that bothers you. You know, Alba will be nineteen next month."

"It's still not fuckin' right, Bella. I'm a grown-ass man lusting after a goddamn kid. There is nothing okay about that shit."

"Gabriel," I say, waiting for him to look at me. "I don't know you that well, but I believe you're a good man. My sister would be lucky to have you."

Standing up I decide to wait with Quinn and Alba while he finishes the drawing. I go to walk away but decide to leave him with a bit of advice. "I understand the whole age thing Gabriel, but don't take too long deciding what you want. My sister is a beautiful girl. It won't take long before she catches someone else's attention." With that, I let him be. I've said my piece and given my blessing.

The sting and burn of getting a tattoo is a little painful, but bearable. Since this is my first tattoo, Gabriel recommended that I might not want to get it on the base of my neck, but I was adamant.

"It's going to be beautiful, Bella," Alba says from right beside me.

"Have you ever thought about getting inked, sweetheart?" Quinn asks Alba.

"Yeah, one day," she tells him.

"I know exactly what your first tattoo should be." Quinn flirts.

I know what he's doing. I try making eye contact with him to warn him not to poke the bear, but nope, he keeps right on going.

"What should it be?" she asks.

I can tell by my sister's tone that she knows Quinn is joking with her.

"You should get Quinn right across—"

He doesn't get to finish his sentence before Gabriel cuts him off. "Not fuckin' happening, brother," his voice booms. "She won't be getting any prick's name on her body, least of all yours."

My sister's cheeks are flushed red, and I can tell she doesn't quite know what to make of the situation. Looking over my shoulder, I nudge Gabriel's leg to get his attention. "Hey big guy, take it easy."

Then I turn to the shit-stirrer, pointing the finger at him. "Quinn, knock it off."

"I don't know what you're talking about," Quinn feigns.

"Yeah, you do."

"Alright, alright, I'll be good."

Turning my attention back to Gabriel, I say, "Now, can we please finish my tattoo? I want to get home sometime tonight."

We make it back to the clubhouse a little after ten. I don't see Logan's bike, so I know he's not back from whatever club business he's on. Alba goes straight up to her room while I head for the kitchen. I haven't eaten since lunch, and my stomach has been growling for a couple of hours now. When I walk in, I see Liz. She's one of the club girls, who was also Cassie's little sidekick. Ever since Logan kicked Cassie out Liz hasn't caused any problems, but that doesn't mean anything. I don't trust the chick. By the look she is giving me, I'd say she doesn't care too much for me either. I go on about my business ignoring her, and she's smart enough to do the same.

After I finish my grilled cheese sandwich, I head up to Logan's and my room for a shower. Gabriel said getting the tattoo wet was fine, but to use a mild soap. Since it's at the base of my neck, I pile my hair on the top of my head, deciding not to wash it. I don't want to take a chance of my shampoo irritating anything.

Once I finish showering, I pull one of Logan's t-shirts from his drawer and slip it on—not even bothering with panties. Logan will tear them off anyway.

Propping my foot on the edge of the bed, I grab my favorite lotion off the bedside table and begin applying it to my legs. I hear the click of the door lock and glance up to see Logan and smile.

21

LOGAN

I am hands down the luckiest fuckin' man in the world. Coming back to the clubhouse, knowing my girl would be here waiting for me, is the only thing that got me through this fucked up day. When I open the door to our room, I'm greeted by Bella's sweet smile. Fuckin' perfect. I love seeing her wearing my t-shirt. Since she's been staying here, it's the only thing she'll sleep in.

Bella doesn't waste any time walking over and wrapping her arms around me. I bury my face in her neck, inhaling the sweet vanilla scent of the lotion she put on, and close my eyes and hold her for a few moments.

"I'm going to take a shower. Come talk to me, tell me about your day," I say, kissing her. She follows me into the bathroom, then lifts herself back to sit on the counter.

I turn the shower on and strip out of my clothes, not missing the heated look on her face. "How did everything go at Gabriel's tonight?"

"Good," she answers cryptically.

Bella refuses to tell me what her tattoo is. I wanted to be the one to take her to get it done, but she insisted it was a surprise. I've appraised her from head to toe since walking into the room, but haven't seen a sliver of ink yet.

"Did things go well with your dad and brother?" she asks, changing the subject.

"Yeah," I sigh. "It went pretty good. I'm still trying to process it all, but I'm glad I talked to them."

"I'm happy for you, Logan. I know learning what happened to your mom was horrible. I can't even begin to imagine what that's like, but also to discover you have a dad and a brother that both want to be a part of your life. I'd say that's pretty amazing."

Getting out of the shower and drying off, I let Bella's words sink in. She's right. I may never get over what happened to my mother, but I could try and make things work with my father. The past is the past. There's nothing I can do to change it. And after hearing his side of things, I can understand why he waited to contact me.

"You know what else I think, Logan?"

Walking up to her, I stand between her legs and wrap my arms around her waist. "What's that, Angel?"

"You deciding to give your dad and brother a chance, the three of you moving forward, it shows that you win. Your grandfather may be dead, but he didn't succeed in keeping you apart."

Placing my forehead against hers, I let out a deep breath. Leave it to Bella to show me the bigger picture, showing me the good in a tough situation.

Reaching down, I cup my hands under Bella's ass, lifting her. She responds by wrapping her legs around my waist as I carry her out of the bathroom and set her down next to the bed. Seeking the heat of her body, I swiftly rid her of the shirt she is wearing.

Her gorgeous eyes fall on mine. I can't ever remember wanting something so much. "You have no fucking idea what you do to me," I rasp, with my mouth hovering over hers.

Bella's breaths are coming out in pants, and I can feel her body shiver with anticipation.

Giving her what she needs, I claim her mouth with mine. My hand trails down her stomach until I reach her slick folds, slipping two fingers inside her pussy. Bella brings her arms up around my neck as I continue to move in and out of her. Moments later, her hips jerk forward, and her pussy clamps down on my fingers while my mouth swallows the moan of her orgasm.

Pulling away, I look into her dazed eyes. She watches intently as I put my fingers in my mouth. "The best thing I ever fuckin' tasted," I tell her.

"Now, I want you on your hands and knees," I command.

Without hesitation, she climbs onto the bed. Dropping the towel from around my waist, I settle in behind her. I run my hand up the curve of her perfect ass, then back down to her wet pussy. Grabbing the base of my cock, I slide the head back and forth between her wet folds, teasing her. Growling with frustration, Bella begins rocking her hips back, seeking what her body craves. Deciding to show her who's running this show, I bring my palm down on her ass, slapping it. I love the look of my reddened handprint on her flawless skin. "You'll take what I give you. Now be still," I order.

"Logan, please," she begs. "I need you inside me."

"You can wait," I say reaching down to run my finger through her pussy.

"Fuckin' soaked. You love it when I spank your ass, don't you?" I ask, slipping my finger inside, causing her to moan, and the walls of her hot pussy clamp down on my fingers. One thing I found out about my girl early on is she loves when I punish her. Deciding I've teased her enough, I grab the base of my cock, and bring the tip to her entrance. Closing my eyes, I grab Bella's hips and slowly sink into her tight heat and relish the feel of the best thing I've ever had.

Undaunted

"Fuck, you feel so damn good," I rasp.

Turning her head, she looks at me over her shoulder. Her face flushed red, and her eyes filled with lust. The sounds of her moans echoing off the walls fuel me as I drive into her harder and harder. Reaching for the hair lying against her sweaty back, I grab hold, wrapping the long strands around my hand. That's when I see it. My movement falters, my breath getting stuck in my throat. Bella stills. She knows I've just seen it and is waiting for my reaction.

At the base of her neck, between her shoulders, is a pair of blue and green angel wings, with the scripture 'His Angel' written across the top. Seeing a part of me on her causes my dick to grow even harder. With Bella's hair still in my hand, I tug her head back, making her look at me.

"You like having my mark on you, don't you, Angel?" I ask with a hard thrust. Causing her to cry out. "Answer me."

"Yes," she moans with pleasure.

Her answer causes a deep growl to vibrate through my chest as I continue to fuck her perfect pussy.

Feeling the tingle at the base of my spine, I bring my hand around, finding her swollen clit. I feel the flutter of her pussy, and it's all I can do to hold off my release.

"Come with me. I want to feel your pussy squeezing my cock."

She comes, sending me right over the edge with her.

Collapsing on the bed, I grab her around the waist, pulling her toward me. We lie there for a few minutes in silence, collecting our breaths before I speak.

"Why blue and green?"

I have a feeling what her answer will be, but I want her to say it. Bella twists herself around to face me.

"Blue and green are the colors of the most beautiful eyes I've ever seen."

THE NEXT MORNING after our shower, Bella and I head downstairs to eat. In the kitchen, we find Lisa and Alba already at work, cooking breakfast.

"Good morning, you two, you're just in time," Lisa says, bringing the food over to the table.

"I'm so sorry I overslept and didn't come down in time to help you, Lisa," Bella tells her.

"Oh, sweetheart, I don't want to hear any of that," she says, waving her hand. "Besides, Alba has been a tremendous help. You two come on and sit."

When we're done eating, I stand from the table, grabbing Bella's hand. "Come on, babe. I've got something to show you."

"Okay?" she wonders, while I lead her out of the kitchen and through the main room. Passing Quinn, he gives me a nod telling me my surprise is ready.

I take her outside, and we walk around to the side of the clubhouse. Turning the corner, Bella lets out a gasp, freezing in place with her hand covering her mouth. Right in front of us is her 1968 Mustang. Only it looks completely different, with a new vinyl top, fresh paint, and brand-new tires. We swapped the old blue interior for a floral white. I'd say Bella's car is very different from the rusted-up piece of shit it was before.

Standing behind her, I bring my arms around her and hold her while whispering in her ear. "You didn't think I would forget your birthday did you, Angel?"

"Is that my car?" she asks in a shaky voice.

"Yeah, babe, that's your car."

Bella walks up to her car, running her hand up the hood and down the driver's side before opening the door and sliding in. "When did you do all this?"

"It wasn't just me; all the brothers helped."

Bella turns to me with tears running down her face. "I can't believe you all did this for me."

Using the pad of my thumb, I swipe her tears. "There's nothing I won't do for you, Angel."

"I love it! You all did an amazing job. It's perfect!" she says, brushing her lips softly against mine.

"Can we go for a ride?" she asks excitedly.

I take the keys from my front pocket, handing them over.

"Hell yeah, babe, let's go."

22

BELLA

I've got major butterflies, standing here in front of the bathroom mirror. While Logan and I were out earlier, driving my beautifully restored Mustang, I made a quick stop at a lingerie store downtown.

Logan is out there in the bedroom, waiting to see what I bought. So, here I am, wearing a black and purple lace corset, matching g-string, black thigh-high stockings, and some ridiculous stiletto heels I let the saleswoman talk me into. I don't know the first thing about being sexy. I'm afraid I might walk out there and make a fool of myself.

Glancing in the mirror one final time, I reach down to slowly turn the knob and pull the bathroom door open.

Logan is sitting shirtless on the edge of the bed as I step out into the bedroom. I stop a few feet from him. He's quiet a little too long, and I start to feel anxious.

"Come here, babe, let me get a closer look at you," he demands, in a husky tone.

Slowly, I walk the last few feet separating us.

Needing to touch him, I rest my hands on his shoulders. "Do you like it?"

Bringing his hand up, he traces his finger over the top of both breasts, causing my skin to shiver. "Fuck babe, you are so damn sexy."

He makes me feel sexy. The way my body reacts to him, it does all the talking for me.

Walking behind me, with his chest pressing against my back, Logan brushes my hair to the side and kisses along my neck, sending shivers down my spine.

"Put your hands on the bed, Bella."

As I place my hands onto the mattress, I hear the rustling of clothes, and his belt buckle hitting the floor. I look over my shoulder and watch as he hooks his thumbs through the strings of my panties and drags them down over my ass, stopping just above my knees. His hands glide up my thighs and splay over my hips, gripping them firmly. "Spread your legs, Angel."

The raw sound of his voice alone makes me wet as I part my legs, and the tip of his cock caresses my opening.

"Fuck, you're already wet for me," he growls.

My legs tremble when his finger starts to manipulate my clit, and in one thrust, he buries himself inside me. His pace never lets up, driving into me with such force, I have to grip the edge of the bed to keep from moving.

I feel my walls tighten around his cock as my climax builds with every thrust and every stroke of his finger before my orgasm explodes. Grabbing my hips tighter, he bears down chasing his release.

THE NEXT MORNING I'm sitting behind the wheel of my car, about to take Alba to school, feeling deliciously used from the night before. Austin is on his bike, riding behind us as we pull out of the gate.

"You ready to get back to school today?" I smile at my sister. She seemed to be eager to leave this morning, which isn't normal for her.

"Yes, I'm so bored. At least at school, I have more to look at than a bunch of hairy bikers all day," she admits, reaching up to pull the visor down, applying her lipstick.

"Listen, Blake will be sitting in the parking lot across from the school. They still want us watched, even though things seem to have died down," I inform her.

Logan didn't tell me too much, just that there hasn't been any activity lately—here in town or from where Los Demonios had been staying. He still feels better having a member watch over us for now, and I do too. The presence of his dad might have something to do with them leaving town. My mom hasn't seen or heard from Lee either, and that's good news too. Either way, I'm glad to see things might be getting back to normal.

My sister acknowledges with a sigh, "Okay."

"You want to be brought to the shop or taken back to the compound after school?" I question while coming to a stop at a stop sign.

"I don't know. I might go over to my friend's house after school. I haven't got to hang with her in a couple of weeks."

I feel bad that she hasn't been able to come and go more freely since staying at the clubhouse.

"Give me a call after school, so I don't worry. Please," I add.

We're pulling up to the high school parking lot when I notice Gabriel sitting across the street. My sister peers over in the same direction.

"I thought you said Blake was going to be out here today?"

"Yeah, that's what Logan said. I guess there was a change of plans."

Undaunted

I'm pretty sure that Gabriel had a hand in that. He probably insisted he is the one to keep watch of my sister. He has murder in his eyes every time Blake gets anywhere near her.

After dropping Alba off at the front of the school, I ride across the street and pull up alongside Gabriel. "Morning, Gabriel," I sing-song. I can't help myself. I'm in a good mood today, plus, I like Gabriel. I'd rather him watch over my sister than anyone else anyway.

"Bella," he says, crossing his arms.

"Will you make sure my sister doesn't forget to call me after school? She might want to visit her friend today but hasn't made definite plans. I don't want to worry."

"You got it," he nods, before adding, "she'll be safe."

"I know, big guy. Thanks."

As I'm pulling into the parking lot at work, my phone rings with an incoming call. Removing it from my purse, the display is lit with a picture of Mila and Ava. Swiping the screen, I answer the call. "Hey!"

"Hey, Bella. I'm calling to ask you to lunch today. Mine and Ava's treat. Can you meet us at the park around noon?" Mila inquiries, with a giggling Ava in the background.

"I'd love to."

"You still being driven around everywhere?" she questions.

"Not today, Logan is letting me drive myself. You have got to see what the guys did to my car. Mila, it's beautiful."

"See you in a few hours, then?" she asks.

"Definitely!" I reply.

When we hang up, I send a text to Logan, letting him know my lunch plans with Mila and where. He texted back, telling me he would inform Austin. It's been forever since I could visit with my friend, so I'm glad I get the chance to catch up with her today. As soon as lunchtime rolls around, Austin grabs himself something to eat and mounts his bike to follow me to the park a few blocks from the shop. He decides to hang back near a table by the parking lot. I make my way over to Mila, who has set lunch up over near the playground area. Ava spots me first and comes running with her long, blonde curls wildly bouncy everywhere.

"Bella!" she squeals, jumping into my arms.

Laughing, twirling, and giving her a big hug, I smile, "I've missed you, pretty girl."

Giggling, she takes her little hands and squishes my cheeks, telling me in her sweet little three-year-old voice, "I missed you."

Looking up, I see her momma watching, with a smile on her face. "You two come on, it's time to eat. You don't have long until you need to get back to work, so let's make the most of our time," she says.

Opening the cooler, she pulls out some sandwiches, apple slices, and juice boxes. "Ava made us a picnic lunch today. Isn't that right, Ava?" she says, placing some food on a paper plate, sitting it in front of her daughter.

"I did it all by myself," Ava proudly announces.

"And you did a wonderful job." I beam at her.

I take a bite of my sandwich when Mila looks at me, smiling. "You look happy," she says.

"I am."

"How's Alba doing with all this?" Mila asks.

I finish chewing on an apple slice that Ava handed me before answering, "She's doing good. The guys in the club have been nice to her, to both of us."

Ava announces she's done and asks if she can play. As soon as Mila cleans her little face, she's running off toward two other kids. I can't help but think about the possibilities of having kids with Logan someday. What would they look like, how many would he like to have, if any? We haven't gotten that far into our relationship to be talking about kids or marriage. I know I want these things. I wonder if Logan wants a family someday? No need to daydream or worry about that kind of stuff now. We have plenty of time to figure it all out.

I turn my attention to Mila, "How've you been doing, with your Grandma and school?"

Mila is going to nursing school. It's something she's wanted to do her whole life. I admire her. She has a lot going on, doing it all by herself, and is still finding ways and making sacrifices to chase her dream. I would love to do that someday—go to school that is. One day I'll get the chance to pursue my dreams too.

"I'm good, and so is Grandma. I think I'll have to either put her in a home or get a sitter for her soon. She's starting to forget where she is sometimes. I worry that she'll wander off one day, and get lost, possibly hurt herself."

I start helping clean the food up and put the trash in the bin nearby. "I'm sorry, that must be hard, especially with going to night school and having to pay a sitter for Ava. As soon as things get back to normal, and everything's safe, I can at least help watch Ava sometimes when you're at night school. I know Alba would too," I tell her.

"Thanks, that means a lot," she says, as she puts the leftover sandwiches and apples back into the cooler, "and on a good note, I got the job at the hospital. They said they would keep me in mind for a nursing position after I graduate later this year."

"That's fantastic! I'm so excited for you."

I grab the phone from my pocket to check the time and notice I need to head back to the shop.

Thinking about the BBQ this weekend, I say, "We're having a BBQ out at the clubhouse this weekend. I'd like it if you would come out and meet Logan."

Looking unsure, she wipes her hands on a napkin before throwing it in the trash. "I'm not sure that's a good idea."

"It's a family get-together. Nothing wild. You can even bring

Ava. Some of the other members have kids she can play with. Come on. It will be fun. Please," I beg.

I know she would enjoy herself if she gives herself a chance. She never takes the time to relax. She has so much on her plate these days. "You deserve to have some fun, Mila. Come on." I grab her hands, pleading with her again.

Finally, caving, she agrees. "Okay, I'll go. Promise me you won't leave me hanging by myself with a bunch of bikers."

"Promise," I smile.

I'M in the kitchen with Lisa and my sister cleaning and preparing for the spring BBQ the club has for the families every year. The guys are outside doing all the grilling today. From what I've heard, it turns into a big competition every year between Quinn and Reid. I can't wait to see that.

"Lisa, if there isn't anything more you need me to do, I want to head upstairs and change," I tell her, looking down at myself.

"I'll finish up here, sweetie. Go on and get prettied up for your man," she encourages, with a wink.

Once upstairs, I quickly change into some black leggings and a comfy lightweight flannel that I can roll the sleeves down on later if the temperature changes. Spring around here changes by the hour but typically stays around the upper fifties. I bought the top while out shopping with Alba and Mila on Friday afternoon. I pair it with some tan combat boots and pull my hair up into a high ponytail. Logan likes my hair up away from my neck. He enjoys coming up behind me and placing kisses just under my earlobe, so he can see goosebumps prickle my skin.

I've been looking forward to this BBQ ever since Logan and the guys started talking about it a few days ago. Mila and her daughter coming to the party adds to my excitement. I also get to meet some of the other members and their families today, along with Logan's dad and brother.

I walk over to the bedroom window and peer outside. Our window has a view of the back of the compound. Scanning the yard, I find Logan building a massive bonfire for later tonight. I hope his dad and brother show up today. It was a significant step on his part to invite them, and I'm happy he did.

As I'm coming down the stairs, Alba is walking toward me. "Oh, there you are. I was coming to tell you; Blake just let Mila through the gate."

"Great! Thanks, Alba."

I walk outside just as she's pulling her little girl out of her car seat. She wore the new sweater dress I talked her into buying for herself, along with a pair of kickass boots.

"Hey! We were just about to get things started. You showed up just in time."

Taking Ava from her, I place her on my hip. At the same time Logan, Reid, and Quinn come walking around, carrying some lawn chairs and coolers. Mila stands a little closer as they walk up.

"Jesus, Bella. What the hell do they put in the water around here? Those men are hot."

Ava clings tight to my shirt as Logan steps up and kisses my forehead.

"Ava, Mila, this is Logan."

Logan smiles, "Bella talks about you and Ava often. Glad you could make it."

"She's told me a lot about you too," Mila quietly remarks, cutting her eyes at me with a smile. I give her a poke in her side, silently telling her to be quiet.

"Oh, and this is Quinn and Reid," I point out who is who in the process.

Ava decides she has been ignored long enough and cheerfully proclaims, "Mommy, he's pretty!" Pointing her little finger right at

Reid, causing all of us to laugh, including Reid, who shakes his head and chuckles.

Mila smiles as a blush creeps up her face while she tries to avoid eye contact with Reid.

"Ava, it's not nice to point," she tries to explain to her three-year-old daughter.

"But, Mommy, he is," she says, looking serious. I've got to give it to the kid; he is nice to look at. Especially with his bright green eyes, tanned skin, and hair the color of honey. It always seems like he's just rolled out of bed. But Reid makes it work.

Logan bends down, kissing my lips. "Gotta go, babe. Why don't you take your friend out back, introducing her to the other members and their families, then come find me later."

"I will," I sigh.

Gathering up all the things Mila brought, we head around back to where the men are firing up the grills and setting up the tables. Other kids are already in the yard blowing bubbles and playing.

"I'm thrilled you came, Mila."

I visibly see her shoulders relax, and a smile spreads across her face as she watches Ava run off to play.

"Yeah, me too," she replies.

23

LOGAN

I woke up this morning to cold and empty sheets. I scrub my palm down my face. Without Bella here to distract my thoughts, I think back to the other day when Reid and I rode out to Dixon to see if we could get an idea of what those bastards Los Demonios are up to.

Reid and I park our bikes in the brush off the side of the road about half a mile from their compound. We make the trek through the woods until we spot their clubhouse.

As we get closer, I notice everything is quiet, and I don't see so much as a bike—in fact, it looks abandoned. I can tell Reid has made the same observation.

Still being cautious, I draw my piece from my cut as I slowly make my way around the side of the building. Reid stays back, covering me, as I walk toward the front of the clubhouse.

Peering around the corner, I see the front door is wide open, exposing an empty room. I give Reid the signal all is clear as I walk into the clubhouse.

"Damn, brother, I wasn't expecting this. Do you think those pussies

got scared and ran after stealing from us? Maybe they got wind that the Russians are in town."

"I don't know, man. Let's look around, see if we find anything, then head back." I pull my phone from my cut and call Jake.

He answers, "What you got?"

"Nothing Prez. Their clubhouse is empty, fucker's just up and left."

"Son of a bitch," he hisses. "You two get your asses back; I'm calling church."

"You got it, Prez. See you in thirty."

"Logan," he stops me before I hang up. "I want to bring Demetri in on this. You going to have a problem with that?"

I sigh. "No, Prez, I think bringing him in is a good idea. I want to be done with this shit."

"Alright, son, I'll make the call."

When Reid and I return to the clubhouse, I see my father's black SUV parked out front. I agree with Jake, bringing the Russians in on this is smart. First Lee disappears, and now with Los Demonios in the wind, there will be no more waiting around. My woman and her sister's life are at stake.

It's time to end this shit.

Walking into church I see Jake, my father, and my brother, Nikolai, waiting for us. Reid walks in behind me, taking his seat while I walk around the table, taking my place next to Prez.

With Quinn at the shop with Bella, Gabriel on watch at the school, and the other brothers out trying to find Lee, it's only the five of us.

I turn to my right to acknowledge my father and brother. "I appreciate you two coming to meet with us."

"Anything for you, son," Demetri replies.

Over the next forty-five minutes, I give them a rundown of the situation. Los Demonios taking our shipment, the arrangement Bella's stepfather made with them to cover his debt—all of it.

"When was the last time anyone has seen Lee?" Nikolai asks.

"Weeks," I tell him. "That motherfucker disappeared after the girls' mom kicked his ass to the curb. We've torn this town apart looking for him. He's the only reason we've not made a move on Los Demonios. We were hoping they would lead us to him."

"Does Bella know of the threat against her and her sister?" Demetri asks.

I shake my head. "No, I decided against telling her. I didn't want to put that kind of stress on her. Bella already has enough bullshit to deal with."

"I understand, but I believe it would be wise to inform her. If she knows of the danger she and her sister are in, it would help her in being more vigilant."

"I agree," Jake cuts in.

Blowing out a frustrated breath, I nod. I didn't want it to come down to me having to tell Bella the whole truth, but my father and Jake make an excellent point. If she knew everything, she would understand why I always have a brother with her and Alba. I also agree she needs to be more cautious.

"I'll talk to her this weekend after the family BBQ. Bella's been looking forward to it, and I don't want to ruin it for her. I'll tell her after the party."

By the time our meeting is over, my father has vowed to use his contacts and whatever resources needed to bring every one of those motherfuckers down.

"Fuck," I groan and pull myself from my thoughts. According to the clock on the table beside the bed, it's 8:00 am, and I know exactly where my girl is. Usually, I'd be pissed she left our bed before I got my morning fix, but seeing how excited she has been about the party I can't be mad. It's all she's talked about this week. Rolling out of bed I head to the bathroom to take care of business before heading downstairs to seek out my woman. As expected, I find her in the kitchen with Lisa and her sister.

"Mornin', Angel," I say, walking up behind her, wrapping my arms around her waist and kissing her neck.

"Good morning, Logan. You hungry?"

"I'm good, just some coffee for now," I tell her before slapping her on her ass, causing her to shriek.

"I'll be out back helping the brothers set up if you need anything, beautiful," I tell her as I head out of the kitchen.

Today, the weather is a little chilly, but we're going to have an above-average temperature today of sixty. Perfect for a BBQ, and later tonight we'll light some bonfires.

I see the prospects setting up tables and chairs, while Quinn is busy arguing with Reid about whose grilling skills are better. Those two have the same disagreement every time we have a cookout.

It's become some tradition. First, they will argue overusing gas or charcoal, then who has the best sauce. Eventually, the whole thing will turn into a cook-off, where the brothers will be forced to choose a winner between the two. I don't think the idiots realize we swap winner's titles back and forth.

Last time Quinn won the title, so today the winner will be Reid. Hell, maybe they do know how we vote and are keeping up the facade like the rest of us, because like I said, it's tradition.

Scanning the yard, I spot Gabriel sitting on a patio chair surveying the yard while drinking coffee. Out of the corner of my eye, I catch Bella and her sister walking toward Blake carrying bags of ice. Blake jogs over to them, taking the bags from their hands. Bella turns, making her way over to me while Alba continues to chat up the prospect.

"Baby, you could've had one of the brothers carry that ice for you."

"Logan, I'm perfectly capable of doing things myself," she tells me with her usual sass.

"Prospect," Gabriel gravelly voice hollers from across the yard, causing Bella and me to snap our heads in his direction.

"Get your ass back to work," he orders Blake.

I watch as the prospect puts his hand on Alba, giving her shoulder a light squeeze before returning to work. The fucking kid has no idea he's stirring the damn pot. He just gave Gabriel a reason to ride his ass. Bella and I watch as her sister walks back inside.

"Well, I better get back in there. You boys play nice."

"Hey, it's not me you need to worry about," I tell her.

"I know, but do me a favor, don't let the big guy over there be too hard on Blake."

"Sorry, babe, I'm not getting in the middle of that shit," I say, chuckling.

"Fine, I guess I'll pray for him, I'm sure he's going to need it."

The sun is shining, and the brothers and their families are beginning to show up. My brother Nikolai sent me a text about twenty minutes ago telling me he and my father were on their way as well.

Bella is anxious to meet them officially. Having her by my side through this whole fucked up ordeal has made things easier. Word has gotten around about Demetri being my father, and the club has been nothing but supportive.

Jake has been the only father figure in my life, and no matter what happens between Demetri and me, Jake will always be that for me.

I've been sitting here bullshitting with Bennett awhile when my girl nudges me. I look at her, then in the direction she's pointing. My father and brother have arrived and made their way across the yard in my direction. Standing up I grab Bella's hand.

"Come on, Beautiful, I want to introduce you."

I meet them halfway across the yard, "Demetri, Nikolai, I'd like you to meet Bella."

"It's nice to meet you, Bella. Logan has told me so much about you," Demetri says, shaking Bella's offered hand.

"It's nice to meet you too."

She then turns her attention to my brother. "Good to see you again, Nikolai."

"You as well, Myshka," he replies. I'm about to ask him what the hell Myshka means when Bella beats me to it.

"What does Myshka mean?"

"It's a term of endearment, meaning little mouse." Nikolai turns to me, "I'm sorry, I should have explained that to you the first time I said it. My apologies, Logan. I would never disrespect your lady."

"We're good, brother," I say with a chin lift, "now, come on, I'd like to introduce you guys to the rest of the members."

Bella excuses herself when she sees her friend approaching. "I'll be back in a minute, Logan."

We make our rounds, giving introductions to the rest of the brothers and their families. I was wondering how they were going to fit in. My father and brother are designer clothes and reek of money. As for The Kings, we're ripped jeans and motorcycle boots. They shock the hell out of me when they sit down at the table with their plates piled with ribs and dig in using their hands to eat.

The sun is starting to set, painting the sky with a yellow and orange glow. Feeling a chill, we decide it's time to light a fire. "Anybody got any matches?" I yell.

"I saw some inside earlier," Bella tells me, getting up from her chair. "I'll go get them. I want to check on Alba anyway. She went in a few minutes ago but hasn't come back out."

I watch my woman's perfect fuckin' ass sway as she makes her way inside.

"She's stunning, Logan, you're a lucky man," my brother says, coming up beside me.

"You'll get no arguments from me. I know how lucky I am to have Bella. What about you, Nikolai? You got a woman back home?"

"Hell no, I'm too young to be tied down."

"Famous last words, brother," I mumble with a head shake. "I was saying the same thing a short time ago, but Bella changed my mind."

My conversation with Nikolai is cut short when I notice Bella running across the yard toward the front of the compound near the gate, screaming her sister's name.

Everything happens in slow motion.

The beer bottle I have halfway to my mouth drops to the ground when I see two men fighting with a struggling Alba, trying to force her into a white van, and Bella running straight for them. A second van pulls up with the side door open, as shots begin to ring out. Men and women scramble to take cover. Women are shielding their children, and husbands are covering their women while returning fire.

"Bella!" I roar while running toward her.

"Logan!" Bennett hollers from my left, "Get down," he warns me just as I see one of the men throw something in my direction. I'm suddenly thrown to the ground, then blinded by a flash of light, followed by a loud bang. A minute later, I feel disoriented and realize it was my father who knocked me to the ground, shielding me.

"Bella!" I shout, getting to my feet. My brothers come running up behind me, as we rush through the dust and fog, but I already know it's too late. I feel it in the pit of my stomach. Those motherfuckers got Bella and Alba. They took my woman and her sister. Looking over at my brothers, my family, there's only one thing to say. "Time for war."

24

BELLA

Waking up, I groan at the pain behind my eyes. My head feels like it's going to explode, and my body feels heavy. I go to bring my hand up to my head, but my arms won't move. I realize my hands are tied behind my back. "What the hell?"

Then my memory comes flooding back. Being at the clubhouse, helping Lisa cook, the party, then nothing but pure chaos. Men were shooting at us. Seeing my sister trying to fight off two men as they began shoving her into a van.

Oh god, this cannot be happening.

I sit on the cold floor, ignoring the soreness in my body and the pounding in my head. I begin to look around frantically.

"Alba!" I listen for her to answer, getting nothing but silence.

I'm almost positive I'm in a basement. Besides a few boxes, there's nothing in the space surrounding me. I can hear footsteps and murmured voices above me. Okay, Bella, think. What the hell are you going to do? My phone! Please let it still be in my back pocket.

My hands tied behind my back ends up working to my advantage. I have easy access to try and reach for my phone. I strain and stretch as far as I can, reaching the tips of my fingers into my right back pocket.

YES!

I let my phone drop to the floor, and with a shaky hand, I reach down and swipe the screen. I start searching for Logan's number. When I find it, I press the call button, then lay my body down on the floor close to the phone so that I can hear. It only rings once before I hear his voice.

"Bella!" Logan shouts into the phone, his voice full of anguish.

I can no longer hold back the tears pricking my eyes. What if this is the last time I hear his voice?

"Angel, please don't cry, I need you to be strong. Can you tell me anything about where you and Alba are?"

"I'm in the basement...I think. I can hear footsteps above me. I'm pretty sure I'm in a house. They must have drugged me because I don't remember how I got here. I just woke up, and my hands have been tied behind my back."

"That's good, Angel, you're doing good. I'm having Reid track your phone right now. Hold on for me, baby. I'm coming for you guys. I promise."

"Logan, Alba's not with me, she's not here. I don't know what they did with her. You have to find her Logan, please," I cry.

With a loud bang, the basement door opens, and my heart stops. "Logan, someone's coming. Oh god, what do I do? Please, Logan, tell me what to do," I whisper and plead.

"FUCK, FUCK, FUCK!" I hear him chanting. "I'm coming for you, Bella, I promise."

I scramble to sit up. I push my phone behind me so they won't see it, but it's too late.

"What the fuck you got there, you little puta, *bitch*?" A man with a Spanish accent spits.

He's wearing a cut that reads Los Demonios. Shit, that's the club Logan and Jake have been talking about, the one Lee has been associating with.

"Fuck you!" I scream at the asshole.

Walking over to me, the man takes his booted foot and knocks me out of the way, exposing my phone lying on the floor behind me. He stomps on it, busting it into pieces.

Turning back toward the stairs, he yells out something in Spanish. Two more men come rushing down into the basement. All three of the men speak rapidly back and forth with each other, and I have no idea what they're saying. One of the men strides toward me, pulling something from his cut. I hold my breath—the first thing that comes to mind is a gun, but it's not. When he gets closer to me, I see it's a needle.

"Get away from me!" I yell while trying to scoot away from him, with nowhere to go.

Grabbing me by my hair, he gets in my face, telling me, "Shut the fuck up." The stench of his breath makes me gag.

Without warning, he sticks the needle in my neck. Seconds later, darkness takes me.

I AWAKEN AGAIN with another familiar headache. I blink a few times, willing my heavy eyes to open. I realize my hands are still tied—this time, above my head—and I'm lying on a bed in what looks to be a bedroom. To my left is a door, and to my right, a window that's been boarded up. Directly in front of me is a small dresser with an older TV with a busted screen sitting on top of it.

The only positive thing in this whole situation is that I still have all my clothes on.

My thoughts turn to my sister. I start letting my imagination run wild on all the things these men might be doing to her. Closing my eyes, I take a few deep breaths to try and calm my nerves. This is not the time to be having a panic attack. I pray that Logan finds us.

I've been lying here for what feels like forever. My arms are killing me, and my hands are starting to go numb.

I haven't heard any sounds coming from the other side of the door. I wonder if they left me here alone, should I scream for help? I quickly decided against it because I don't want to do anything that will draw attention to myself.

A few minutes later, I hear the click of the door and a man walks in. He is not one of the men from before, but he is wearing the same cut. I notice the VP patch as he gets closer to the bed. He's only about five feet ten with long hair pulled back in a ponytail. He also has a large jagged scar running the length of his right cheek, but it's his soulless black eyes that have a chill running down my spine.

"Where the hell is my sister?"

"You know it's a shame my father has plans for you," he says, completely ignoring my question.

He comes to a stop right next to me, and then slowly runs his finger down my arm, then down my chest between my breasts. My breathing picks up, and I start tugging on my tied hands.

"Don't fucking touch me," I seethe while trying to keep the tremble out of my voice but fail.

"I want to know where my sister is."

Leaning in close to my ear, he whispers, "I can smell your fear."

It's all I can do to keep the bile from rising in my throat as he starts to work the buttons on my shirt. I open my mouth to scream, but we're both cut off by the ringing of his phone.

"Mierda, *Shit*," he hisses, digging his phone out of his pocket and putting it to his ear "Qué, *What*?" he barks out.

After listening to whoever is on the other end, he hangs up. Turning his attention back to me, with seedy eyes that make my skin crawl, he says, "I'll get my taste puta, *bitch*."

The promise of his words has me shutting my eyes tightly, praying Logan finds me before he makes good on his word.

What feels like hours later, a different man walks in the room with a young girl trailing behind him, carrying what looks like fast food, and my stomach instantly growls at the smell of fries. She can't be any older than sixteen. She's short, about my height with long, reddish-brown hair and honey-colored eyes. Walking over she places the bags on the table beside the bed.

"I brought you something to eat," she speaks so softly I can hardly hear her.

"I need to use the bathroom," I tell her. I've been holding it for so long, and refuse to go on myself.

The man that came in with the young girl comes over and proceeds to uncuff my hands from the headboard. They immediately begin to burn and tingle from lack of blood flow.

"Don't even think about being stupid. You try anything, and next time I'll let you piss yourself."

Walking me to the bathroom, the man stands in the doorway. I wait expectantly for him to at least turn around and give me a little privacy, but he only grins and appraises me from head to toe.

I try my best to act indifferent about the total lack of privacy. When I've finished my business, he walks me back over to the bed, where the girl has begun taking food out of the bags. He sits in a chair on the other side of the room and ignores us for the most part, with his attention on his phone.

"What's your name?" I ask the girl sitting in front of me.

She bites her lip for a minute like she's unsure if she should talk to me. "Sofia," she responds quietly.

"That's a beautiful name, Sofia. My name's Bella."

I don't miss the small smile on her face.

"Do you know where my sister is, Sofia? Did they bring in another girl?"

She shakes her head no, and her eyes dart over to the man in

Undaunted

the chair making sure he can't hear our exchange. I decide not to push her into talking anymore; she's clearly scared.

While eating the food Sofia brought, I take notice of the bruises on her arms and neck. I have no doubt in my mind this poor girl is not here willingly. My heart is breaking for her. I make a vow when Logan finds me, I'll do whatever I can to bring her with me. There is no way I could live with myself knowing what will happen to her if I leave her behind.

When I'm finished eating, the guy cuffs me back to the bed. My heart breaks as I witness the rough way he grabs Sofia by the arm and pulls her out of the room.

I'm again left alone. Eventually, my eyes grow heavy. I try hard not to fall asleep. I'm too afraid of what will happen if I don't stay awake and alert. A few short minutes later, I lose the battle and drift off to sleep.

The click of the bedroom door startles me awake. I don't know how long I've been asleep. The fact that there is no sunlight seeping through the crack of the boarded-up window lets me know it's nighttime.

I only hope it's not the VP coming back to finish what he started earlier. I sigh in relief when I see Sofia come in. She quietly shuts the door and pads across the bedroom with bare feet. Sitting on the bed next to me, "I want to help you get out of here," she whispers.

"What do you mean, do you have the key for the cuffs?" I ask, getting my hopes up.

"No, I'm sorry I don't have a key," she says, dashing my hopes. Sofia notices my defeated look. "I'm sorry, Bella," she says sadly, hanging her head.

"Hey, it's okay. None of this is your fault. I don't want anything to happen to you for trying to help me. You shouldn't be here."

"It's okay. I want to help you. If you can give me a phone number, maybe I can call someone for you. Sometimes Antonio leaves his phone out on the table before falling asleep.

"Which one is Antonio?" I ask.

"He's the man that came in with me before," she tells me. "I think I can sneak it and call someone for you."

"Sofia, you can't do something like that. I won't let you risk your life for mine."

"I'll be careful, I promise. I'll wait until he's had too much to drink. Antonio doesn't hear a thing after he passes out."

I contemplate letting her do this for me. I would never want Sofia to put herself in danger, but her doing this might be my only hope.

"I'm going to give you a number. His name is Logan. All you need to do is tell him you're helping me, and then give him the address."

I give her Logan's number, then she stands, making her way to the door.

"Sofia," I call out to her. She stops and turns back toward me.

"I won't be leaving here without you, I promise. Logan, the man you're going to call, he'll come for me, and when he does, you're coming too."

Sofia nods her head, but I can tell by the sad smile on her face that she doesn't believe me.

The next day goes pretty much the same with me mostly being left alone, except for the guy I now know as Antonio coming in a few times a day with Sofia to bring food and to uncuff me so I can use the bathroom.

I feel disgusting because it's been a few days since I've had a shower. Antonio watching me use the bathroom is bad enough. There is no way I'd want him watching me shower.

I'm thankful the guy who put his hands on me the first day

hasn't been back. I asked Sofia earlier who he was, and she told me his name is Jorge, the President's son. She told me he's been gone since yesterday and is not sure when he'll be back. I can only hope he stays gone.

Sofia and I are sitting on the bed eating when Antonio gets up from his chair and goes into the bathroom. She glances over her shoulder, making sure he can't hear us.

"Antonio has been drinking all day. He'll be passed out tonight for sure."

I nod my head at her as he comes out of the bathroom, and we continue eating in silence. I hate that I can't have a real conversation with this sweet girl. I'm desperate to know all about her and how she ended up here. The only thing I've been able to find out so far is that she's seventeen. I wonder where she's from? How long has she been here? Does she have a family that misses her? Why would she risk her life to help me and not herself?

I can't imagine what she has gone through.

Knowing what these men are probably doing to her makes me want to kill every one of them myself.

After I'm done eating, Antonio is once again placing me back in the cuffs. He sneers at me when I give him my best 'fuck you' look. "Too bad your new owner wants you unmarked, I'd love nothing more than to wipe that look off your face and teach you some respect puta, *bitch*."

My stomach drops at the mention of the words 'new owner'. Refusing to let him see the effect his words have on me, I lift my chin defiantly and seethe, "Go to hell."

Antonio swiftly punches me in the stomach, knocking the wind out of me and causing me to double over sideways in the bed, bringing my knees up to my chest. It's all I can do not to throw up the food I just ate.

"Lucky for me, I know how not to leave marks," he says into my ear, right before he grabs Sofia and leaves.

25

LOGAN

"**B**ella!" I holler into my phone. The room goes deathly silent, apart from Reid frantically typing away on his computer, and I know he's begun tracking her phone. I put her on speaker, and she quickly starts giving me what information she can. She's doing her best to describe where she is.

"That's good, Angel, you're doing good. I'm having Reid track your phone right now. Hold on for me, baby. I'm coming for you guys. I promise."

She goes on telling me Alba is not with her. She pleads for us to find her sister. Her sobs filling the room are making me feel helpless. And the next moment is what has me losing my shit.

"Logan, someone's coming. Oh god, what do I do?" she whispers. "Please, Logan, tell me what to do."

"FUCK, FUCK, FUCK!" I chant.

"I'm coming for you, Bella, I promise," I holler out before the connection is lost.

"GODDAMMIT! SON OF A BITCH!" I roar, picking up a chair next to me and hurling it across the room, causing it to shatter into *pieces as it hits the wall, barely missing Quinn's head. He's smart enough not to say a word. The room goes quiet once again.*

"Got her location," Reid says, breaking the silence.

"Where?" I bark out.

"I tracked her cell to a house in Ronan, about twenty minutes out. If we haul ass, we can make it in fifteen." Reid doesn't even finish his sentence before I'm out the door with Gabriel at my side and the rest of my brothers trailing behind.

We make it to the house in Ronan only to find it empty. Bella getting caught with her phone had the fuckers fleeing. They knew we would be here in no time. I make my way down to the basement where I know she was kept. I see her busted cell phone on the floor. I walk back outside to find my brothers' defeated looks mirroring my own.

The loud crack of the gavel slamming down on the table, bringing me back to the present. Fuck, I haven't been able to stop replaying Bella's frantic phone call since yesterday. I glance around the room to see all the members, including my brother and father, here. The voices in the room start to bleed together creating a dull throb in my head.

"Unless one of you has some useful information, you need to shut the fuck up," Jake bellows.

One of my father's men who arrived moments ago steps forward. "I got a lead this afternoon on the girls' stepfather. He was spotted last night in Dixon with a young woman driving a red Camaro.

"That bitch Cassie has a car matching that description," Quinn indicates. "Could be a coincidence, but my gut says no. She's had it out for Bella since she started working for the club," he adds.

"Found her," Reid cuts in. I look over to him, typing away on his laptop. "Her credit card activity had her checking in at some piece of shit motel just outside of Dixon last night, paying for two nights. My guess is she's still there."

"I'm heading to Dixon to follow up on this lead we have on Lee. It's the only thing we have to go on at this point," I say, standing.

"I'm with Logan," Gabriel declares, snubbing his cigarette out.

We don't bother waiting for anyone's response. All I care about is finding my woman. I can't lose another person I love. Walking out of the clubhouse together we mount our bikes and head toward Dixon.

Gabriel and I park our bikes at a gas station next door to the motel where Reid said Cassie is, and sure enough, I see her car parked out front. My father's guy said they spotted Lee with some chick in a red Camaro. I should have known that cunt was going to try something to get back at Bella. What better way than to hook up with Lee, helping him seal the deal with Los Demonios.

I wait outside the office while Gabriel, in a not so friendly way, asks the greasy lookin' fucker behind the counter for a card to Cassie's room. We walk up the stairs toward room 128. Stopping, I listen for a second; all is quiet. Giving Gabriel the signal he inserts the key into the door. Opening it, we both have our guns drawn. We immediately spot the low life himself asleep in the bed. Gabriel slams the door behind us. When Lee opens his eyes, he's met with the barrel of my gun. He looks scared as fuck but tries to mask it when he asks, "What the hell do you want?"

I cock my gun, "I'm askin' the fuckin' questions around here," I inform him. I watch him visibly swallow, and beads of sweat drip down his face. Lee's eyes cut over to the bathroom door when it opens. Cassie walks out with a towel wrapped around her, letting out a shriek when she notices the scene in front of her. "Get your ass over here, you stupid fuckin' cunt, and sit next to your boyfriend here."

"Logan, it's not what you think, baby, I can explain."

"There's nothing to explain. I know what the fuck is goin' on. The only time either one of you is allowed to speak is to answer my questions," I advise them. "First, I want to know where Bella and her sister are."

Lee is the first to speak. "I don't know about Bella, but Alba is being held at a place over in Somers. Some suit is paying big bucks for the little shit, that's all I know."

At Lee's confession, Gabriel lets out a growl from behind me. "What about Los Demonios, where are they at?"

"Hell if I know. I went to their clubhouse the other day, but everyone was gone. The only reason I know about Alba is that I overheard one of those Mexicans talking on the phone with someone."

Turning to Cassie, I ask, "What part did you play in all this?"

She looks over to Lee, silently asking for help. The coward shakes his head and looks away. Knowing that there is no way out of this shitstorm, she caves. "I've been keeping tabs on the club through Liz. She told me about the party the club was having, and I gave that information to him," Cassie says pointing at Lee. "That bitch took you from me, Logan. If it weren't for her you would be mine."

This chick is fuckin' delusional. "Cassie, I was never going to be yours. A whore like you has nothing on a woman like Bella." With those parting words, I pull the trigger. Her limp body falls onto the bed next to Lee whose face has turned deathly pale. I set my gun on the cocksucker himself that started all this shit with Los Demonios.

"What the hell are you doing? I told you what you wanted to know." Lee turns his wide eyes to Gabriel. "Please don't let him kill me!"

With his black, unblinking eyes, Gabriel says, "Decirle al diablo que dije hola, *Tell the devil I said hello*," and I pull the trigger.

We leave the motel, not giving two fucks about the mess we're leaving behind. We'll have some brothers come out and take care of it. Gabriel already contacted Prez telling him what we found out about Alba, so he's sending Quinn and Reid to meet us in Somers. We didn't have an exact address for Alba's location, but tracking a few of Los Demonios members down wasn't hard. One of my father's men went and scoped out the small town. It didn't take long before a few of those assholes were spotted at a bar. They lead Volkov's men straight to a house we're hoping Alba is being held. We parked our bikes a few blocks away, not wanting to take a chance of anyone hearing us. Quinn drove the van here, so Gabriel, Reid, and I hop in, and ride with him over to the house.

My father's men are already set up at the house, awaiting my instructions. Once we're all in position, I give the signal. Using my foot, I kick in the front door. I fire my first shot at the man sitting on the couch. I get a sick sense of satisfaction at seeing his brains paint the wall behind him. Gabriel fires the second shot from behind me at a guy rounding the corner of the hallway. I walk into the kitchen as Gabriel heads down the hall toward the bedroom. I see the back door is wide open, and two bodies are lying on the ground next to Quinn and Reid.

"All clear out here, brother," Quinn tells me. I give him a chin lift and walk back through the kitchen and into the living room in search of Gabriel. Walking down the hall to the bedroom, I find him scooping a crying Alba up off the floor of an empty room. The only thing in here is pieces of rope, which I'm assuming was used to tie her up. Gabriel strides past me, whispering words I can't make out to Alba as she holds onto him like he's her lifeline.

The drive back to our bikes is quiet. This is a small victory for us, but the battle is far from over. Bella's still out there, and we won't rest until we bring her home. Gabriel refused to leave Alba, so Reid offered to ride his bike back to Polson. My father's men said they would stay behind and take care of the mess. I'm mounting my motorcycle when I hear an explosion and see an orange glow and smoke in my side mirror.

Back at the clubhouse, Gabriel takes Alba straight to his room

Undaunted

with Bennett and Lisa in tow. I'm desperate for any information she may have, but I know she needs to be checked out by Doc first. Giving them privacy for a few minutes, I head to Jake's office to see if we have any new leads. He's sitting behind his desk nursing a tumbler of whiskey when I walk in. "Anything new?" I ask, letting out a sigh.

"No, son, nothing new."

"Bennett's in with Alba now, maybe she knows something," I tell him. We're interrupted when Lisa knocks on the door. "I wanted to let you know Bennett's done with Alba if you wanted to come to speak with her." Not wasting any time, I leave Jakes office, heading to Gabriel's room. Bennett is stepping out into the hall as I approach the door.

"How is she Doc?" I ask.

"Physically, she's good. Whatever drugs they gave her to knock her out have worn off. There are no signs of abuse, but mentally she's a mess. She's asking about Bella. Gabriel told her the club has men out looking. She also said she doesn't remember anything, the last thing she remembers is the party, and some men throwing her into the van, and then waking up in an empty room. I'm sorry Logan, I don't think she's going to be able to tell us anything that will help us find Bella."

"Alright, thanks, brother. I'm going to go in to see her."

"Good luck with her guard dog in there," Bennett mutters as he walks away.

Stepping into Gabriel's room, I find him sitting in a chair by the bed watching Alba. "Doc gave her something to help her sleep."

"Yeah, I just talked to him, he said she was going to be fine. I wanted to check on her myself. I'm going to go see Demetri, see if he's gotten any new leads on Bella." Before walking out of his room, I stop and turn to Gabriel, saying, "Thanks for having my back today, brother."

"Anytime, Logan."

FIVE LONG FUCKING DAYS.

That's how many days Bella's been gone. After tearing the state of Montana apart, we're no closer to finding her. I'm walking back into the clubhouse after returning from yet another useless trip to Dixon when my phone rings.

"What," I snap.

"Hello, is this Logan?" a shaky female voice asks, causing me to stop in my tracks.

"Who the hell is this?" The bite in my tone has several of my brothers looking in my direction on high alert. "My name is Sofia. I got your number from Bella," she speaks so softly I can hardly hear.

"Can you tell me where she is, Sofia?" I listen intently as she does her best to give me her location. She doesn't know the exact address but can tell me the name of the town and a description of the house. Several minutes into the call I hear a man's voice in the background.

"What the fuck you doin' you little puta, *bitch*?" I hear the girl scream before the line goes dead.

26

BELLA

Several days have passed, or so I think. I have no way of judging the time except for the rise and fall of the sun.

Sofia said she was going to sneak the phone tonight and call Logan. I can only hope she can do all this without getting herself hurt. I hate to think of my sister, alone and just as scared as I am. We've always had each other to get through a terrifying situation in the past. We've both made it this far in life. I'm not about to give up now. I know Logan and the others will find us.

I tried hard to keep my eyes open and not to fall asleep while waiting for Sofia to return hopefully, but exhaustion won that battle. I jolt, hearing a commotion outside the bedroom door. The door flies open, and a gasp escapes my lips when Jorge strides in, his eyes trained on me.

"So," he draws out, "it seems my little bird was planning to fly away?" He walks over to the edge of the bed.

Malice drips from his voice with his next words, "First, I hear that your buyer has backed out of the deal, seems he found out you're not so pure after all." He runs a cold, clammy hand over my breast before squeezing, then rips my shirt open. "Then, you conspire with our little whore to help you escape."

My heart sinks. They must have caught Sofia. My only hope in someone finding me, gone. I clench my eyes shut, turning my head away—the fear of him doing more, making my skin crawl, causing me to tremble visibly.

"We caught the whore talking to someone on the phone. Heard her say the name Logan," he sneers, not once taking his cold, dead eyes off of me as he peers down.

My head snaps up, looking at him. Giving away the recognition of the name he just said.

"So, this must be the gringo that you belong to," he states. Pulling a knife from his boot, he begins to run the long blade down my cheek and along the side of my neck. I'm frozen with fear. The sound of my heart pounding in my ears is so loud it's deafening.

"Oh, your biker is probably on his way, but we have plenty of time to have some fun before I go."

There is absolutely nothing I can do when he takes the knife and cuts my bra, exposing me. I'm tugging on the restraints so hard that my skin has torn and started to bleed. I watch as he traces the blade around the curve of one breast, then drags it along the curve of the other, this time applying pressure. Immediately I feel the sting of my skin being sliced. Tears fall from my eyes as I beg him. "Please, please don't do this."

His eyes stay transfixed on where he has sliced me and the blood that is dripping down my ribs. His expression is blank, like he's not even here. Blinking, he reaches out, dragging a finger through the blood on my flesh. "Your blood is all I want. Nothing more. There is no better high than watching the life slowly drain from someone."

His blade begins to trail my body again. The rise and fall of my chest quickening as panic quickly takes hold of me. He pauses, the tip of the knife resting along my side, on top of my ribs, then slashes into me once more. This time I scream, the pain much worse than the first cut. He doesn't let up. The knife digs into my flesh again and again. I lose count after a few moments. The pain is unbearable.

"Hermosa, *beautiful*." I barely hear him say through my screams.

I faintly hear a knock on the door and turn my head to watch Jorge get up and walk over to open it. He starts speaking, in Spanish, words I don't understand. With his back turned, I look around, trying to figure out any way to help myself get out of here. I notice his knife lying on the bed, but it's impossible to reach with my hands above my head. I try once again to tug on my restraints. The pain is excruciating. I look down to see my skin is gashed open in several places with blood seeping from each wound. It's no use. My struggles do nothing but further weaken what strength I still have.

A few more words are spoken between the two men before Jorge closes the door, making his way back over to the bed.

I watch as he picks the knife up again. "Your biker is almost here. I'm going to make sure he sees you die before I kill him myself." He puts the knife back in his boot, just as another man wearing the same cut walks through the door.

"Help me take her down to the basement. We will wait for them down there. Order the men to their posts. I want to know the moment he arrives."

Jorge uncuffs both my wrists before hoisting me over his shoulder, sending intense, shooting pain through my entire body. Flashes of lights and shadows dance behind my eyes just before I pass out.

When I came to, I'm hanging upright with my hands tied above my head, wearing nothing but my panties. My eyes dart around the room, taking in my surroundings. The lack of light makes it hard to see much of anything. I hear a noise to my right. Straining my eyes, I can make out a figure lying on the ground. "Who's there?" I stammer.

No one answers.

The lights come on without warning, and sitting on a chair in the middle of the room is Jorge.

I scan over to where I heard the noise seconds before and gasp when I see Sofia, chained to the floor, beaten so severely her eyes are completely swollen shut.

"He'll kill you," I seethe.

"Good, I see you're ready to fight. I'm going to enjoy watching the light fade from your eyes."

Striding over, he places the tip of the blade on my inner thigh. "Be still now. If you move, it will be much worse."

Of course, I don't listen. I try to kick him, but it's no use I'm too weak. I unwillingly scream as I feel a burning, sharp pain. His blade sinks into the flesh of my leg.

"Just inside the inner thigh is the main artery, and if you puncture it just right, the blood will slowly leave your body. If I cut any deeper, you'll die within minutes," he boasts, satisfaction in his eyes as he watches the blade sink in.

The tears continuously flow down my face as I sob. I tell myself to stay strong, but the pain is winning. Looking down I watch my blood slowly trickle from my inner thigh, forming a small puddle at my feet.

"Now, we sit and wait," he declares, with his arms spread wide.

Instead of pleading for my life, which at this point would be useless, I concentrate on my breathing. I do my best to calm myself and clear my head. Logan is on his way, this much I know. I need to make sure I hold on that long.

27

LOGAN

It hadn't taken long for the club to put a plan into motion. As soon as my call with Sofia was cut off, my brothers, along with my father, organized a course of action. We now know Bella is in Fairfield, Washington. Demetri has arranged for his private plane to take us to Spokane. Drive time would have taken well over two hours, with flying it cuts that two hours down to about thirty minutes. Once we arrive at the airport in Spokane, we will make a forty-minute drive to Fairfield. Even though we don't have an exact address where Bella is being held, my father informed us his men are very good at finding people, and has assured me that we will have the information by the time we reach Spokane.

Jake, Quinn, Reid, and Demetri will be making the trip with me, while Gabriel and my brother, Nikolai, will stay behind watching over the clubhouse while we're away. With the President of Los Demonios dead, there's not much of a threat, but we're not taking any chances. We still have no clue as to who Alba's buyer was, or if he has any hurt feelings at not getting what he's paid for. People who are sick and crazy enough to buy another human being, for whatever reason, don't usually give up too easily on their obsession.

Walking out of the clubhouse toward my father's SUV, I see Victor, his driver, loading several duffel bags into the back. An advantage of flying private is we're able to bring our artillery. Speaking of, I see Bennett striding over to Reid carrying a familiar black case that holds his .300 Win Mag; he passes it off to him with a lift of his chin.

The drive to the airport is silent. My wandering thoughts have me on edge. Is she okay? What are those motherfuckers doing to her? I clench my hands into fists with the idea of anyone putting their hands on my woman. "Don't let your head go there, son," my father speaks from beside me. "Focus on their blood—on vengeance." He's right; I need to keep my shit together. I'm no good to Bella if I let my emotions cloud my judgment.

Sitting inside Demetri's plane, I can't help but think about the kind of wealth he has. My mother was a single parent who sometimes struggled to make ends meet on her nurse's salary, while my father was able to afford whatever his heart desired. Logically I know it's not his fault, but it still hurts to know that my grandfather, my blood, didn't think I was good enough; that my mother wasn't good enough for his son. Cutting my eyes over to my father, I see him staring at me like he knows exactly what I'm thinking, and I'm startled by the look of devastation on his face. At that moment, I realize he's hurting just as much as I am, and I need to let my anger go. Bella told me I was lucky to have this second chance with my father. He has shown me nothing but love, patience, and loyalty since coming into my life. I owe it to myself and my mother to give him the same. Something tells me my mom would have wanted it this way.

When we land in Spokane, I watch as my brothers file out of the plane, then I turn to look behind me to see my father talking to the pilot.

"Dad," I call out.

Pivoting his head in shock, Demetri answers, "Son."

"Thank you," I say sincerely.

"You're welcome, Logan," he answers back with noticeable emotion in his voice. With those parting words, I walk off the plane, leaving the ghost of my grandfather behind.

True to his word, my father's men found the address where Bella is being held. We pull off to the side of a secluded road about a mile from the abandoned house where we know Jorge, and at least a dozen of his men are located. Jake, Quinn, and I climb out of the SUV along with Demetri and Victor. We remain silent as we ready ourselves. As I'm sliding my 9mm into my shoulder holster, Jake speaks up. "Chances are that these motherfuckers will be expecting us. I'm sure they know by now we killed their president, who happened to be the VP's father. They'll be looking for blood," he cautions us.

Prez is right. There will be no sneaking up this time. We'll have to go in hot and make this shit quick. I watch as Reid pulls out the black case Bennett handed him before we left the clubhouse out of the back of the SUV, and takes off in a jog. The dirt road we are on is situated directly behind the abandoned house the sons of bitches are held up in, and Reid is headed off to get in position. The .300 Win Mag that Reid is carrying is the same one Bennett taught us to shoot when we were younger. Reid is an excellent shot, and he's excellent at not being seen. My brother is a ghost when need be.

"Alright, it's showtime," Jake announces as Victor speeds up the dirt road, stopping directly in front of the house. We're barely out of the vehicle when shots are fired in our direction. Demetri is the first to return fire, catching a man on top of the roof, as Jake takes out a man who crept up on the side of the house. I hear several more shots as Quinn and Victor make their way around back, while Jake and I settle up by the front door. Prez gives the signal and on three, he boots in the door as I cover him from behind and drill two holes into some fucker's back as the coward tries to run away. Rushing down the hall, I quickly start checking rooms. They're all empty, except for what I find in the third one that almost brings me to my knees. Blood! Blood-soaked sheets covering the bed, and my first thought is *I'm too late*. There's no way anybody can still be breathing after losing that much blood. "Fuck," Jake hisses from behind me.

"Jake," I choke out.

"We don't know nothin' for sure, Logan, so don't let your head go there." I hear Jake's phone ping. He looks at his message. "Let's go, Reid has eyes through a window of the basement. He says there's movement down there."

Running back into the kitchen, I jerk open the door I know leads to the basement. The squeak of the stairs no doubt alerts whoever is down here to my arrival, but I don't have it in me to give a shit, I'm on a mission. With my pistol raised, I round the corner, and I'm met with the worst sight I've ever witnessed. My angel is hanging from the ceiling, covered in lacerations, and with a pool of blood at her feet. It takes me all of two seconds to notice the motherfucker sitting in the chair to my left with his gun trained on me. He's spewing some shit about how our club killed his father, and now he wants me to watch the woman I love die right in front of me.

Catching the small red light coming through the window, I sneer at him, "Motherfucker, your father was a spineless coward who was caught trying to flee instead of fighting like a man. The barrel of the gun that was pressed between his eyes as he stared death in the face is the same one your sorry ass is staring down right now. The only one dying here today is you." By this point, we both have our guns trained on each other, but before he has a chance to react to my statement, Reid's single shot hits Jorge right

Undaunted

between the eyes, and I'm at Bella's side before his body reaches the floor.

Taking a knife from my pocket, I cut her loose and Bella's limp body falls into my arms as I quickly cut her down. She's still conscious but can't hold herself up. Her lips are turning blue, and her skin is pale. Laying her on the basement floor, I slip my cut off and cover her exposed body as she slurs, "I love you, Logan."

"I love you too, Angel. Stay with me," I say in return.

With shaky hands, I take my belt and tie it above the puncture wound on the inside of her thigh. Scooping her up in my arms, I wince. With the number of cuts on her body, there is no way of moving her that's going to be painless. Behind me, I hear pounding feet making their way down the stairs. When I turn, I see Jake and Quinn.

"Oh shit, brother," Quinn mutters when he sees the state Bella is in, "and who the hell is that?" he curses, pointing to the small shadowy figure lying on the floor in the corner of the room. Quinn swiftly strides over to the unmoving person. "It's a fuckin' kid," he announces, "and she's beaten all to hell."

"We've got to move now. Bring her with," I exclaim.

Taking the stairs two at a time, I practically run out of the house with Bella in my arms. By the time we load up into the truck, she passed out. "Go! Go! Go!" I shout at Victor.

"Hospital is ten minutes out," he clips.

"Baby, please," I chant as I rock her limp body in my arms. "You've got to stay with me, okay? Babe, please. You can't leave me now. Come on, what the fuck is taking so long?" I bellow. I look around at my brothers, and I hate seeing the look of pity on their faces—like it's over, like she's already gone. Fuck that shit. I'm not giving up on her.

With the screeching of tires, we pull up to the emergency room. I jump out, still holding Bella in my arms, and jog through the sliding doors while Quinn carries in the other girl we found down in the basement with her. "We need a fucking doctor now!" I yell, drawing the attention of several patients in the waiting room, along with a few staff members milling around. A tall, lean man wearing scrubs comes running toward me with a short, black-haired girl wearing a white coat. No way is she a fuckin' doctor. She doesn't look like she's old enough to be out of high school yet. "I said I wanted a goddamn doctor!" I growl at the woman who is attempting to assist the nurse in getting me to let go of Bella and lay her down on a gurney.

"I am the doctor," she hisses back at me. "Now, you need to let her go so I can assess her," she calmly insists, cutting her eyes to Bella, whom I still have a death grip on. "What's your name?" she questions me.

"Logan," I snap at her.

"I'm Dr. Evans, and I promise I'm going to do everything I can to help..." she pauses.

"Bella, her name is Bella," I inform her.

"I'm going to help Bella, but first, we need you to let her go." Relenting, I place Bella on the gurney and watch as they rush her away.

I can't move. I'm frozen to this spot watching as more nurses surround her, poking and prodding as they hook her up to machines. Dr. Evans is giving out instructions left and right. I watch as one nurse runs over carrying units of blood. My brothers stand silently behind me. There's nothing to be said at this point. A second later, the shrill sound of monitors going off fills the emergency room.

"She's crashing!" the skinny male nurse calls out. My heart feels like it's stuck in my throat as my legs begin to move on their own accord toward the chaos. I'm halfway across the room when two security guards stop me.

"I'm sorry, sir, but you can't be here," they inform me.

"I need to get to my woman," I snap.

"Sir, you're not allowed, but if you go to the waiting room, someone will be with you shortly." Seeing me about to protest again, the other guard cuts in.

"Look, man. I got a wife, I understand. I promise someone will be with you as soon as possible. Let them do their job. Dr. Evans is one of the best. Your girl is in good hands." Giving in, I allow Jake to lead me back to the waiting area.

Two hours later, a nurse approaches us, "Excuse me, sir, Dr. Evans asks that I bring you all to a private family room."

"What the hell for? Why can't she come to talk to us here?"

"Sir, please."

"Fuck, no! I know why doctors take people in the family rooms, I'm not havin' that shit. She's not telling me my girl is dead, you hear me?"

"Logan, come on, son, let's go," my father urges me.

"No, they're not going to tell me she fuckin' gone!"

"Logan," Dr. Evans cuts in. Calmly walking over to me, she places her hand on my arm. "Bella is in surgery and stable for now. I wanted to bring you to the family room so we could discuss her condition in private. I'm sorry that my instruction alarmed you."

I slump my shoulders in relief, "Is she going to be okay?" I ask.

"Right now, Bella is stable, but she's not out of the woods yet. If you all will follow me, I will explain her condition to you."

Nodding, we follow the doctor into a private room. I sit and listen to her describe Bella's injuries. "She has seven lacerations to her chest and torso that will require at least 200 or more stitches; she's being sewn up now. I repaired the femoral artery in her leg. Whoever tied the belt around her thigh saved her life. Had it not been for that, she wouldn't have made it to the hospital. She's still unconscious and will most likely remain that way for a while. I want you to keep in mind that even though she's stable, she is still in serious condition and will be admitted to the ICU for a few days. Bella also had some bruising on her hips and along the inside of her thighs indicating possible sexual assault."

My body tenses at the mention of rape. "And?" I ask.

"The examination determined she wasn't raped," Dr. Evans assures.

"When can I see her?"

"Once Bella is moved to the ICU, she will be allowed one visitor at a time. I'm also going to suggest a counselor talk to her when she is awake. Bella will most likely have some issues and trouble dealing with the level of damage that has been done to her body. Recovery will be a challenging road for her. I called in a favor and had the best plastic surgeon in the state come in. He's the one working on Bella now. I'll go check on his progress and send someone to take you to her as soon as possible."

"What about the girl that was brought in with Bella? How's she doing?" Reid inquires. Shit, I completely forgot about her. My only focus has been on my woman.

"Sofia has a broken arm and a significant amount of bumps and bruises. She's awake now and was able to tell us her name and give some information about what's happened to her. She seems to be a strong girl. I'm going to work on finding her family."

"Thanks, Dr. Evans," I say offering her my hand, "and I'm sorry about before. When we first arrived, I meant no disrespect."

Accepting, she replies, "You're welcome, Logan. Given the situation, your actions were to be expected. You only wanted what was best for the person you care for and believe me, you're not the first person to question my credibility, and you won't be the last," she says in a bit of a teasing tone to lighten the mood. Standing up, Dr. Evans makes her way to the door and adds, "There are a couple of detectives in the waiting area asking to speak with someone about the incident involving Bella and Sofia."

Before I can reply, my father cuts in. "I'll take care of it," he says, immediately leaving the room.

"Excuse me there, Dr. Pretty," Quinn drawls from the corner of the room. "Would you mind showing me where I can get some coffee?"

The doctor's face flushes red as she stammers, "Um, sure." I watch as he walks out of the room, throwing a wink over his shoulder as he trails behind the poor unsuspecting woman.

"Fucking Quinn. Can't take his ass anywhere," Reid scoffs.

IT'S BEEN TWO DAYS, and Bella still hasn't woken up. The plus is that she is no longer considered critical and has been moved to a regular room. Dr. Evans has been coming by every few hours to check on her progress and assures me Bella will wake up when she's ready. My father has arranged for Bella to have a private room while she's here, and he's gotten Jake, Quinn, and Reid situated in a local hotel. With things quiet back home, they refuse to leave until Bella can come home.

It's almost 9:00 am. At any moment, the men will be here for their first visit of the day. When the door opens, I'm expecting to see my brothers walk through, but instead, I see Alba—a furious Alba. She appraises her sister for a moment before she turns her fiery eyes to me. This is not the sweet, timid little sister we have come to know. "You," she seethes pointing the finger at me. "TWO DAYS my sister has been laid up in this hospital without me. TWO DAYS you assholes have instructed Gabriel to keep me home."

"Alba—" I begin to speak, but she cuts me off.

"No! If any of you ever try to keep me from my sister again, I will nut-punch every single one of you!"

With a brow lift and amused look on my face, I look over at Gabriel, who is quietly standing by the door, and I can't help but chuckle. Her attempt at being intimidating is about as effective as Bella's.

"She has a fire," he states.

Whipping her head around, Alba growls, "Gabriel!"

"Cariño, *sweetie,*" he rasps, drawing out the 'r,' making his accent sound even stronger. I watch in amusement as she turns red. Deciding to give up on her intimidation tactic, Alba turns her attention back to Bella. Walking over to the bed she sets her purse down and then very carefully crawls into bed with her sister.

28

BELLA

Day Three
A low murmur of what sounds like a TV starts to pull at me, rousing me from sleep.

"Alba, I'm heading down the hall to grab a coffee. I'll be right back. You want anything?" I hear Logan's hoarse voice say.

"No, thank you, Logan," Alba tells him.

I feel pressure on my lips the moment Logan presses his to mine, then hear booted footsteps as he walks away.

I struggle to pry my eyes open, and a bright flash of light breaks through. I feel like I did when I experienced my first hangover in high school. The brightness hurts at first, but I keep forcing them to open more. My vision is blurry, like looking through a fogged-up window in the wintertime, so I blink a couple of times slowly. It feels like the inside of my eyelids are lined with sandpaper, but soon I'm able to bring everything into focus.

Every muscle in my neck feels stiff as I turn my head and see my sister curled up next to me, her nose in her Kindle. I reach my hand out, or at least try to. Peering down at my side, I notice the IV line, which explains the slight tug I felt when I tried to move.

Without warning, flashes of images flood my memory—the BBQ and running after my sister. Her and I being taken by Los Demonios. Jorge repeatedly cutting my flesh. Logan saving me. It all crashes into me—wave after wave of flashbacks. The last thing I remember was Logan telling me Alba was safe. I can't recall anything else after that.

When I try to lift my hand again, I hear a gasp. I look back up to find my sister staring at me.

"Oh, my God! Bella?"

Her Kindle falls to the floor as she turns, putting her head in my lap, and begins to sob. I reach my hand up and softly stroke her hair. My emotions are getting the better of me, as well. My sister is everything to me. I can't begin to describe the relief I feel knowing she's okay.

"It's okay, Alba," I croak out, my voice sounding uneven and raw.

I continue to stroke her hair, trying to calm her down as I do my best to compose myself.

I glance around at my surroundings, taking everything in. The hospital room I'm in is big. The walls aren't the ordinarily cold, sterile white. They're a soft blue. The light shining through the big window hurts my eyes still, but it's much more bearable than before. Flowers and balloons line the window seal.

I turn my head to look to the other side of the room, and the door opens with Logan stepping in, holding a cup of coffee. My breathing falters the moment our eyes meet. I give him an unsure smile.

"Bella," his husky voice croaks out. He sounds every bit as emotional as I am now, but he is hiding most of it well as he takes a few strides before stopping right beside me. Placing the coffee on the table, Logan grabs my empty hand and places it over his heart. Using his other hand, he brushes the tears from under my eyes.

He rests his forehead on mine—both of us feeling the weight

of everything. I thought I would never get the chance to see him again, have his arms hold me, feel his lips against mine one more time, yet here we are.

"I love you," I whisper in his ear as he pulls me close.

"I love you," he rasps with so much emotion his voice betrays him.

My sister lifts her head from my lap, and Logan moves to the side, letting her lean forward to give me a light hug.

"I'm going to go clean my face in the bathroom. When I come out, I'll ask the nurse for some warm tea with honey. It should help your throat," she says, and smiles warmly at me while wiping her eyes with the back of her hands.

"Bella," she adds, turning back around just as she opens the bathroom door, "I love you."

Crying all over again, I tell her the same before she closes the door.

Reaching down, Logan pushes a button and tells the nurse I'm awake. Before I have time to catch another breath, a young woman with black hair, I'm assuming is the doctor, and a couple of nurses in pink scrubs come walking in after a brief knock on the door.

The doctor walks up and begins checking all the monitors they have hooked up to me before speaking. "Well, Bella. I'm happy to see you're finally awake. I'm Dr. Evans. I've been treating you since you arrived a few days ago," she says, holding a clipboard against her chest.

"How many days have I been here? How long have I been out of it? Where's Sofia?" I question her with a hoarse voice.

Dr. Evans smiles warmly at me. "Sofia was admitted and is doing great. She has a broken arm, along with some bumps and bruises, but she is going to make a full recovery."

I relax a bit and close my eyes while letting out a sigh of relief.

"You've been here and under my care for three days. If you're up to it, I want to go over everything with you. I want to make sure you understand what your body has been through and your recovery process."

I feel Logan stiffen at my side. "Do we need to do this now, doc? Can it wait? She just woke up," he huffs out, sounding irritated.

The bathroom door opens, and my sister walks back into the room. I hate being the center of attention and right now, everyone's eyes are on me. I'm starting to feel very uncomfortable. I want to get the prodding over with. I remember everything I went through before being brought to the hospital, but nothing more up until now. I don't want people to look at me differently like they are right now.

Pulling up a chair beside my bed, the doctor sits, crossing her legs while folding her hands in her lap.

"Everyone in this room knows that you went through a horrible ordeal, Bella. I'm sure you remember everything so that I won't repeat it."

I close my eyes. How can I forget? Logan has my hand in his, and my sister is now holding my other hand, both giving me the support I need as the doctor continues.

"You lost a lot of blood, and your heart stopped not long after you were brought to us. We had to give you more than one transfusion during surgery. You have Type O negative blood, and being O negative, you can only receive the same. We didn't have much of that in supply. Thankfully, one of your friends was O negative as well and donated."

I look to Logan for clarification on who helped save my life.

"Quinn donated, Angel," Logan says.

I feel very overwhelmed, but I'm pretty sure from the look on her face she's not done telling me everything. "Could I get something to drink? My throat is so dry," I ask.

Alba leaves my side to get the hot tea she mentioned a few moments ago. My mind is running a mile a minute. My heart stopped beating? Did I die?

Undaunted

"We called in one of the best plastic surgeons in the area to take care of the lacerations you received. The worst ones were on your ribcage. I assure you the scarring will fade in time. I repaired the damage to your femoral artery as well. That's where most of your blood loss came from."

Scars. I'm left with permanent marks on my body from that monster. Alba walks back in with my tea and hands it to me. I sip on it slowly, and the warmth instantly soothes the scratchiness in the back of my throat. I'm also drained. I slept for three days, and I already need another nap. That's insane.

"I can see you're tired. That is just your body's way of healing, but before you sleep, I want to change your bandages and get you to eat something light. Okay?" Dr. Evans informs me.

I cut my eyes at Logan. Instantly I have anxiety about him seeing me. I don't understand my hesitation myself. Why would I suddenly feel this way? He's seen my body several times. All I know is, right now, at this moment, I want nothing more than to hide from him.

"Babe, what's wrong?" Logan inquires.

I hate to tell him to leave while they tend to me, but I can't handle him seeing me this way right now. I know what I'm about to say will not go over well.

"Logan. Would you please step outside while they change the bandages?"

He's taken aback by my request. Hurt and anger appear on his face, just before he masks it. "I'll be downstairs, having a smoke and calling the guys." He stands up and bends down, pressing his lips softly to mine. "I love you."

"I love you," I tell him before he walks out the door.

Turning back to the doctor, I ask her, "When can I shower?"

"With help, you can take one first thing in the morning. Now, let's change those bandages. I'll warn you; it's going to hurt. The gauze will stick to the stitches. I'll be as careful as possible."

I lay still in the bed as they carefully set me up and remove my hospital gown. The pull of the skin on my side hits me instantly. I grit my teeth and push through it.

The gauze is wrapped around my torso, and the nurses who accompanied Dr. Evans earlier start to unwrap it carefully. The doctor takes over, carefully pulling the tape off my skin. It feels like the skin's going with it. When she gets to the bandage that covers the larger area and starts peeling it away, I can't help but flinch.

"It looks good. No signs of infection. Don't be afraid to move. It will hurt, but the movement will help the skin stay loose. We don't want it to become tight. Physical therapy can help with that."

Not being able to bring myself to look down at it, I keep my eyes focused on my sister.

I'm pulling strength from her right now. It shouldn't be that way; big sister needing her baby sister to take care of her. I don't know how to let that sink in. Right now, though, it feels like the most natural thing to do.

The nurses help me into a new gown before leaving, and Dr. Evans asks if I feel like I need anything for the pain. Truthfully, I hurt. I ache all over, but I only ask for a mild pain reliever. I don't like taking medicine if I don't have to.

Finally settled, I sip some more on my tea. The whole time my sister has been sitting right next to me. Quiet.

"Alba, are you okay? Did they hurt you in any way?" I've needed to ask her this question since I first woke up. The thought of her going through anything makes me shiver.

"They manhandled me, told me what awful things they wanted to do to me, but they didn't do anything else." She grabs my hand and holds it in hers. "Promise," she whispers.

I hear a knock at the door and Logan's voice asking, "Angel, are you dressed? I brought visitors."

I'm a mess, and he brings visitors? I look over at Alba, and she sees the worried look on my face. "I'm sure I look hideous," I tell her.

"Do you want me to make them leave? I'll do it. It's probably the guys, but if you want them gone, just say so."

She makes me laugh. I know she means every word she says, but I'm not used to her being so boisterous. The laugh hurts like hell but feels good at the same time.

"I think we can spare them your wrath for now," I smile at her.

"Come in," I try and call out, but my voice comes out as a little squeak.

The door slides open, and in walks Logan, followed by Gabriel, Quinn, Reid, and Jake. All have big smiles on their faces.

"The guys just needed to put eyes on you, Angel. Soon as I told them you were awake, they showed up."

Walking over, he takes the seat he was in before, right by my side. One by one, the guys come over and kiss my forehead.

I grab Logan's hand. I'm overwhelmed with emotions. I'm scared, happy—but mostly grateful. Every man standing in front of me helped save my life and my sister's. I have no idea how to thank them or repay anyone for what they did for us.

With tears threatening to spill and a shaky voice, I try my best to say something anyway.

"Umm, I want to say thank you for everything, but I feel it's not enough guys. What you all did for my sister and me—" I can't even finish. My lips tremble. What I was trying to hold in breaks free, and I bury my face in my hands.

"Angel, don't cry. I told you. You belong to me, and that makes you family. There isn't a damn thing we wouldn't do for you or your sister."

I try my best to wipe my face dry with the bed sheet before peering up at everyone. I see nothing but pure love and devotion on every one of their faces.

A nurse walks in with a tray and sets it down in front of me. I'm not hungry. From the looks of it, it's just some simple chicken broth and a pack of crackers, so maybe sipping on the broth won't be so bad.

The guys don't stay long. They say their goodbyes and leave.

I insist Alba leave and get a good night's rest in a decent bed instead of cramming herself into the one I'm lying on right now. She finally relents, only because Gabriel promises to have her up here early tomorrow morning.

Yawning, I push the button on the bed to let the head down. Logan decides to climb in beside me once I've gotten myself comfortable.

His tall frame barely fits with his feet hanging over the end of the bed. I let him hold me. I snuggle into his warmth, calming the storm brewing inside. I've put a brave face on all day, no one realizing that I felt uneasy. Then again, maybe they did, and I'm just fooling myself. I can't get the image of Jorge out of my mind. I don't even have to close my eyes, and he's there. I can still hear his sadistic voice ringing in my ears.

As if knowing he needs to drown out the noises in my head, Logan puts his lips next to my ear, whispering in his deep raspy voice, "I've got you, beautiful. I'll be here when you wake up."

That's exactly what I needed to hear. My pulse steadies, my body relaxes, and my eyelids slowly close.

THE NEXT MORNING, I wake up to the smell of cinnamon rolls and coffee. I sit up in bed and watch as Logan places a roll on a plate sitting it in front of me before dumping several packs of creamer and sugar into my coffee, then stirring it. "Morning, Angel."

"Morning." I rub my eyes.

We sit and eat quietly, up until my sister comes bursting through the door, holding a shopping bag. "Went shopping last night. I got you some comfy clothes to put on. I figured you'd like to get out of that hospital gown once you took a shower this morning. I picked up some of your favorite hair shampoos and body lotion." She beams.

My sister seems to be in a good mood this morning.

"I can't wait to get a shower. I feel so gross."

I slowly swing my legs over the side of the bed and sit on the edge. Feeling a little lightheaded, I grab onto the side rail.

Logan helps me to my feet. "You wanna take a shower now, babe? Just let me get the nurse to bring in some fresh bandages, and I'll help you," he says.

"Logan, would you mind if my sister helps me shower?" I ask him hesitantly.

I can tell he wants to argue but doesn't. He sits back down in his chair and pulls out his phone. My sister walks over and helps me to the bathroom. I look over my shoulder to peer at Logan, and he's watching my every move with hurt written on his face. My heart sinks to my stomach.

Alba turns on the shower as I slowly start to undress.

"I brought your iPad. I know you like to listen to music in the shower," she softly tells me.

"Thank you."

I pull up my playlist so I can hit random play before stepping into the shower. Hesitantly I let Alba help me unwrap the gauze, then gently peel the bandage off my side. I don't look down, and I can't look in a mirror because the only one in the bathroom is above the sink.

Hating myself for putting her in this situation, I carefully gauge her reaction. She tries to mask her emotions, but she quickly falters. Silently, tears run down her face. My own tears spill, cascading down my cheeks, making me feel pathetic and small. We both stay silent as my sister helps me into the stall. I press play and stand under the spray of the water.

Music fills the room.

My heart is pounding, and fresh tears wash down the drain when Christina Perri's 'Arms' is the next song to play. The emotions that I feel when this one line repeats throughout the song has my emotions spilling over—*'You put your arms around me, and I'm home.'*

I couldn't be sure, but I almost thought I heard my sister's sobs mixed in with the words of the song. I stand there under the hot stream of water and try to make sense of all the mixed-up emotions I'm feeling, trying to wash away my pain.

29

LOGAN

Stepping out of Bella's hospital room, I lean against the door and blow out a frustrated breath. She's refusing to let me help her do anything that involves me seeing her wounds. Part of me understands why she's this way, but the other part of me wants to take care of my woman. Dr. Evans has assured us the scars will fade significantly over time, but right now they are red and swollen. She explained to Bella she could have plastic surgery in the future, but in her professional opinion the surgeon who stitched her up did an excellent job, so any more operations are highly unlikely. Dr. Evans also has scheduled a counselor to speak with Bella later this afternoon.

"You okay, brother?" Gabriel asks from beside me. He's been keeping guard of Bella's hospital room since he and Alba showed up yesterday.

Looking down at him sitting in a chair nursing a cup of coffee, I respond while running my hand down my face, "Fuck man, I don't know."

"Bella's a strong woman, Logan. She'll get through this shit," Gabriel assures.

"Yeah, brother, you're right," I tell him, pushing off the door. "I'm going to check on the kid, be back in a few."

I talked to Sofia for the first time yesterday. She told me she was the one who called letting me know about Bella. The poor kid took a beating for trying to help my woman. Because of that the club is indebted to her.

Coming up to her room, I see Dr. Evans walking out. "Hey, doc, how's she doin'?"

Smiling, she answers, "Sofia is doing much better today."

"Have you been able to locate any of her family?" I ask.

Shaking her head sadly, she says, "No, Sofia said her parents are dead, and she doesn't have any family. I'm afraid I'll have to call child protective services."

"That won't be necessary," I argue. "She'll be coming home with Bella. She and I will take care of the kid."

"Legally, I have to inform child protective services in a situation like this," Dr. Evans informs me.

I go to interrupt her, but she cuts me off by holding up her hand. "Unofficially, Sofia has no family, but officially if I had the name of, let's say a cousin, someone I can put on the paperwork. Preferably someone of Latin descent, being that Sofia is from Mexico."

To say I was shocked at the doc's suggestion was an understatement. I fully expected this situation to go in the other direction. I don't give two fucks about the system, but the doctor helping us out saves the club from having to handle shit. She has no doubt noticed a certain broody Cuban outside Bella's door lately, and in a roundabout way just told me how to solve our problem regarding Sofia.

"Can I ask why you're doing this?"

Sighing, Dr. Evans darts her eyes around making sure we're not overheard. "Sofia has been through hell, the kind of hell nobody should ever have to go through, let alone a seventeen-year-old girl. The system will no doubt fail her. If I can, in some way, help avoid that then I will, even if it goes against the rules of this hospital. I have a feeling about you and Bella. I see the way those men are—the ones that have been coming to visit. My gut tells me she will be well taken care of."

"She will be," I promise.

"Okay then, I'll have some paperwork that needs to be filled out. I'll bring it by later when I come to check on Bella."

Knocking on Sofia's door, I wait for her to answer before going in. "Hey, kid. How's it goin'?"

"Hey, Logan," she says quietly.

I take in her appearance. She looks better today than yesterday. She's still covered in bruises and is now sporting a bright pink cast on her left arm. The swelling on her face has gone down considerably, as well. At the end of her bed is an array of magazines, books, and an iPad. I sent Quinn out yesterday to pick up some shit I thought Sofia might enjoy while being stuck sitting in this hospital room. She's also underweight, and since hospital food fuckin' sucks, Quinn's been bringing her treats, mostly ice cream. The first time he asked her what she wanted, she shyly told him she missed ice cream, so every day this week he has brought a different flavor.

"How are you feelin' today?"

"Better, how's Bella?"

"Good, she'll be here in a bit to see you."

"Really?" Sofia asks with excitement, sitting up a little straighter in her bed.

"Yeah, kid, she's been asking about you nonstop since she woke up yesterday."

I can't help but grin at the smile on Sofia's face.

"So, you guys will get to go home soon now that Bella is getting better," she says sadly while looking down at her fidgeting hands.

"Hey," I say, walking over and lifting her chin with my finger. "You're going to be going home soon too."

"No, I won't, I don't have a home."

Damn, this kid is playing on my heartstrings. Bella told me about her promise to Sofia to save her. I'm not going to tell Sofia she'll be coming home with us, that's Bella's place. "Don't you worry about all that okay, it'll all work out, you'll see."

"Hey, sweetheart, it's Chunky Monkey day." Quinn singsongs walking through the door. I've never been more grateful for the interruption.

"Hey, brother. I just came from seeing your girl, and she's itching to come see Little Bit here," he tells me, using the nickname he's given Sofia. "Okay, I'll go get her and bring her down."

Walking back into Bella's room, I motion for Gabriel to follow. I see her and Alba sitting on the edge of the bed, talking in hushed tones while giggling. I'll admit having her sister here is the best thing for her.

"Hey, beautiful," I say, greeting her with a kiss. I watch as Gabriel takes a seat by the window while I pull a chair up next to the bed. "I've got some news to tell you before we go see Sofia."

"Okay..." Bella draws outs skeptically like she's preparing for me to say something terrible.

"It's good news, babe," I assure her. I watch as she visibly relaxes. "I spoke with Dr. Evans, and she informed me Sofia has no living relatives. She was able to gather a little information from her. We know both of Sofia's parents have passed, and she has no family in the States."

Bella interrupts me. "Logan, what's going to happen to her? We have to do something."

"Hold on; I'm getting to that. In cases like this, child services would get involved. Dr. Evans has come up with a solution. What

I'm about to say doesn't leave this room, unless it's one of the brothers we're telling." I wait a moment for Bella and Alba to nod their heads in understanding. "She suggested Sofia may have a cousin to claim her as family. Preferably someone who is Latino, since Sofia is from Mexico. It would make it more believable." I wait for what I said to click. It only takes about three seconds for their heads to turn in Gabriel's direction.

Grinning and rolling his eyes, he asks, "What do I have to do?"

I never doubted my brother. He would do anything for the club. We all already consider Sofia family for what she did for Bella. "You'll have to sign some papers; Dr. Evans will bring all that shit by later."

"So," Bella chimes in. "She gets to come home with us?"

"Yeah, babe, she's coming with us. Figured you'd want to be the one to tell her."

We're interrupted by a knock on the door, followed by Dr. Evans and an older lady. She looks to be in her late fifties with short gray hair and a warm smile. "If you've got a minute, Bella, I have someone who'd like to talk with you," Dr. Evans' requests. "Her name is Helen. She is a counselor who specializes in PTSD." I notice Bella's body visibly stiffen when the word PTSD is spoken. "I also want to go over your discharge instructions since we're letting you go home tomorrow."

As introductions are made, I notice Gabriel quietly leading Alba out to give us some privacy.

Over the next hour, we listen to Helen give us tons of information on post-traumatic stress disorder, as well as the names and phone numbers of specialists near Polson. I can tell Bella has shut down and is not paying attention to Helen's advice. She's nodding her head while giving a polite smile, but she has a wall up, I see it in her eyes.

Once Helen has left, and doc gives Bella her aftercare

instructions, I decide now is not the time to press her on her dismissive attitude toward counseling. Instead, I'm going to help her focus on something positive. "How about we go see Sofia? She's probably wondering where we're at." Smiling at me, a real one, not the fake bullshit smile she had plastered on her face moments ago, she nods.

30

BELLA

Refusing to use a wheelchair, I let Logan help me make my slow trek down the hall to Sofia's room. I'm so excited to get to see her finally. The last time I laid eyes on her she was a bloody beaten mess on the basement floor. I remember not knowing if she was even alive. When I woke up after being in the hospital for three days, one of my first thoughts was of Sofia. I felt so much relief when Logan told me they had gotten her out of that house, and she was safe, right here in the hospital. When we walk into her room, she is so engrossed in the iPad she's holding that it takes a minute for her to register that we're even here. "Bella!" Sofia beams.

"Hey, sweetie," I exclaim. Offering me his hand, Logan helps me sit on the side of Sofia's bed. "How are you feeling? The guys treating you good?" Quickly nodding her head, Sofia affirms.

"Yes, everyone has been nice to me. Logan brought me this iPad, and Quinn brings me ice cream every day."

"That's great. I knew they'd take good care of you."

"How about you?" Sofia asks. "Logan said you get to go home soon."

"Yup, we sure do. I'll have one of the guys come to help you get all your stuff together tomorrow." It's all I can do to be nonchalant. I bite the inside of my cheek to keep from smiling. It only takes a few seconds for her to catch on to what I said.

Snapping her head up from staring at her lap. "What do you mean help me get my stuff together?"

"Well, we are going home tomorrow."

"Home? We?" she asks, confused.

"Yes, sweet girl, you're coming home with us tomorrow."

"Really?!" Sofia screeches. I can't help but bust out laughing at her excitement. I ignore the way laughing causes my body to hurt.

"We're going to go so you can get some rest. We have a long day ahead of us tomorrow," I announce patting Sofia's leg.

"Okay, Bella, thank you so much," she hiccups, trying to hold back her tears.

"You're welcome, baby girl."

I'm utterly exhausted after Logan helps me get settled back in my hospital room. I hate how a short walk down the hall leaves me worn out and breathless. Dr. Evans told me that was to be expected. She said not to overdo it, to give my body a chance to heal properly.

Then there's Logan. He's been nothing but patient toward me; even though I know it kills him I won't let him help. I can't help it, though. The thought of him seeing me, seeing what my body looks like under my clothes. I cringe at the thought of what he will think. Will he be disgusted? Will he still want to be with someone who's body is covered in scars?

"What are you thinkin' about, babe?" Logan asks, bringing me out of my sulking thoughts. "Nothing," I say. "I'm just tired." By the look on his face I know he doesn't believe me but he decides not to call me out on it. "Okay, you get some rest. I'll call the guys and get shit straight for tomorrow." Walking over, he gives me a light kiss, and I close my eyes, breathing in his scent, letting it comfort me.

Undaunted

THE NEXT DAY is a bit of a frenzy. I'm so over being in this damn hospital. Finally, Logan has Quinn round up one of the nurses to bring me my discharge papers so we can go. Demetri is flying us home on his plane, which I'm grateful for. I'm not in the mood to be stuck inside a car for a couple of hours. Alba and Gabriel left yesterday, so they could get the house ready for us. We needed groceries and some things for Sofia. My sister was ecstatic at the mention of shopping, but poor Gabriel looked like he'd rather take a bullet. When Alba sassed off saying she would do it herself, the big guy quickly shot that idea down.

A minute later, Quinn strides back into the room, followed by a nurse pushing a wheelchair. I don't want to ride in that damn thing, but it's hospital policy. Sucking it up, I sit my ass in the chair. I'll do anything if it means getting the hell out of here and going home.

Walking into Logan's house we're met with silence. Logan said everyone was anxious to see me. He refused, telling them to let me get settled first. When I was ready, they could come for a short visit. I'm thankful to have him looking out for me. I'm definitely not up for company right now, except for my sister. She's the one I need. "Come on," I say grabbing Sofia's hand from beside me. "I'll give you the grand tour."

Her eyes go big as she takes in the house. After making our way from room to room, I bring her outside, showing her the lake. "Oh my god," she gasps. "Is this real? Do I get to live here?"

"Yes, you get to live here."

Standing at the edge of the water for a moment, I close my eyes, embracing the wind on my face and breathe in the fresh air. Turning my head, I look at the young girl beside me to see her doing the same. I squeeze Sofia's hand, "Come on; let's go inside."

"Would it be okay if I stay out here a few more minutes?" she asks.

"Sure, come in when you're ready."

Back inside, I find Logan in the kitchen, making tea. "Hey, babe, you get Sofia settled?"

"Yeah, she's out by the lake. She'll be in soon."

He nods his head, motioning toward the table. "Come sit, and I'll fix you a cup."

"I need to use your phone to call my sister," I tell him as I pull a chair out and sit. "I want to ask her what time she'll be home."

Peering at me with a tight jaw, he grinds out. "If you need help with something, I'll do it. You're my woman, no more pushing me away."

I flinch when he slams the spoon he's holding down on the counter.

"Logan—" I start before he cuts me off.

"Fuck no, I'm sick of this shit. You need help changing your bandages; I'll change them. You need help taking a shower; I'll help," he states with conviction.

Feeling a rage bubble in my gut, I stand up from the table. "You know what, Logan, it's not really up to you now is it?" I calmly challenge, not taking my eyes off him. If he thinks he's going to take over telling me how things are going to be, he's got another thing coming.

"Angel," he says. His face softening.

Bracing my hands on the table, I hang my head. "I'm not ready," I whisper.

In seconds Logan is beside me holding my head in his hands. I notice the defeated posture of his body as he uses his thumb to brush away my tears, then kisses my lips. "I'll call your sister," he murmurs with a sigh.

I wake up in Logan's and my bed a while later to see Alba lying

Undaunted

next to me. After our little feud earlier, I told Logan I needed a nap. "How long have you been here?"

"About thirty minutes," my sister replies as we engage in a stare-off.

"Just say it," I huff.

"He loves you. You have to let him in. I know you're afraid."

I shake my head, "You don't understand."

"I may not understand what you went through, but I understand being afraid."

My eyes soften at her declaration. Alba, thankfully, came out of this whole nightmare unharmed, but she does indeed understand my feelings on some level. "I need more time, that's all I'm asking."

Climbing off the bed, she walks over to my side. Taking hold of her hands, she helps me stand. My stitches don't feel as tight, just sore. The doctor said I have another week before they can be removed, and I no longer have to keep them bandaged. Walking into the bathroom with my sister I refuse to look in the mirror as she starts the water for my shower. I'll be glad when I can take a real shower, five minutes just isn't cutting it, and my legs needed a razor-like four days ago. Alba catches my horrified look aimed toward my legs and giggles.

"Sit," she commands, pointing to the closed lid of the toilet. "I'm going to shave those hairy beasts you call legs." I hear her snicker when she catches me, flipping her the bird.

It feels so odd having the sister roles reversed. My whole life I've been the one taking care of Alba, so much that it sometimes felt as if she were my child. Now the table has turned, and my baby sister is taking care of me. The first time she saw my cuts, it seemed as though it was harder for her than me. She tried to hide her sadness, but Alba has never been able to mask her feelings very well, especially not from me. Still, she took a deep breath, held the tears back, and became the strong one. At that moment, she knew that's exactly what I needed from her.

Walking downstairs, feeling somewhat human again, I'm hit with the smell of Chinese food, causing my stomach to rumble. "Hey, you two hungry?" Logan questions, when Alba and I walk into the kitchen.

"Yes," we both spill out in unison. I smile when I walk into the kitchen and find Sofia helping him set the table. Sitting down, I immediately dig in while Logan grabs us a couple of beers, and the girls a Coke. Conversation flows freely, mostly about the guys and how things are at the shop. Alba tells me how she talked to Mom the other day, but didn't tell her anything that had happened. No one has mentioned Lee, or what happened to him. The only thing Logan said was it was taken care of. That's good enough for me. The bastard is an afterthought at this point. I hope he's rotting in hell, although even that would be too good for him. When we finish eating, Alba and Sofia excuse themselves to go upstairs. I insist on washing the dishes. I told Logan I need some normalcy.

Once finished, I let him lead me upstairs to our room. "I'm taking a shower, and then we're going to talk," Logan insists, leaving no room for argument.

Not in the mood for being forced into doing something I've voiced I wasn't ready for, I decide to ignore him. If that man thinks I'm going to roll over at his demands, then he's sorely mistaken.

Hours later, I'm woken by someone shaking me and calling out my name. When I open my eyes, it takes me a moment to register where I am and who is holding me. My heart is racing, my body aching and drenched with sweat. I then notice Logan is holding on to me. He has several bloody scratches on his face and chest. I gasp at the realization. I did that. Oh my god. A sobbing noise has me cutting my eyes over to the bedroom door. My sister is standing there, with a tear-streaked face and her hand covering her mouth.

31

LOGAN

Being woken by Bella screaming in her sleep gutted me. I reached out to pull her into my side, in the hope she would calm down and rest. Instead, it has the complete opposite effect. She starts kicking, screaming, and flailing her hands everywhere.

"No-No-No!" she screams.

She's putting all she's got into the struggle as I try to wake her up. "Babe. Wake up. It's me. It's Logan," I plead with her. I grab at her wrists to keep her from scratching at my face anymore.

"Angel, it's okay. You're home. Come on, beautiful," I whisper into her ear.

Her actions slow, and her breathing calms. It's not too dark in the room. The moon's reflection off the waters has cast a blue-gray gleam over most of the bedroom. I start to see the subtle changes in her expression as she comes around. Hearing her gasp, I look down and see tears pooling in her eyes.

"Oh my god. I'm so sorry," she cries.

She has nothing to be sorry for. I understand all too well about having nightmares. I go to say something but don't get the chance to respond.

"Your face," she sobs, bringing her soft hand to my cheek, then running the tip of her finger over my eyebrow. "You're bleeding."

Still holding her, I kiss her forehead, and I calmly ask, "Are you okay?"

I look over toward the door when I hear crying. I see Alba standing in the doorway. She brings her hand to her mouth. No doubt shocked by the commotion that was coming from the room. I hold onto Bella a few minutes longer to soothe her. I want to kill that motherfucker all over again for what he put her through. I motion to her sister who has already taken a few more steps into the room. I catch a glimpse of Sofia peering around the door frame and tell her to come in as well.

"Would the two of you mind sitting with Bella, so I can go clean my face?" I ask them.

"Sure," her sister says in a hushed tone. Sofia doesn't speak. Only nods.

I slip my arms from around Bella's waist and stand, making my way to the master bathroom, and close the door behind me. I'm exhausted. Between the plane ride home, helping the club and my father deal with some loose ends here in town, and now this. She had one while she was still in the hospital, but it wasn't anywhere near the intensity.

I stand in front of the mirror. The scratches on my face aren't that bad. I turn the water on, giving my face a good splash and collect myself before going back out there. I'm trying my best to understand and let her go at her own pace, but fuck if it isn't frustrating as hell at the same time. Every little advance I've made toward her to help has gone ignored. If it involves talking about what happened or even helping her change her bandages, she completely shuts me out.

I'm trying to help the woman I love.

I'm torn.

Do I watch her spiral down that rabbit hole, or should I force her to let me in?

Walking back into the room, I watch as Bella sips on some tea. It seems to calm her nerves, so I've made sure we have plenty of the herbal stuff in the house. Personally, I don't like the shit. She loves it, and that's what matters.

Alba and Sofia hug her, telling her goodnight, before turning to me. "Logan, if you need anything, please come get me. I'll do what I can to help," her sister says.

I know she means well. I give her a nod, and a look that I hope conveys I appreciate her, but this is my job.

They leave the room, closing the door behind them. I walk over and turn the bedside lamp on and flip the overhead switch, turning those lights off.

Bella reaches over, setting her tea down as I climb back into bed. She looks a little unsure and starts twisting the sheets in her hands. I reach over and pull her into my side. I feel her body tense for just a moment before melting into me, laying her head on my chest.

"I'm so sorry I scratched you," she whispers.

I can feel the tears silently falling onto my skin and her warm breaths as they caress my flesh. I will my body not to react in the way it naturally does when I'm around her. The smell of her hair, the softness of her skin against my rough, calloused hands.

Fuck.

Taking a cleansing breath, I gain some self-control over other parts of my body. "I'm okay, babe. Nothing to worry yourself with. Do you want to talk about it? The nightmare?"

"No. I'm tired. Could you just hold me awhile?" she asks in a soft, shaky voice.

"Yeah, beautiful. I can do that," I declare, pulling her tighter.

I lay there for the next couple hours, holding on to the best thing to ever walk into my life. Eventually, I'm lulled to sleep, listening to her soft, relaxed breaths.

"Yo, Quinn!" I holler from across the shop.

I'm stripping down an old Harley that a customer salvaged from the boneyard. He came in last week, wanting to convert it to a bobber style. It'll be a nice-looking ride when I'm done with it. The guy is a Navy SEAL vet. He's not looking for anything over-the-top, just a classic-lookin' smooth ride.

"What ya need, man?" Quinn fires back at me as he continues to work on a big twin that was brought in yesterday.

"I need you to close up shop this evening. I got some shit I need to do."

"Not a problem, brother. Listen. The guys are throwing a party tonight. You comin'?"

Relaxing and having a few drinks sounds like a pretty good idea. The last few weeks have been stressful as hell. I've been bustin' my ass here at work. Mainly because I don't feel needed anywhere else. So, I come to work, staying late most nights, before heading home to shower and sleep. "Yeah, man, I'll be there."

Throwing myself into work is the only way I can deal with my stress and the pent-up tension. That, or drink, and I've been doing my damnedest not to chase the bottom of a bottle lately.

I finish up my day, leaving Quinn to wrap things up at the shop. I step outside and mount my bike. I make my way out to my father's estate. Nikolai, my brother, called me a couple of days ago asking if I could ride out sometime. He wanted to discuss a few things with me but didn't want to do it over the phone. I pull up to the gate, and I'm immediately let through. I still can't get used to the wealth my dad has. He made it quite clear on the plane ride to save my woman that 'what is his, is now mine.' The thought of

Undaunted

having disposable money and endless resources at my fingertips is overwhelming. I've always worked hard to get what I want. Nothing has ever been handed to me. For now, I'm happy with the way things are.

Nikolai comes walking out as I'm getting off my bike. "Logan, glad you came. I have lunch ready out back."

I follow him through the house and out the back patio door. It smells fuckin' good out here. I span over to my left, and he has the lid of a BBQ grill open, taking off some big ass ribeyes.

"Fuck, brother. I wasn't hungry before, but now..."

Laughing, he points to a cooler sitting on the ground by the patio table and chairs. "Grab us a beer. I'll bring these over in a minute. I like grilling. It relaxes me. It makes me feel normal."

After slapping the steaks onto some plates, he carries them over and sits one in front of me with a big ass bowl of seasoned fries. Damn. I'm not going to complain. Meat and potatoes. I can handle that.

"By normal, you mean pretending you're not the son of Russian Mafia?" I pick at him, handing him a beer.

"Exactly. I was born into this life. I didn't choose it. It can be very unsatisfying. Sometimes I want to be alone. Left to do as I wish. Not what's expected of me, which brings me to what I wanted to discuss today." He pauses, taking a bite of his food.

After taking a few bites of the steak, that would give Reid and Quinn a run for their money. I take a sip of beer. Nikolai continues with his conversation as I stuff some fries in my mouth. "I want to stay here in Polson, and I would like you to help me convince my —our father that it would be a good idea."

Little brother feels like rebelling. I smile. It could be a very good idea or go very badly. Either way, everyone should get to experience life out from under someone's thumb.

"You wanna stick around, huh? You got a plan on what you want to do while you're here?"

"I was planning on staying here at the estate, but I was hoping to maybe look for some normal work. Something I could be proud of. Learn and feel accomplished at," he boasts, with a look of determination and eagerness.

"Hell yeah! I can get behind that. You want to be your own man. I get it. I'll do what I can to help you out."

Raising his bottle of beer to me, with a big fuckin' smile, he tells me, "Thank you, brother."

We finish lunch with easy conversation. Getting to know each other a little better before I head out. The sun is starting to set, so I pull out my phone, giving Bella a call. She answers on the first ring. I let her know I'll be late again tonight. Mostly, I just wanted to hear her sweet voice say, 'I love you.'

It's almost dark when I get to the clubhouse and park my bike. The party has just started as I walk through the doors, and make my way to the bar. Gabriel is sitting in his usual spot, nursing a beer, as I pull up a stool and ask for one of my own, along with a shot of whiskey.

"Hey, brother, you doin' okay?" Gabriel's inquires in a low murmur while staring at me.

"Yeah, man. I just wanted to swing by and unwind for a bit."

Nodding his head, Gabriel doesn't say anymore. He gets up, making his way upstairs.

As I'm nursing my second beer and my third shot, Reid sits down beside me. "Logan, haven't seen you hang out around here for a while. You doing okay?"

If there is one person I can talk to about some deep shit, it's Reid. I've known him longer than any of my brothers. Hell, he practically is my brother. We grew up together. I consider all this before opening my mouth. "Reid, man, I don't know what to do. She won't open up to me. She's pushing me away."

I sound like a pussy right now. Fuck it. I take another shot. Enjoying the burn as it slides down my throat.

"Do you think going home to her drunk is going to help the situation?" Reid cautions.

"I can sleep it off here. Trust me. She won't even care if I'm not there, brother. She has her sister and Sofia."

I hear him sigh beside me. "Logan, maybe she needs some time. Someone tortured her, mentally and physically. My guess is your woman feels lost, damaged, and possibly even unattractive. It's not easy dealing with scars of any kind. It's taken me a long time to accept that my body is different. I still feel the need to hide it. In a way, I understand what she is going through."

Fuck. He's right. I drag my hand down my face. I've watched him struggle since the accident. Not only with losing his brother but his leg as well. He hides it well, always wearing jeans. He may understand where she's coming from, but I'm fighting the battle too. How the fuck can I be there for her when she doesn't let me in? How can I help her to get better if all she wants to do is ignore the situation altogether? I love her, but it's hard to fight demons you can't physically see. I can beat the hell out of anyone any day. Hell, even pull the fuckin' trigger if I had to for her, but the ghosts.

"I don't see her any different than I did before. She is still the same beautiful woman I love," I say, frustration laced on every word, but it's the truth. What I see hasn't changed one bit.

"She doesn't feel beautiful, and she's not going to ever be the same, on the inside. Until she does, all you can do is wait. Be there for her when she does let you in," Reid finishes, as he motions to Blake for another beer.

Releasing a breath, I raise my head, looking at my reflection in the mirror that hangs on the wall behind the bar. She doesn't deserve to see me like this.

I clasp my hand on the back of Reid's neck. "Thanks, brother. It felt good to talk to someone. I'm going to head to the kitchen, make some coffee. I don't want to go home shit-faced."

"I'll join you. I'm not feeling the party atmosphere tonight," he mumbles.

It's around midnight once I make it home. Reid and I bullshitted for a couple of hours. Reliving some good times and sharing memories from our childhoods.

I'm too beat to shower, so I strip out of my clothes and climb into bed. Bella tenses for a moment as I pull her into me. The touch of her soft skin as I wrap my arms around her quiets the noise in my head.

"I love you, Angel," I quietly whisper in her ear.

"I love you," she says in a sleepy voice, almost too low to hear.

I'M RIDING out to the lake today to try and clear my head. The conversation I had with Reid last night is on a continuous loop, and I'm finding it hard to concentrate on anything else.

I can't get my mind to focus on anything but Bella, and the distance she's putting between us, so I told her that I had club shit to deal with. I shouldn't lie, but I need some breathing room and space to think.

She's still having nightmares at least once a week but refuses to talk to me about them. To top it off, she is still hiding her body from me.

"Fuck!" I yell into the wind while driving down the road.

Riding down a dirt road that leads to the lake where my mom and aunt are buried, I notice a blacked-out SUV parked a few yards ahead. I roll to a stop, and the driver's door opens and out steps Victor, my Dad's driver and right-hand man.

I kill my bike's engine and put the kickstand down. "Victor. Is my dad in there?" I point to the vehicle.

"No. He is over there," he says in his thick Russian accent, pointing to the right.

Undaunted

When I scan over in the direction Victor is pointing, I see my father knelt directly in front of my mom's headstone. He has his palm splayed over the top.

Letting out a ragged breath, I make my way to him. As I get closer, I notice the subtle shake of his shoulders, showing he's having a moment. I hang back, letting the man collect himself.

Taking a deep breath and letting it back out, he speaks without turning around. "I heard the rumble of your bike as you pulled up, son. I apologize for my current state. I could no longer stay away. I had to pay my respects to the only woman I have ever loved."

Walking up behind him, I place my right hand on his left shoulder, giving it a light squeeze, letting him know I understand; that I'm here for him. My gesture, though unspoken, is loud and clear. His shoulders slump, and he hangs his head.

"Thank you, son."

Standing a few seconds later, he reaches into his pocket and pulls out a gold coin, placing it on top of the headstone. I've heard about customs like this where people leave coins on the graves of loved ones. Greek mythology. It's a toll of some sort, also a sign of respect.

Turning toward me, my father appraises me. "You look tired, Logan. Is everything okay?" he questions.

Shit. I wasn't aware that my appearance matches how I felt on the inside. I run my hand through my hair and rub the back of my neck, my muscles tight with tension.

"I'm good, Dad. Nothing to worry about," I try to assure him.

"How is your woman, Bella? I'm sorry I haven't been around much. I didn't want to overstep my welcome by prying into your personal life. Is she adjusting well at home?"

We start walking toward the waterfront, stopping to take a seat on an old tree log. I contemplate sharing anything. "She could be doing better. The nightmares are getting fewer, though," I divulge.

"And you? How are you doing?"

I let out a long sigh before giving him a clipped, short answer, "Tired."

"Yes. She is worth it, though. Am I right?" my dad asks.

As exhausted as I am mentally over the whole situation, I can honestly say that my woman is worth it. I'm just hoping one day she will see her worth too. I plan on showing her unconditionally every day that she is loved. I won't give up on her. Even if she wants to give up on herself, "Yes, she's worth it."

"You're both strong. Give her your strength when she needs it, and she will return it tenfold. Women are much stronger than we could ever be. She will rise. Give her time."

Time.

We both continue staring out over the clear waters that mirror the blue sky above, without speaking another word.

Both searching for answers. Both seeking comfort in the silence and solitude.

32

BELLA

Two months later

It's been two months since Logan carried me out of that basement. I feel like I'm walking through life like a zombie. Adjusting hasn't been easy. Some people look at me with pity, while others treat me as if nothing happened. I don't know which is worse. Many things have changed since coming home from the hospital. As for Logan and me, we've been stuck in some limbo.

The nightmares are few and far between. My stitches came out. The scars, although significant, have started to lose a bit of the angry red appearance. Logan has been nothing but patient with me, even though I still haven't shown him my scars yet. Sometimes I let the guilt eat at me. We've hardly touched each other in these past months. I know he has needs. There have been nights where he's called, saying he's working late, and I'll wonder if he's working or if he's hooking up with one of the club girls. I feel self-conscious all the time, and I let negative thoughts take over. Deep down, I know he wouldn't cheat on me.

"You okay?" Sofia asks, plopping down on the couch beside me.

"Yeah, I'm fine. Had my head in the clouds is all."

"Do you want to talk about it?"

I wave a dismissive hand at her, "There really isn't anything to talk about."

I don't feel like talking to anyone. I haven't even been talking to my sister about my struggles with my body image.

"I know I'm just a kid, but you can talk to me. I see things, and I know you're having a tough time."

I lean over, squeezing her hand. "I'm fine. Really, you don't need to worry about me." I plaster a fake smile on my face to hopefully avoid any further discussion.

Turning her body to face me, she continues, "Well, can I ask you a question?"

"Yes, of course. You can ask me anything."

After a few beats, she begins, "Do you think one day a man will want to date me, to be with me? I mean, once they find out what happened, will they think I'm ugly or damaged?"

Though Sofia hasn't talked about it yet, I know she was raped multiple times. Dr. Evans confirmed it in the hospital. My heart aches that she even thinks those things about herself.

"Sofia, a good man—the right man—will see you as nothing but the beautiful, amazing girl you are. What happened to you will not change that," I say with certainty.

With a severe and stern look, she regards me. "If you're so certain of that for me, then why can't you believe those things about yourself?"

I go to open my mouth, but I have nothing to say. She's right. I wear my scars on the outside. Sofia wears hers on the inside. Scars are scars, regardless if they are visible or not.

She stands up and heads upstairs, leaving me speechless.

That sneaky, smart girl. I shouldn't be surprised. Sofia is slowly opening up to us. A few weeks after coming home from the hospital, Logan and I took Dr. Evans' advice about getting her a therapist. She has sessions with Dr. Kendrick twice a week now.

I'm amazed at Sofia's progress. Logan and my sister have expressed on several occasions they'd like for me to schedule an appointment. Given the positive change I've seen in Sofia, maybe I should consider it. Perhaps it's time I dealt with everything I've been avoiding.

Deciding I can't sit around and do nothing any longer, I grab my phone and shoot Lisa a text. I want to plan a graduation party for Alba. This is the distraction I need. I don't even wait for her reply before I'm walking over to the kitchen counter in search of my car keys. If I know Lisa, she'll be game. That woman lives for anything that involves cooking or parties. I'm also hoping to talk to Jake about going back to work.

"Sofia," I shout up the stairs. "I'm heading over to the clubhouse, want to come?"

Peeking her head from around the corner, she says, "Yeah, let me grab my bag."

Sofia doesn't go anywhere without her messenger bag Alba gave her, along with several books and a Kindle. Leave it to my sister to get her addicted to reading. Alba loves that she now has a book buddy.

I smile as she sprints down the stairs in a white baby doll dress, bronze gladiator sandals, and her bag slung over her shoulders. "I'm ready," she huffs out breathlessly, once she makes it down the stairs.

"You didn't have to rush. I would have waited for you," I chuckle.

Returning my smile, she asks, "You think Alba will be there?"

Looking down at my watch, I reply, "She'll probably get there in about the same time we do if we leave now. Let me send a quick text to Logan telling him to bring her to the clubhouse instead of home."

This is her last week of school, followed by graduation in two weeks. Sofia has expressed how excited she is to get back to school. She's missed most of this past year and will be a grade behind the other kids her age, but it doesn't seem to bother her, she's only focused on a fresh start.

We arrive at the clubhouse at the same time Gabriel pulls up with my sister. Stepping out of my car, I walk over to where he's parked.

"Hey, I thought Logan was picking Alba up today," I question.

He leans against his bike, smoking a cigarette.

"Had some club business to take care of, asked me to pick her up," he offers.

"Yeah, sure," I mumble, turning to walk away.

"Bella," Gabriel stops me.

I come to a halt, refusing to look at him. I know I'm letting my insecurities show. It's not like me to be this way, but lately, I can't help it. I'm always worried that I'm not good enough, that I'm not what Logan wants anymore. I drive myself crazy with all the thoughts that run through my head.

"You've got nothin' to worry about with Logan."

Turning my head slightly, I cut my eyes towards Gabriel, giving him a nod.

When I step inside the clubhouse, I smile when I see Quinn sitting at the bar. "Hey, darlin', come over here and have a drink with me," he drawls.

Taking a seat next to him, he taps the counter, getting Liz's attention. "Get Bella something to drink," he clips. Losing the sweet tone, he had with me moments ago.

Liz has been on thin ice with the club ever since we found out she was feeding information back to Cassie. She insisted she didn't know what Cassie was up to, and the boys decided on giving her a second chance. Either way, I don't trust the bitch.

Bringing his attention back to me, Quinn asks, "What brings you here today?"

"I'm going nuts, sitting around the house all day, so I came to

Undaunted

talk to Lisa about a graduation party for Alba. And to also talk to Jake about going back to work."

"Really? You talk with Logan about that?"

"No, Quinn, I didn't. I wasn't aware that I needed his permission," I deadpan, crossing my arms.

"Hey, I'm on your side, sweetheart. Without you there, I'm forced to eat day-old pizza and shit. I'm literally starving, Bella. What I wouldn't give for some of your fried chicken," he says with his head tilted back and a dreamy look on his face.

Poking him in his rock-hard stomach, I laugh, "Yeah, you look like you're wasting away, Quinn."

"Let me go talk to Jake. Hopefully, I'll be back to filling your belly soon," I jest.

I really do miss working. I can't stand sitting around the house all day. I need to be busy doing something. I've always been busy either taking care of someone or working. I need to get back to work. Hopefully, that will be soon.

Rewarding me with his signature smile, Quinn says, "Looking forward to it, darlin'."

Walking to Jake's office, I see his door is open, and he's sitting at his desk.

"Hey, Jake," I greet, tapping on the door.

"Bella? What you are doing here. Everything okay?"

"Everything's fine. I wanted to come to talk to you about coming back to work," I say, taking a seat.

"Work? You think you're ready for that?"

"It's been two months, Jake. Seriously, you guys have got to quit treating me with kid gloves all the time. I'm ready, I promise. I wouldn't have come to you if I wasn't."

"Well, you know you can come back to the garage anytime you want. We all miss having you there. Especially Quinn. The dipshit won't shut up about not having a decent meal to eat. I swear, kid. You've spoiled the man."

"Great! How about I start back on Monday. Put Quinn out of his misery," I chuckle.

"Sounds great, Bella. Just one thing; have you talked to Logan about this?"

"Why does everyone keep asking me that?" First Quinn, now Jake. What makes anyone think I should ask him first. I don't need permission from Logan to go back to work.

He holds his hands up in surrender. "Sorry, I was only asking. Though maybe you should discuss it with him before Monday," Jake suggests.

"I'm sure Logan could care less. I'll mention it to him later, okay?" I say, getting up from the chair. "I appreciate you agreeing to me coming back, Jake."

"Anytime, sweetheart. If I don't see you later, then I'll see you on Monday at the garage."

After leaving Jake's office, I head in the direction of the room Alba has here. Turning the corner, I run straight into Logan as he's exiting his room. I thought he had club shit to deal with, at least that's what I had been told. I stand here looking at him and cross my arms.

"Hey, babe. What are you doing here?" he says, looking a bit confused, and I'm sure he doesn't miss the same expression, mixed with growing anger on my face as well.

"I came to see Jake. What are you doing here? Gabriel said you had some club business to take care of, and that's why you didn't pick Alba up from school," I say suspiciously.

"I did. I just got back. What did you need to see Jake for?"

"I'm ready to go back to work. I was making sure he was cool with it."

"Go back? Do you think you're ready?"

I swear I'm so damn tired of that question. Are you okay? How are you feeling? Do you think you're ready? It's my damn choice when I'm ready and what I do.

Undaunted

"I wouldn't have told Jake I was ready to come back if I weren't ready, Logan." I can't help the bitchy way my words come out.

"Don't start, Bella," he clips.

"Start what, Logan?" I feign like I don't know what he's talking about.

"This shit where you turn everything into an argument. I'm sick of it, and it stops now."

"I don't know what the hell you're talking about."

I do, and I hate that he's calling me out on it.

"You're always avoiding any real issue, Bella. So instead of dealing, you look for any reason to start a fight with me. Over stupid shit too. Like today. You knew going behind my back, asking Jake to go back to work, without talking to me first would start a fight. Only today, it's not working. Today we're dealing with our problem," Logan declares through gritted teeth.

By the set line in his jaw and fire in his eyes, I know he's done. There will be no more hiding. No more distance. He has had enough.

"Fine," I snap. "I'll go get the girls, and meet you at home."

"No, they can stay here tonight. I'll let the guys know so that they can keep an eye on them."

Without replying, I brush past him, continuing down the hall. There is no arguing with him when he's like this.

When I get home, I decide to take a shower before Logan gets here. Since coming home, I have avoided talking about what happened in that basement. Talking about it is not going to make anything better; it's not going to make the scars go away. He needs to understand what's done is done. We can both talk till we're blue in the face, but in the end, it won't change a damn thing.

After stepping out of the shower and drying off, I realize I forgot to bring a change of clothes. Wrapping a towel around my body, I open the bathroom door to go to my closet and grab my pajamas. I stop in my tracks when I notice Logan standing in the middle of our room, his eyes tracking my every move.

Once I retrieve my clothes, I try stepping around him to get back to the bathroom, only to have him block my path. "Logan. Let me get dressed; then we can talk."

"No," he says flatly.

"What do you mean, no? I'm not having a conversation with you in my towel."

Shit. I know where he's going with this, and I'm not sure I'm ready for it. I KNOW I'm not prepared for it. My whole body gets warm, and I start to get the jitters. My hands are clammy, my breaths are quickening, and my pulse is racing. I am working up to a full-blown panic attack. I have avoided this very moment for months now, and he has let me.

"If you need to get dressed, you can do so in front of me, Bella. No more hiding."

My stomach drops. He can't be serious. I was prepared to talk. Not this.

"I'm not ready," I say, gripping the towel tighter around me.

"Yes, you are. You're strong, baby. You just don't know it."

"Don't tell me what I am. Stop trying to force me into doing something I don't want!" I yell.

At this point, I'm so worked up—so angry—my body is vibrating.

Logan is standing five feet in front of me, nose flaring, and a look of fury on his face. "I was there. I saw what that motherfucker did to you. I carried your bloodied, almost lifeless body in my arms, Bella!" he yells back, pacing the floor, pulling at his hair.

"Is this what you wanted to see?" I cry at him, dropping my towel to the floor, keeping my arms at my sides, resisting the urge to cover myself. I'm facing my fears head on while battling the voices in my head to do the complete opposite—to run and hide.

"Tell me, Logan! You come in here making demands like you

have the right. Newsflash. This," I say, pointing at my scars, "didn't happen to you! It happened to me! I'm the one who was kidnapped! I'm the one who had that filthy motherfucker's hands all over my body! I was the one who was screaming in pain while being sliced open!" I yell with tears rolling down my face.

"And it's my fucking fault!" Logan bellows, cutting me off, pacing back and forth and running his hands through his hair.

"What?" I ask, stunned, losing some of my anger. He's mad because he thinks he didn't protect me. I was expecting pity or a look of disgust. Instead, Logan is looking at me like he could care less about my scars.

He looks defeated, tired.

"It's my job to protect you. If I had protected you better, none of this would have happened."

This whole time I've been so focused on my demons, I didn't stop to think about how this whole fucked up situation affected him. He's been battling demons of his own, and I was too selfish to see it.

"It's not your fault this happened to me. It's because of you, I'm alive," I challenge.

In three strides, Logan is in front of me, gripping my face in his hands. "It is my fault, Bella, and I'll spend the rest of my life making it up to you, starting right now, starting by telling you how beautiful you are. You are the most beautiful woman I have ever seen. Your scars are a part of you now. I love everything about you."

Picking me up, Logan holds me as if I'm the most precious thing in the world. Carrying me across the room, he gently lies me down on the bed. "I'm going to show you just how beautiful you are," Logan says, his tone a promise.

Starting at my feet, he slowly kisses his way up until he reaches the inside of my thigh. He places a gentle kiss on the first scar. The smallest one, but that's the cut that nearly cost me my life. Next, he trails his rough calloused hands along the jagged scarring on my ribs. I feel another array of soft kisses, this time along the edge of my breast. I have no doubt he doesn't miss the tremble in my skin, as I try with everything I am to suppress a sob. I feel the heat of his body hovering above me, but refuse to open my eyes. I'm scared of what I might see now that he's seen me, touched me.

"Open your gorgeous eyes for me, Angel."

Fisting the sheets in my hands, I shake my head, refusing.

"Yes," he whispers softly, his mouth against my ear.

Opening my eyes, I'm not prepared for what I see—no, what I feel. Love, and I can't hold back any longer. The pain I've been holding onto for so long is released through tears that are streaming down my face.

"Beautiful." Logan softly repeats over and over while he continues to kiss and caress every inch of my body. It doesn't take long for my sobs to turn into pants when he runs his tongue over my nipple, causing me to gasp. It's been forever since I've felt Logan's touch, and I'm desperate for it. Rising off of the bed, I watch him rid himself of his clothes. "I need to taste you."

Kneeling before me, he grabs my legs, pulling me to the edge of the bed and spreading my legs, Logan peers at me. His eyes dark with desire before lowering his head. I moan loudly at the feel of his hot, wet mouth on my pussy. It feels so good I nearly come right then.

"Not yet, Bella. When you come, it's going to be with me inside you."

"Logan, please," I beg.

"Please, what, Bella? What do you want?"

I lower my head, looking at him between my legs, "I want you inside me," I urge with fire in my voice.

When Logan stands, my mouth waters at the sight of his cock.

Climbing over me, he takes my legs and urges me to wrap them around his waist.

Leaning down, Logan takes my mouth. I open to him, allowing his tongue entrance at the same time his cock fills me.

As he lazily moves in and out of me, placing soft unhurried kisses along my neck and down over my collarbone I start to realize, the sex this time is different.

This time Logan is delivering on his promise. He's making love to me and showing me how beautiful I am, that he loves me—ALL of me.

33

LOGAN

Things have been fuckin' great since Bella and I had our little 'come to Jesus moment' a few weeks ago. Now we're facing everything head-on together. I can't begin to explain what it was like to finally touch her, kiss her, taste her after so long. I'm fuckin' addicted to Bella Jameson. She owns my heart, holds it right in the palm of her little hand.

It's July already. Bella's sister graduated a couple of weeks ago but wanted to wait on celebrating until it was closer to her birthday, which is today. So, we are having Alba's birthday and graduation party at the clubhouse this afternoon. Everyone's involved with making sure it's a big blowout. The smell of food grilling is floating on the breeze as I help set up the tables and chairs out back. Bella and the other women are inside preparing the rest of the food.

My brother Nikolai is manning one of the grills alongside Reid and Quinn. He's been hanging around the clubhouse more than he has his place since our father went back home to take care of some business. I thought it would be harder than it was to talk him into letting my brother stay behind, but surprisingly he felt it could do him some good.

The brothers seem to have adopted him. Jake even gave him a room of his own to crash here at the clubhouse. He seems to be enjoying his freedom and a new-found sense of family.

I watch as Bella comes walking out the sliding glass doors, carrying a large bowl of food, followed by a couple of the other brother's women. One by one, they place the food down on the tables, along with paper plates and plasticware.

She's nothin' but smiles today, as I stand here and take her in.

"Man, you've got it bad," Quinn laughs as he comes to stand beside me, looking in the current direction my attention is fixated on.

"Yeah, brother, I do."

Bella turns to see me watching her, her eyes telling me that my heated stare is having its intended effect, and begins to walk my way. She's wearing a white sundress today with her favorite pair of boots and has left her hair down. The sun reflecting off her beautiful face is making the gold speckles in her hazel eyes flicker, hypnotizing me, making me fuckin' speechless as she comes to a stop in front of me.

"Brother, you're droolin'," Quinn says.

Hearing Quinn's outburst, Bella laughs. Damn, it's good to see her happy again.

"Fuck off, Quinn," I say as I take hold of my woman.

I watch him walk off, satisfied with himself.

Looking down, I speak to Bella. "Hey, beautiful."

"Hey." she beams up at me.

"Looks like everything is about ready to kick off. Where's the birthday girl?" I ask her.

"She's up in her old room, getting ready with Sofia. Has someone gone to get her present yet?"

"Yeah, babe. Gabriel should be here any minute with it. I

figured we should give it to her first thing. There's no way we're gonna be able to hide it," I inform her.

"I'm so excited! She's going to love it." She reaches up, wrapping her arms around my neck, pulling me down for a kiss. "I'm going back inside to help her get ready. I'll bring her out when Gabriel gets here."

"Okay, babe."

I release my hold on her and watch her ass sway as she makes her way inside. Jake walks up and hands me a cold beer.

"Hey, son. She's looking much better. Gabriel on his way yet?"

"Yeah, he'll be here soon. Glad you found me. I wanted to see if you and the guys could do without me for a few days toward the end of the month. I want to take Bella out of town after her sister leaves for school. I know we've been bogged down with builds at the shop lately, so I want to make sure I won't be leaving you in a tight spot," I explain to him.

"That shouldn't be a problem. I'll get my sorry ass out there and do some work for a change. I need the distraction anyway," Jake says, running a hand down his beard.

I don't ask questions about what's bothering him. Jake doesn't share much, and meddling only pisses him off. "Thanks, Jake." My phone rings. Taking it out of my pocket I answer it. "Yeah?"

"I'm down the road, brother. Everyone ready?"

"Yeah, I'll get Bella to bring Alba down."

I hang up the phone and text Bella.

Me: Gabriel is pulling up. Get your sweet ass down here.
Bella: Yay! On our way.

Less than a minute later, Bella comes walking out with her sister and Sofia in tow. I stand back and watch the excitement on Bella's sweet face as Gabriel comes cruising around the side of the building in a black lifted Chevy four-door pickup truck, coming to a stop beside the girls.

Undaunted

"Oh my god! You guys got me a truck!" Alba screams with delight as she squeezes her sister.

Gabriel slides out of the truck, and Alba runs over, wrapping her arms around his neck and jumping into his arms. No one misses the sweet kiss she plants on his cheek before letting go and climbing into the truck.

The rest of the day goes smoothly. With all previous threats being taken care of, we can relax and have a good time. Music is playing, and the smell of the wood burning in the huge bonfire has filled the air. Quinn even got out his guitar, playing a few songs, which he hasn't done in a long time. Sitting back, I take it all in.

Most everyone ended up staying at the clubhouse to sleep for the night, even the brothers with kids. They pushed the pool tables in the common room off to the sides and set up some rollaway beds we had stashed in the building out back. The kids loved the idea.

LYING IN BED, I trace over Bella's scars. They're looking much better, and she's more at ease, letting me see them. "You know, babe, you could tattoo over them if you wanted to. People do it all the time," I inform her.

I don't see anything wrong with them myself, but maybe putting something over them would help her feel better.

"Really? I've never thought of that. I don't know if I could let someone look at me, though. At least, not right now," she sighs.

"You do what's right for you, babe. You're beautiful, no matter what you decide." I kiss her lips and trace my hands down her body.

With a full house, I quietly make love to my woman. Showing her that everything about her is beautiful.

I'M SITTING HERE, watching my woman nervously let Gabriel look at her scars.

Since I expressed to her that she could always have a tattoo cover them, she hasn't stopped talking about it. I spoke with Gabriel beforehand and set up a time for us to come into the shop. The only person I trust to do the job right is my brother, Gabriel. He's done cover-ups like this before.

It took her about a week to get the courage to come in. My woman is a fighter, though, facing those demons head-on, and I couldn't be prouder. She's not healed up enough to have the needle on her skin, but will be soon enough.

She glances over her shoulder at me as she lays on her side, her shirt scrunched under her breasts, as he examines the area. She knocks the wind out of me every time she looks at me that way. With love. Nothing but pure, unfiltered love.

A few weeks ago, she was pushing me away, but she's been going to counseling twice a week now, and since then has only had two nightmares. Things between us are stronger than ever.

She and Gabriel have wrapped things up, and she's walking over to me, wearing a beautiful smile on her face. "Gabriel said that he shouldn't have any issues covering my scars. That he'll make them fade into the background like they aren't even there. Afterward, I should wear my scars with pride, not disgust, because I'm no longer a victim, but a survivor," she says to me with tears pooling in her eyes.

I look over at my brother, quietly thanking him for giving my woman strength with his words. Standing on her tiptoes, she presses her lips against mine, giving me a soft kiss. I grab her around the waist, pulling her tighter.

"Fuck, I love you," I say after my lips leave hers.

Once we walk out and mount my bike, I tell her we're going for a ride, but don't tell her where. I'm cruising down the highway with Bella tucked into my back, her hands wrapped around my waist, and it's the best fuckin' feeling in the world.

I pull off onto the dirt road leading to the lake—our lake. The sun's peeking through the canopy of trees as we make our way down the narrow path until it opens to a perfect view of colored fields and the crystal blue water.

Over the past few weeks, the lake has become a place of healing for both of us. We try to make it out here at least once a week. Getting away from everyday life has given both of us a newfound sense of peace.

I pull to a stop, parking the bike and lifting her off after I stand. I unstrap the small rolled up blanket I have fastened to my bike, grab her hand, and lead us to our favorite spot on the water's edge. Spreading the blanket, I guide her to sit.

"I'll never get tired of coming out here. It's beautiful," Bella says, breathing in the warm fresh air.

I stare at her as she closes her eyes, soaking up the rays of sunshine hitting her face. At that moment I see an image of her, sitting in this exact spot, belly swollen with my son, and a little girl running around with deep, brown curls bouncing around as she picks wildflowers. The image is so vivid I reach out, putting my hand on her stomach.

"Logan, are you okay?" She laughs.

I blink. *Where the hell did that thought come from?*

The words leave my mouth before I can even think about what it is I'm saying. "I want to have a family with you, Angel."

She looks surprised, a little caught off guard by my statement, but doesn't falter as she reaches up, cupping my face in her tiny hand, telling me, "I'd like to have a family with you too, Logan."

The loving, sincere smile that overtakes her face is my undoing. I crush my lips to hers, stealing her breath, making it my own.

Pulling her into my lap, I break our connection to reach into my cut. I hear Bella gasp as she watches me pull out a small, blue ring box. Opening it, I look at her. She hasn't taken her eyes off the ring nestled inside. It's a vintage-cut chocolate diamond, encased with small champagne diamonds, mounted on a rose gold band.

My father insisted that when the time came, he wanted to provide the ring. I didn't refuse. He and Jake are the only ones who know what I'm doing today.

"Bella, I'm not perfect, but you make me want to be a better man every day. You've shown me the kind of love and acceptance I never knew I was missing in my life. I'm a man who knows what he wants, and that's you—right by my side, or on the back of my bike. Be my old lady. Marry me." It's not a question but a statement.

Tears are falling from her eyes as she gives me her hand to slip the ring on her finger.

"I love you! Yes, I'll marry you!" She beams, full of excitement.

I stand up, pulling her up with me, lifting her off the ground. The sun shines behind her, casting a golden halo.

I'm at a loss for words.

My future is within this beautiful, strong woman I'm holding in my arms.

Her love warms my once cold fuckin' heart and feeds my soul.

"Angel, I will spend the rest of my life and the one after, lovin' you."

EPILOGUE

BELLA

As I stare out the living room window at the ice-covered lake, and the white snow that blankets the ground, I can't help the smile taking over my face. It's almost Christmas, my favorite time of year. To top it all off, my sister will be coming home in three days.

Alba has been away at college since August. I miss her terribly, but I'm proud of her. Alba was given a full ride to Montana State University in Bozeman. She's only been home once since leaving, always making up excuses as to why she can't visit. I can't help but wonder if she's okay. Alba quickly squashes any doubts, telling me she's just busy with assignments.

Sofia has been thriving. She started her junior year of high school at the end of August and has made lots of friends. The guys in the club have become very protective of her. She can't even go to the movies with her friends without at least one of the prospects watching over her. I don't think she minds, though. I think it makes her feel good knowing she has a dozen big brothers looking out for her.

I've been busy decorating the house. Logan took me the other day to get a tree, only to come home with a truckload of decorations. He didn't understand the magnitude of how seriously I take Christmas. While in the checkout line he asked, "Babe, do you really need all this shit?"

I turned and gave him my best 'you're kidding, right' look. Although, he did draw the line when he saw me hauling boxes of decorations into the clubhouse.

"Hell fuckin' no, Bella. I love you, babe, but the brothers will never let me live that shit down."

The next night Logan and I decide to go to the clubhouse and have a few drinks with the guys. I'm sitting on Logan's lap, listening to all the endless banter when the door opens. Looking over, I'm shocked when I see my sister. She wasn't due to arrive for two more days.

"Alba!" I screech. Leaping off Logan's lap, ignoring the groan that leaves his mouth when I not so gracefully got up.

Running up to her, my steps falter a bit when I take in her red, blotchy, tear-stained face. "Alba, what's wrong?" I question, picking up my pace. Once she's within arm's reach, I grab a hold of her, pulling her in for a hug.

Her trembling body sends me on high alert. Stepping back a bit, while keeping a hold of her shoulders, I plead with her again, "Tell me what's wrong. Are you okay?"

Feeling a looming presence behind me, I glance over my shoulder and find Gabriel's tall frame standing there.

"Cariño, *sweetheart*?" he tenderly addresses her.

I watch as Alba's face goes deathly pale, and she begins to pull her heavy winter coat tighter around her body. Something is off. I just can't place it. I let my eyes assess her from head to toe, looking for a sign of anything wrong, but I find nothing.

It takes me a couple more seconds to realize what's different. Letting out a small gasp, I cover my mouth.

"What the fuck?" Gabriel growls.

Made in the USA
Columbia, SC
01 July 2025